Praise for Author

Tamara Linse

"Linse writes as if flexing her own ranch-toned muscles, creating intense, original characters and letting them loose. The result could fill a novel—or two. All bodes well for Linse's future work." —Kirkus

"In this winning debut collection of short stories (*How to Be a Man*), Linse presents a vivid portrait of life in the American West. ... readers will be drawn in to the collection's world and will find themselves wanting to read more of Linse's intimate tales." —*Publishers Weekly* (starred review)

"Linse's wide array of believable characters, and her ability to return to the same set of themes without becoming repetitive or predicative, makes her a notable literary force. ... HOW TO BE A MAN is a notable debut from a very promising writer." —IndieReader

Also by Tamara Linse

How to Be a Man (stories)

Deep Down Things

Tamara Linse

willow
words

Cover art: Tree of Life No. 3, *mixed media, courtesy Andrea Pramuk, www.andreapramuk.com*

Print
ISBN: 0991386752
ISBN-13: 978-0-9913867-5-8
Print (Amazon)
ISBN: 0991386736
ISBN-13: 978-0-9913867-3-4

Epub
ISBN: 0991386744
ISBN-13: 978-0-9913867-4-1
Kindle
ISBN: 0991386760
ISBN-13: 978-0-9913867-6-5

Edition 1.1

For Alex, who would have been 18 this year,
and Kelly, the woman who loved him

God's Grandeur

THE WORLD is charged with the grandeur of God.
 It will flame out, like shining from shook foil;
 It gathers to a greatness, like the ooze of oil
Crushed. Why do men then now not reck his rod?
Generations have trod, have trod, have trod;
 And all is seared with trade; bleared, smeared with toil;
 And wears man's smudge and shares man's smell: the soil
Is bare now, nor can foot feel, being shod.

And for all this, nature is never spent;
 There lives the dearest freshness deep down things;
And though the last lights off the black West went
 Oh, morning, at the brown brink eastward, springs—
Because the Holy Ghost over the bent
 World broods with warm breast and with ah! bright wings.

Gerard Manley Hopkins (1844–89)

Deep Down Things

Part 1
January

Maggie

Jackdaw isn't going to make it. I can tell by the way the first jump unseats him. The big white bull lands and then tucks and gathers underneath. Jackdaw curls forward and whips the air with his left hand, but his butt slides off-center. Thirty yards away on the metal bleachers, I involuntarily scoot sideways— as if it would do any good. The bull springs out from under Jackdaw and then arches its back, flipping its hind end.

Jackdaw is tossed wide off the bull's back. In the air he is all red-satin arms and shaggy-chapped legs but then somehow he grabs his black felt hat. He lands squarely on both feet, knees bent to catch his weight. Then he straightens with a grand sweep of his hat. Even from here you can see his smile burst out. There's something about the way he opens his body to the crowd, like a dog rolling over to show its belly, that makes me feel sorry for him but drawn to him too. With him standing there, holding himself halfway between a relaxed slouch and head-high pride, I can see why my brother Tibs admires him.

I haven't actually met Jackdaw before, but he and Tibs hang out together a lot, and they have some English classes together. I haven't run across him on campus.

The crowd on the bleachers goes wild. It doesn't matter that Jackdaw didn't stay on the full eight seconds. They holler and wolf-whistle and shake their programs. Their metallic stomping vibrates my body and brings up dust and the smell of old manure.

With Jackdaw off its back, the bull leaps into the air. It gyrates its hips and flips its head, a long ribbon of snot curling off its nostril and arcing over its back. Then it stops and turns and looks at Jackdaw. It hangs its head low. It shifts its weight onto its front hooves, butt in the air, and pauses. The clown with the black face paint and the big white circles around his eyes runs in front of the bull to distract it, but it shakes its head like it's saying no to dessert.

The crowd hushes.

Then, I can't believe it, Jackdaw takes a step toward the bull. The crowd yells, but not like a crowd, like a bunch of kids on a playground. Some holler encouragement. Others laugh. Some try to warn him. Some egg him on. My heart beats wild in my chest like when my sister CJ and I watch those slasher movies and Freddy's coming after the guy and you know because he's the best friend that he's going to get killed and you want to warn him. "Bastard deserved it," CJ always says, "for being stupid."

It's like Jackdaw doesn't know the bull's right there. He starts walking, not directly to the fence but at a slant toward the loudest of the cheers, which takes him right past the bull.

I turn to Tibs. "What's he doing?"

"He knows his stuff," Tibs says, his voice lower than normal. The look on his face makes me want to give him a hug, but we're not a hugging family, so I nod, even though Tibs isn't looking at me.

Tibs is leaning forward, his eyes focused on Jackdaw, his elbows on his knees, and his shoulders hunched. Tibs is tall and thin, and he always looks a little fragile, a couple of sticks propped together. His face is our dad's, big eyes and not much of a chin, sort of like an alien or an overgrown boy. He has the habit of playing with his fingers, which he's doing now. It's like he wants to reach out and grab something but he can't quite bring himself to. It's the same when he talks—he'll cover his mouth with his hand like he's holding back his words.

Tibs is the tallest of us three kids—CJ, he, and I. CJ's the oldest. I'm the youngest and the shortest. Grandma Rose, Dad's mom, always said I got left with the leftovers. Growing up, it seemed like CJ and Tibs got things and were told things that I was too young to have or to know. It was good though, too, because when Dad and Mom got killed when I was sixteen, I didn't know enough to worry much about money or things. They had saved up some so we could get by. But poor CJ. She in particular had to be the parent, but she was used to babysitting us and she was older anyway—twenty-two, I think.

Like that time when we were kids when CJ was babysitting and I got so sick. Turned out to be pneumonia. I don't know where our parents were. Most likely, they were away on business, but it could have been something else. Grandma Rose had cracked her hip—I remember that—so she couldn't take care of us, but it was only for a couple of days and CJ was thirteen at the time. In general, CJ had started ignoring us, claiming she was a teenager now and didn't want to play with babies any more, like kids do, which really got Tibs, though he didn't do much besides sulk about it. But that day she was playing with us like she was a little kid too.

We had been playing in an irrigation ditch making a dam. I pretended to be a beaver, and Tibs pretended to be an engineer on the Hoover Dam. I don't remember CJ pretending to be anything, just helping us arrange sticks and slop mud and then flopping in the water to cool down. I started feeling pretty bad. Over the course of the day, I had a cough that got worse and then I got really hot and then really cold and my body ached. My lungs started wheezing when I breathed. I remember thinking someone had punched a hole in me, like a balloon, and all my air was leaking out. CJ felt my head and then felt it again and then grabbed my arm and dragged me to the house, Tibs trailing behind. All I wanted to do was lie down, but she bundled me in a blanket and put me in a wagon, and between them she and Tibs pulled me down the driveway and out onto the highway. We lived twelve miles from town, in the house where I live now. I don't know why CJ didn't just call 911. But here we were, rattling down the middle of the highway. A woman in a truck stopped and gave us a ride to the hospital here in Loveland. Can you imagine it? A skinny muddy thirteen-year-old girl in her brown bikini and her skinny nine-year-old brother, taller than her but no bigger around than a stick and wearing red, white, and blue swim trunks, hauling their six-year-old sister through the sliding doors of the emergency room in a little red wagon. What those nurses must've thought.

On the bleachers, I glance from Tibs back out to Jackdaw. The bull doesn't know what's going on either. It shakes its lowered head and snorts, blowing up dust from the ground.

Jackdaw bows his head and slips on his hat. Then the bull decides and launches itself at Jackdaw. Just as the bull charges down on Jackdaw, the white-eyed clown runs between him and the bull and slaps the bull's nose. Jackdaw turns toward them just as the bull plants its front feet, turns, and charges after the running clown.

Pure foolishness and bravery. My hands are shaking. I want to go down and take Jackdaw's hand and lead him out of the arena. A thought like a little alarm bell—who'd want to care about somebody who'd walk a nose-length from an angry bull? But something about the awkward hang of his arms and the flip of his chaps and the way his hat sets cockeyed on his head makes me want to be with him.

The clown runs toward a padded barrel in the center of the arena, his white-stockinged calves flipping the split legs of his suspendered oversized jeans. He jumps into the barrel feet-first and ducks his head below the rim. The crowd gasps and murmurs as the charging bull hooks the barrel over onto its side and bats it this way and that for twenty yards. The bull stops and turns and faces the crowd, head high, tail cocked and twitching. He tips his snout up once, twice, and snorts.

While the bull chases the clown, Jackdaw walks to the fence and climbs the boards.

The clown pops his head out of the sideways barrel where he can see the bull from the rear. He pushes himself out and then scrambles crabwise around behind. He turns to face the bull, his hands braced on the barrel. The bull's anger still bubbling, it turns back toward the clown and charges. As the bull hooks at the barrel and butts it forward, the clown scoots backwards, keeping the barrel between him and the bull, something I'm sure he's done many times. He keeps scooting as the bull bats at the barrel. But then something happens—the clown trips and falls over backwards. The barrel rolls half over him as he turns sideways and tries to push himself up. The bull stops for a split second, as if to gloat, and then stomps on the clown's franticly scrambling body and hooks the horns on its tilted head into the clown's side, flipping the clown over onto his back.

Why do rodeo clowns do it? Put their lives on the line for other people? I don't understand it.

The pickup men on the horses are there, but a second too late. They charge the bull, their horses shouldering into it. They yell and whip with quirts and kick with stirruped boots. Tail still cocked, the reluctant bull is hazed away and into the gathering pen at the end of the arena. The metal gate clangs shut behind it.

Head thrown back and arms splayed, the clown isn't moving. Men jump off the rails and run toward him, and the huge doors at the end of the arena open and an ambulance comes in. It stops beside the clown. The EMTs jump out, pull out a gurney, and then huddle around the prone body. One goes back to the vehicle and brings some equipment. There's frantic activity, and with the help of the other men, they place him on the gurney and slide him into the ambulance. It pulls out the doors and disappears, and the siren wails and recedes.

Tibs stands up, looks at me, and jerks his head, saying *come on, let's go.* I stand and follow him.

Tibs

The clown. Such athleticism and courage. I hope he'll be all right.

But before that grim scene, my man Jackdaw. Spectacular, the manner with which he flourished his hat, James Bond-esque. His second ride ever, his second. He didn't best Father Time, *id est* stay mounted for eight seconds, but who cares?

Maggie and I connect with him behind the stalls. It's frigid outside, with burgeoning gunbarrel-gray clouds over the mountains to the west. Now, beyond the reach of the crowd, Jackdaw's glasses rest on his nose, ruining the film-star cowboy effect. It's humorous, really: only Jackdaw would place himself near-sightless in a ring with a thousand pounds of murderous Charlais in order to look the part.

Sure, Jackdaw isn't the clown, but nonetheless, he was in there, just as fearless. He'll do anything for the crowd. He's always the epicenter of things. If there's a group, his charisma pulls everyone into a vortex. He has this ideal of perfection, of what the world should become, and he must embody that and shape the world. This is why he started riding bulls, I think. He likes the black-and-white cut-and-dried nature of it. You win, you lose; perfection or death.

Don't get the wrong idea. I'm not gay—I'm attracted to girls. He's just cool, that's all.

Jackdaw's life, his goals, his quest, is much like Hemingway's. Hemingway did everything and went everywhere. He volunteered as an ambulance driver for the war in Spain; he lived, loved, and wrote in Paris; he hunted—for big game, but also for himself—in Africa; he tried his hand at bullfighting in Spain; he fished and adopted the war effort off Cuba; he lived—and died—in Idaho. But no matter his physical location, there was always a group with Hemingway at its vortex. Hemingway was courageous, though he was also a bit of a bumbler. Courage fascinated him. Most of all, he was brave to lay bare the warts and pimples of his life for all the world to see. He had the courage of brutal honesty. He put himself out there, made a decision, affected the world—I want to be more like them, like Jackdaw, like Hemingway.

Face serious, Jackdaw converses with this old guy near the corrals and flips his bull rope as Maggie and I approach. He says, "See you later, Dick," to the gentleman, and then all three of us walk to his gear bag.

"Jackdaw, my man," I say, "you were looking good."

"Two seconds worth of good," Jackdaw says.

"No, man. You didn't stay on for the required eight seconds, but I bet your style points exceeded everyone else's."

"I don't know. All the style in the world, but if you can't get the job done."

We're all quiet for a long minute. I don't know about Jackdaw and Maggie, but the fate of the clown leaps to my mind. The way he didn't move, not even to curl in pain. It did not bode well for him. I wonder briefly if Jackdaw feels any responsibility, but then I am pulled back into the present by the silence.

"Jackdaw. I would like to introduce my sister Maggie," I say and glance at her. She's pretty—not beautiful, not handsome, but pretty—standing there with her gold-red locks glowing in the sunlight, her frame so small and slight. She's curvaceous, though, and her pale skin is dotted with freckles. Her iridescent green eyes appear tinted by contacts, but they are genuine. One thing you can say about Maggie—she's genuine. Naively so. Not that she hasn't dated. I imagine it's because she's so intent on pleasing everyone. She's just got the freshness and gleaming health of a Mormon girl—except, I don't know, purer.

"Maggie, I would like to introduce Jackdaw."

"Hi," Maggie says.

"Hey," Jackdaw says. A change comes over him. His face smooths out and opens up. "Maggie," he says, as if he's tasting the word.

Maggie looks at him, though I cannot read her expression. Her eyes are on him but she has this thoughtfulness too.

I turn to Maggie. "Did I tell you, Jackdaw attends my nineteenth century lit class?"

"Do you do cowboy poetry, like Baxter Black?" she says.

Jackdaw is about to say something, but I cut in, "Maggie. Have you ever heard of a literature professor addressing cowboy poetry?" I turn to Jackdaw. "East coast and mid-Fifties is as close as they come to Colorado." I hear my own tone and immediately regret saying it. I force myself to laugh.

Maggie starts to say something and then stops and presses her lips together.

"Do you mean do I write cowboy poetry?" Jackdaw says.

Maggie glances at me as she says, "Yeah."

"I've written cowboy poetry. But mostly I write political poetry, poetry that makes a statement, protest poetry, right Tibs?" Leaning toward her, he glances sideways at me.

I'm not sure what he's talking about.

He smiles and continues. "I'm all about justice and freedom. Taking it to the man. Fighting for the little guy—or gal. Yeah, that's me."

"Like songs?" Maggie says.

"No, limericks." He stands up straight, puffs out his chest, and recites, "There once was a man from Colorado, who was scared of his own shadow, he went when he came, each time just the same, to the relief of the women he'd had, though." He tilts his head in my direction, and looks at me over his glasses. "Eh, Tibs, ol' boy?"

Maggie laughs quietly under her breath. I shake my head but have to laugh too.

"So Maggie," Jackdaw says as he coils his bull rope, "how'd you turn out so pretty, having a brother with such an ugly mug?" He ties the rope with a scrap of leather.

She smiles broadly and looks at me.

He continues, "You must've had a very pretty mailman." He purses his lips and rolls his eyes.

"You must've had a butt-ugly mailman," I say, "either that or your old man looks like Peter Boyle."

"Good one," he says and holds out his fist. I bump it with mine.

"Hey, how about some lunch?" I say. "We could go to the concessions stand for a hotdog."

14

Maggie nods.

"I could down a dog," Jackdaw says, kneeling to tuck his rope into his green canvas gear bag.

Jackdaw

Well, ain't she as pretty as a picture?

Maggie. Have you seen those paintings of pioneer women? Standing beside their man, their faces tilted upwards like they can see heaven. The winds whipping the women's skirts. A fat baby on a hip and a boy in shortpants and girl with braids nearby. A Conestoga wagon and cows and horses so muscled they could've been painted by an old master. They're what women are supposed to be. That's what I think of when I see Maggie.

Tibs, Maggie, and I go back inside the arena and stand in line at the concessions stand. Luckily it's not a long line—I pulled something in my ankle with that landing out in the dirt. Tibs orders a polish sausage with mustard and sauerkraut, Maggie orders a corn dog, and I order a foot-long with jalapenos and nacho cheese, and then I pay for it with my last ten dollars. We sit around a folding table and eat. I make a show of opening my mouth as big as Dallas and shoving in as much dog as I can. Maggie, shaking her head, watches me and nibbles her corn dog. Tibs tells a story about the time I got everyone in a literature class to vote to read Louis L'Amour. The teacher nixed it, though.

"Tell Maggie about the time your dad had you wrestle a pig," Tibs says.

I lick my fingers and swallow the last of the dog. "Well, okay. My dad was a hard ass." I pause. "Still is, I imagine." They're both focused on me, which makes me feel good.

"You imagine?" Maggie says.

"Haven't seen him in a while. He'd say things like, 'Toughen up, boy. No place in this world for a pansy ass.'" As I say it, I can hear his voice in my head, and my stomach knots.

I get an image of him standing over me, his voice surrounding us, a thing all its own. I'm on the ground, and I can feel the cold dirt clods digging into my back as I try to sink into the ruts in the road to the barn. My skull is ringing where he rapped me upside the head because—I don't know because. If I thought I had a reason one time, it didn't work to try to avoid it the next time. It was almost like he didn't want me to guess, so he could keep at it. But there I am, seeing stars too. Some people think it's just a saying—seeing stars—but you really do when you get your clock cleaned. They're little blue twinkle lights that flit mosquito-like around your face. There's something wet on my chin. Later, I'll figure out it's blood from where I lit on my nose when he punched me. I'm hoping he won't stomp on me, and in my mind I see myself like a cur dog, rolling over and fawning because it's afraid of its master. And then I hate myself and push up to standing, even though I know what he's going to do. He's going to hit me again. Which he does.

Maggie and Tibs are looking at me, so, to cover, I say, "He'd do things like have me run along behind the car on the

17

way home and yell at me, 'Keep up, boy.'" I laugh. Tibs chuckles.

"That's awful," Maggie says, all serious.

"Aw, it was all right. Made me the Clint Eastwood you see before you." I hold my hands up like a pistol. "Go ahead, punk—"

Tibs chimes in, "Make my day." We're laughing.

"Oh," Tibs says, "'I tried being reasonable, I didn't like it.'"

I say, "How about, 'There's two kinds of people in this world. Those with loaded guns, and those who dig. You dig.'"

Tibs is way into it, but I'm losing Maggie. She's shaking her head and staring down at the remains of her lunch. I reach over and push her shoulder. She smiles. "Clint doesn't light your fire?" I push her shoulder harder this time, so that she almost tips over. I make my voice high, "'Oh, Clint, you're such a strapping hunk of a man,' admit it."

She laughs. "Tibs went on a Clint Eastwood kick when he was in high school," she says. "We must've watched *Pale Rider* a thousand times."

"At least once too few," Tibs says.

"So you watch chick flicks?" I say. "'Oh, Rhet, please come and sa-a-ave meh.'"

Tibs laughs.

Maggie says, "It's better than blowing people away left and right. They're about things that matter, like love and family."

I lean forward, and I can smell Maggie's perfume—it's something flowery but deeper. "Come on, admit it. There's days when you'd like to take somebody out. Everybody run, Maggie's got a gun."

"No, not really," Maggie says.

"Sorry, Jackdaw," Tibs says, "I'll have to back her up on this one. I've done my share of tormenting her over the years, and she's always turned proverbial cheek. Even to CJ, our sister, who can be quite trying."

"So we have a saint in our midst," I say. "I'm going to have to hang around you more often. Maybe some of it will rub off on me." And as I say it, I really mean it.

As we get up to leave, gathering our paper plates, Tibs says, "You never told the pig story."

"That's all right," I say. "Somehow I don't think it's Maggie's kind of story."

CJ

I should've brought Maggie with me, then maybe I wouldn't feel quite so shitty. But she was going to something today, a rodeo I think, with Tibs. Besides, I haven't told her anything about this crap.

I sit on the exam table in the small examination room, still in the awkward drafty gown, and my butt sticks to the vinyl. The room is chilly and smells like abrasive cleaning fluid.

"Are you okay?" the doctor asks me. He's a nice guy, and over the past couple of months I've gotten to know him way too well. He looks like an aging football player—a few pounds overweight but still carrying himself well. His breath always smells like spearmint and cigarettes.

"Fuck you," I say.

He snorts and then catches himself. "I'm sorry, I shouldn't have laughed."

"No. Laughing's about right," I say. "God's one twisted motherfucker. Good thing I don't believe in Him." I push off the table with a scraping sound as my skin separates from the plastic. Cool air whispers through the slit in the back of the gown and makes me aware of how naked I am.

His voice deepens as he shifts into support mode. "Would you like to talk with one of our grief counselors? We have an infertility support group that meets every other Thursday. Would you like that contact number?"

My turn to snort. "I don't need a dozen other poor bastards like me sniveling in their cups. That's what the bar's for. Besides, they're just infertile. I'm fucking sterile." I shrug. "Naw. I'm all right."

Maggie

The little boy looks at me with eyes like blue-tinted crystal. He's finished eating before his parents and is bored, so he's turned to look at me. All I can see over the back of his chair are those eyes and blonde curls with what looks like a blob of grape jelly pulled through a matted strand.

"It was irresponsible of them," CJ says. "You shouldn't have kids unless you're going to take care of them."

CJ sits opposite me in the orange diner booth. Her short hair molds to her head like a brown helmet, and her makeup is a little heavy for nine a.m. In the morning light, the pupils of her eyes are small, like a bird of prey. She eats the world's largest omelet, attacking with her fork and pulling off pieces and shoveling them into her mouth.

"I'm sorry, but they knew we were safe," I say, my eyes still on the boy. "We were with Grandma Rose." The January chill pushes through the plate glass window next to our booth. Through them I can see the mountains draped with snow that rise above us to the west, but the foothills have been blown bare by the winds off the plains to the east. I cup my hands around my coffee to warm them.

CJ chews and swallows. Then she takes a gulp of orange juice. "You don't think leaving your three kids with a dotty old woman, even if she was their grandmother—you don't think that was irresponsible?"

"Grandma Rose was not dotty," I say. "She was ..." I'm trying to think of the right word. *Dotty* means she was crazy. She wasn't crazy. She was just getting old. "Her mind was starting to go a bit, sure, but she wasn't crazy."

"All those cans she saved up in little pyramids in the garage, in case the price of steel went up?"

"She lived through the Depression."

"The time she met Tibs at the door with the twelve gauge?"

"She thought we were being robbed."

"It was two in the afternoon."

"People get robbed at two in the afternoon. I'm sorry, but they do."

CJ won't let it go. "The whole family is crazy. Naming us Cleopatra, Tiberius, and Magdalene. Who does that? It's like putting a target on our backs, a huge sign that says kick me."

"Grandma Rose wasn't crazy."

"That's not the point, anyway. The point is: Our parents went off to do Dad's archaeology and left us without a second thought."

The little boy's fingers are hooked over the back of his seat, and now he lifts up his right hand and makes a fist and then splays his fingers open wide and then closes them into a fist and then opens and closes, opens and closes. He's waving. He's smiling with his eyes. I can't get over how blue these eyes are. They're darker at the outer edge but in the center they're radiating splinters of blue, prisms from almost white to a shade darker than the sky. He's got long lashes like a girl's. He could be a Gerber baby, his eyes just grab you.

I look back at CJ. "CJ. They did what they thought was best. They had to make money, and that was Dad's profession, even if it was only going on digs. He did what he had to. Mom—"

She cuts me off. "Oh, don't even start with Jane. Dad, ok, he had to work, but Jane. Not even a second glance."

The little boy has lost my attention and he tries to grab it back. He lifts his whole arm and waves it back and forth like he's at a concert and he's waving a flashlight or something. I smile now and wiggle my fingers at him.

"CJ, look at that little boy. Isn't he just the cutest?"

CJ glances at the boy. At first she smiles a little and then it's like she remembers something and her face clenches.

"What?" I say.

CJ doesn't say anything, which is odd coming from CJ. She's got something to say about everything. She looks away.

The little boy sits up straight in his chair, and the bottom half of his face raises above the chair back. His upper lip is exaggeratedly feminine, a cupid bow with tall upside-down Vs on top, and the bottom lip pooches out. There are two slash scars where the edges of the divot under the nose should be. His nostril on one side is wide and high and his nostril on the other is flattened. One side of his face is normal, but the other looks like it's been compressed like the side of an accordion, jaw shorter, the corner of his lips curling up, his nose flattening down.

I'm shocked. A minute before he was beautiful, and now he's ugly and I can't stop looking at him. I'm trying to make what I saw before fit with what I see now.

Then his mother glances at me and sees the look on my face. Her lips press together for an instant and then she leans over and whispers in the little boy's ear. The little boy listens to her but looks at me. He's shy all of a sudden and tucks in his chin and his shoulders curl up. Then he smiles.

There's something about the way the little boy leans back into the cup of his mom's shoulder, the way he takes it for granted that the shoulder will be there without looking, and there's something about the way the mom rests her hand on the little boy's thin neck, not ownership but an intimacy that no one can touch. I take a deep breath. Suddenly, I want something so bad, something so deep I can't name, like I'm in the snow and I'm looking in a window at a roaring fire.

Now the little boy is beautiful like he was before, shining and genuine, but different, deeper, like he's felt pain but it turned out ok. I can't imagine what this boy has been through already in his short life. And how people must look at him every day with these expressions on their faces and what that does to him. I wonder what his mother said to him just now, what she says to him every day to counteract that.

"Moms do what they got to do," I say to CJ and glance outside at the dirty snow piled on the curb. After a minute I say, "Anyway, don't talk ill of the dead. They're family."

Tibs

We stand in a "tube home," a trailer, drinking beer. It rests in a trailer park on the east edge of town, affording a view of the fields beyond. Because it's winter, the fields consist of gray dirt, open to the scouring of stray winds. The land is so flat beyond, blue above, hazy tan below, you can see the earth curve. We're in the bachelor kitchen, bare, wood-paneled, smelling of stale beer and oven gas.

Jackdaw tells a story; he holds everyone in the palm of his hand. He's wearing his ostrich-skin boots—pale and bumpy below, chocolate brown uppers—and his black felt hat. The attending guys form a semicircle around him, arcing like a vast halo. Jackdaw is animated, and everyone laughs. I'm standing behind him, at a remove.

"And that's when that son of a bitch flipped me in the dirt," Jackdaw says. "I had him. I *had* him." He thrusts out his right hand in a grasping motion. "But he didn't think so. Turns out he was right."

"You could've had him," I say quietly. "You did have him." No one looks at me as I speak.

"Yeah, I did have him," Jackdaw says. He chugs his beer. "Too bad about the clown, though."

The guy who owns the trailer says, "I've got a meaner bull than that. I keep him right out back." The guy's body is short and fat but energetic and coordinated in the way of some fat men. Think Jackie Gleason, John Belushi.

Jackdaw's skepticism shows on his face. He nods. "Yeah, right."

"Yep. The neighbors don't care for him, but he's right out back."

"You don't have a bull," another guy retorts.

"Sure I do," the guy says. He jerks his head sideways, indicating we should follow him. He walks down the long hall, past a bedroom strewn with clothes and an echoey bare bathroom. He pushes open the back door with a loud scraping creak. In comes the smell of dog shit. We emerge onto a small redwood deck. In among patches of snow, there's an old fifty-gallon drum, at one time blue, suspended by means of ropes from four round wooden posts. There's a length of rope encircling it, and its paint is worn in gray and brown patches where it's dented across the middle from the rear ends of countless riders.

"You suck," Jackdaw says and grins and jumps off the porch. He approaches it, places his beer on the ground, and mounts the bucking barrel. He grabs the rope and wiggles his butt forward, causing the barrel to jerk back and forth. "You guys couldn't flip a nickel off the back of your own hands," he challenges.

A guy grabs each rope and they all yank, the combined effect causing the barrel to twist and buck. I stand back, watching. Jackdaw hangs on easily.

"You trying to rock me to sleep?" Jackdaw says.

The guys put more into it this time, and by coincidence they all pull at same time, popping the barrel up in the air. It then flips sideways but Jackdaw hangs on with his hand on the rope and his feet around the sides. His legs are long enough to keep the "bucking bronco" to him, so he ends up pulling the barrel over as he topples. He comes to rest on his shoulder, suspended from the barrel by his legs.

"That's a draw, I'd say," Jackdaw says. "Either that or I'm dead." He releases his legs and drops to the ground. "All right. Who's next?" He pushes up to standing with his arms, dusts off his hands on his jeans, and looks at me. "Tibs, my man, get your nose out of a book and mount this sucker."

Hell no! Panic as all eyes turn toward me. "No way in hell," I say.

"Come on, you lily-livered bastard," Jackdaw says, amusement in his voice. He moves like he's going to drag me forth. I back away and shake my head. There's a silence as Jackdaw stands with his arm outstretched.

"I'll do it," the guy who lives here says, glancing at me. "I bet I beat you by five seconds."

In that moment, I have two directly opposing impulses: to punch Jackdaw in the face and to shout out in Jackdaw's defense.

Maggie

The classroom is a square box that echoes when we talk. The student desks, teachers' desk, lectern, and whiteboard just fit in the space. It smells like institutional floor cleaner and burned coffee from the vending machine out in the hall. Tibs has to do a practice teaching in the morning, so he asked me to come be a student for him. I sit in the front row. He stands at the lectern and fiddles with papers like he can't figure out how to get started.

"Didn't you forget to take attendance?" I say and smile at him as I flip open my notebook and click my pen.

"We're not doing the full class, just a lesson," Tibs says and glances at me. "Oh, you're kidding." He laughs at himself and then glances at the door.

"Okay, student is ready," I say.

He turns to the desk and picks a paper up from a pile, walks around the desk, and hands the paper to me. I glance at it. It's the *Declaration of Independence* all typed up. He goes back behind the lectern and then glances at the door again.

"You expecting someone?" I say.

"Well, uh, yeah, I—" Tibs says as Jackdaw walks in and plops into the left-hander desk next to me.

He's wearing his hat, a green Carhart jacket, a red-checkered western shirt, jeans, and boots. He doesn't have a backpack or anything with him. "What's up, teach?" he says as he takes off his jacket.

"Tardy, Mr. Donner," Tibs says, glancing at me and smiling. "That'll cost you."

"You can't start without your star pupil," Jackdaw says. "Let me get set." He glances around and then sees my notebook on my desk. Then he turns his head toward me and sort of relaxes his shoulders and raises his eyebrows. "My, what a pretty lady," he says, his voice high. "And so prepared. My-my, my-my-my." He shakes his head back and forth.

I feel the warmth of his eyes on me and it makes me feel so good. I laugh and glance from him to Tibs and back.

"Um, miss," Jackdaw says, "I seem to have come unprepared. Do you suppose you could lend me your pen?"

"It's my only one," I say but hold it out to him. He delicately takes it from my fingers and turns to his desk as if to write. "Thank you."

"All right, Jackdaw," Tibs says, shaking his head, "let's—"

A poke on my shoulder. "Um, I seem to have misplaced my paper. Could you?" Jackdaw cranes his neck while looking at my notepad.

I snort and glance at Tibs then back to Jackdaw. I look at Jackdaw but tip my head toward Tibs and jab my finger. "We're here to be taught?" I say.

In a loud whisper, he says, "That old chump Jordan couldn't teach his way out of a paper bag." Then he opens his mouth wide and gives an exaggerated wink. Then he turns to look at Tibs. "Oh! Mr. Jordan, I didn't see you there," he says.

I don't want to, but I laugh. Tibs is standing there not smiling, but I can't help myself. I whisper loudly, "I think Mr. Jordan's giving you an F for the day."

"Okay, *class*," Tibs says. He sighs and grabs another paper from the pile on the desk and hands it to Jackdaw. "Today, we'll be addressing primary documents, and as an example we're going to look at the *Declaration of Independence* in the context of its time. How many of you have read the *Declaration of Independence?*" He looks at me, his head tilted my direction, ignoring Jackdaw.

Jackdaw leans over sideways without looking at me and whispers loudly, "I declared independence once, but my mom made me go to bed without supper." Then he focuses on Tibs like he's listening.

I shake my head and raise my hand.

"Yes, Maggie," Tibs says, still ignoring Jackdaw

"We had to read it in high school social studies." I play it straight.

"And what did you think of it?" Tibs says.

I try to think what a student would say. "It's boring," I say, my voice nasal, which brings a snort from Jackdaw but a frown from Tibs. "It's just history," I say with my voice back to normal. We're here for Tibs. I wonder if Jackdaw is like this with Tibs all the time, giving him a bad time. That wouldn't be very nice for Tibs.

Tibs says, "That's what I thought you'd say." A smile reaches his eyes. This is what he prepared for. "Imagine that there's a huge war between say, Washington D.C. and California, and they each send troops into Colorado to fight. The people from D.C. give aid to the Colorado government,

31

while California gives money to the Mexican immigrants to fight against the Colorado government who's at the behest of Washington."

As Tibs talks, Jackdaw scoots his desk just a bit toward me. Then he scoots it a little more, and then a little more until finally it makes a loud scraping noise.

"Yes?" I say, nodding to Tibs but watching Jackdaw out of the corner of my eye.

Tibs continues, "So a bunch of your friends get killed, maybe even family members, with Washington ultimately winning out, but then they have the audacity to charge you what the war cost. Would you be mad?"

By this time, Tibs is slouched down right next to me, his shoulder almost touching mine. I can feel the warmth of his body through his shirt, and a flush goes through me and then circles to my groin. I take a deep breath.

Tibs is still explaining, "That's what happens in the 1750s and 1760s during the Seven Years' War, or what the Colonies called the French and Indian War. The British and the French were fighting over the Americas, and then when the British won, they tried to charge the cost of the war to the Colonies."

Something smells. I wrinkle my nose and try to look around without moving my head. It's getting stronger, strong enough that I quit pretending and look around until I spot Jackdaw's boots sticking out from under his desk. They have manure on them, some of it fresh.

Do I say anything? Tibs is trying to practice, and Jackdaw's being a pain—a funny pain, but still a pain. But I don't have to say anything. As I sit there wondering what to do, Tibs stops and shakes his head. "Jackdaw. What did you do?"

Using his hand, Jackdaw pushes himself up straight. "What?" he says. His shoulder bumps against mine, and I give a sharp intake of breath. But then his shoulder is away, and I get a little mad at Tibs for making Jackdaw move, even though I don't show it.

"I always knew you were full of shit," Tibs says, his voice strained, "but now it's leaking out your boots." As he says this, his hand rises and flutters in front of his mouth.

Jackdaw looks down and then his jaw tightens a little. Then he glances at me and says, "Shit. I hope I haven't offended the lady." He toes off his boots, mud and manure flying, and gets up and carries them to the door in his stocking feet. He sets them outside and comes back and sits down, scooting his desk a little away in the process.

I feel sorry for Jackdaw, then, and I don't like the way Tibs rubs it in. Also, Jackdaw's shoulder is far away. I try to keep the disappointment off my face.

Tibs picks up a paper from the desk behind him and begins reading, "When, in the course of human events, it becomes necessary."

CJ

"Let's get out of this fucking town," I slur at Peter, who's behind the bar. He owns Golddiggers—a small cinderblock bar on a side street, oval neon signs, ten barstools opposite four booths, a big-screen TV, and a pool table. Still smells a little like cigarettes from before the smoking ban. I bartend here, and I drink here.

"Just for the weekend," I say.

Peter's got that seedy look I love, Margaritaville and good-ol-boy all rolled into one. Medium build, a bit of a belly, balding red hair, but that nice leathery tan skin with lots of character wrinkles.

Peter and I are sleeping together, friends with benefits, fuck buddies, whatever you call it. I stay over at Peter's a lot. I don't even know why I have an apartment. His place is a nice, if bland, two-bedroom. Tan carpets, square mirror tile on the walls, white kitchen appliances, a layer of dust over everything. It's always picked up, though, because he's never there. Sometimes we do other things together when we're not working, but usually one or the other of us is working.

Being fuck buddies doesn't affect our work. It's kind of odd, really. I think we both genuinely like each other, but sometimes it feels more like doing the dishes than having sex.

Something you do it because you need to do it. It makes you feel better, relieves stress. Sometimes I feel guilty about it, like I really should have a grand passion for Peter, but I don't, and he doesn't, and we're all right with that. I think that's also what makes it easier at work. We aren't particularly passionate about each other, so we don't get jealous and we separate our work from our sex. Peter's like that, very orderly. He likes things in their places, uncomplicated-like. Maybe that's why I still have an apartment.

"If we go, who'll bartend?" Peter says, wiping down the bar top in front of me with a grayish rag that smells of hops.

"Fuck that. John'll cover. Plus we can get Dan and Dave to pitch in. Just for a weekend. We could go camping up north. Red Feather Lakes maybe. Or the Poudre." I try to imagine us camping. Instead of tents and pine trees, I see us plastered, hanging out on the deck overlooking the rocky river at the Mishawaka bar listening to a blues band.

"Well, let's play it by ear," Peter says and puts another Bud Light in front of me.

I need to get out of this town. I've got too many old drunks in my life, myself included. Too much same old, same old. Loveland's in a rut. It sits in northern Colorado between the straight-backed un-fucking-forgiving Rocky Mountains and the hot and lazy plains, with the Big Thompson River juicing right through the center. That rut is called booze. Loveland is an old drunk, a regular. You always know what drink it'll order. For example, if you say, "You know the guy, black cowboy hat, tall Jack and Coke with two shots," another bartender'll know who you're talking about. But, if you say, "You know, Joe Alexander," they'd say, "Who?"

35

Knowing Loveland for a long time makes it an old friend. One who'll help you carry cases of beer up from the cooler in the basement and one who'll bail you out of jail at four in the morning. One who'll also get drunk and sleep with your wife and feel bad about it but'll do it again given the chance. The Loveland I know would be waiting out front sitting on the curb when the bar opens at seven in the morning. He wouldn't've bathed or shaved in a couple of days. He'd be hunched over with his hands tucked under his belly to keep them warm. First thing, he'd order a Pabst with his coffee. His hands would be shaking as he sipped the coffee and then chugged the beer. "Just to take the edge off," he'd say. In the evening, he'd order a shot of the cheapest whiskey and pay with quarters he won playing pool. That's my Loveland.

If you think of Loveland as female, she'd order slow gin on the rocks and wouldn't wear makeup. She'd sit at the bar slumped over, her head resting in the crook of her arm, her body flabby and pale. She'd lean over and throw up onto the floor, lurch back to center, wipe her lips, and then order a draw to get the taste out of her mouth. That's my Loveland.

Others call it the Sweetheart City because every Valentine's Day people from all over mail in their valentines so they can have a Loveland postmark. That Loveland'd probably order a strawberry daiquiri and get so drunk and wild she'd pass out in the back seat of her car, her panties around her ankles. Some people like to think of Loveland with a sparkling crystal glass of freshly juiced wheatgrass. I haven't ever been able to see that. I don't often get to see Loveland with its pretty face on. I suppose there's others who think it'd order a cosmopolitan, or a shot of rye whiskey, or maybe even a club soda. There's no accounting for taste.

Peter says, "Tell you what. Why don't you take the weekend off? Lay around. Maybe see if your sister wants to do something, eh?"

Jackdaw

Time slips by so fast I can't keep up. Standing on the boards behind the bucking chutes underneath the grandstand. Trying to stay out of the guys' way and watching it all happen. Knowing I could die in a few minutes. On my third ride ever. Not die like "I could've just died when she said that," like girls say. Really die. Hooked by a horn through the guts or stomped into the shit of the arena and have my back broken or land on my head and break my neck or get my arm hung up and be dragged and battered and hooked all the way across the arena. Any of this could happen. Standing here trying not to think about it. Slow down. Slow it down.

Shooting pains going from my shoulders up through my neck and my breathing coming in short sharp bursts. I'm bearing down like I've got to shit. Relax. If you don't relax, if you stiffen up, you ride like driftwood. One jump and you're toast. Relax like a rag doll, keep your balance and your looseness. Try to anticipate but go with it. That's why you see the guys jumping up and down with one hand thrown above their heads. They're stretching and focusing and trying to keep loose.

I close my eyes. Tip my head down to one shoulder and then the other and then roll my shoulders in circles, first one way, then another. I force myself to breathe slower, sucking the air all the way down and then puffing my cheeks to blow it out. *Clang!* and I open my eyes. Time shoots forward.

It's all blurry because I'm not wearing my glasses. The bull runs down the chute with his head cocked to one side so he won't catch his horns on the upright posts. He's done this before and he knows. *Creak* and *wham!* of the guy on the boards standing to my right as he slams down the gate in front of the bull's nose. Followed a split second later by *smack!* and rattle as the bull rams his flat face into the metal bars. He rebounds backwards, but the guy to my left drops the metal gate behind him just in time to catch his hip bones. The gate doesn't make it all the way down before the bull pushes backward, his hips curling under like he's trying to sit down. The guy to my left thrusts an electric prod through the rails, zaps the bull. The bull jumps forward, releasing the gate, which the guy shoves all the way down to the dirt floor. Then the bull relaxes. He doesn't kick the rails or the metal gate. He doesn't ram his horns into the gate in front of him. He settles in. He's not moving, just standing there. He's done this before.

Those horns. They arc out from his head like a bug's mandibles. They're not the short curls, which are pretty much harmless unless they get really close. They're not the long windy ones that catch you just by chance. No. These are what horns were meant to be. Precision instruments to disembowel. Without thinking, I put my hand to my side. Let it drop. That's where he'd stick me. Right there in the side where he'd perforate a bowel and drag the intestine out with a flick of his head. Acute septicemia and massive internal injuries.

The guy to my right drops the tail of my rope down past the bull's ribs. The guy on the outside of the swinging gate pushes the hook through the rails and snags the bottom of the rope and pulls it over and up. They hook it together. The guy next to me nods. I crawl up and over the rails and seesaw my feet down the rails, first left then right. When I get low but still clear of his ribs, I grab the rope with my right hand in its rosined glove and rub up and down, up and down, heating the rosin. I grab the handhold. Then the guy pulls the rope and gets it as snug as I can stand. I wrap the tail back into my fist. The bull hasn't shifted its weight, but now it feels the rope around its chest and humps its back and gives a little crow hop. Adrenaline shoots through me like water through a garden hose. My head feels like it's going to explode. The guys above me are ready, though. They grab me around my body and pull me up out of the way. I keep ahold of the tail of the rope, though.

The bull gives a half-hearted kick against the metal gate and then calms. The guys release me. Again, squatting like a crab, I seesaw down the boards and get my right hand situated. The guy above me grabs the end the rope and helps me get it tight. I wrap it back into my fist like I'm tying a boy scout knot, close and tight. Then I wrap my fingers around the rope, pulling them into the tightest fist I've ever made. I curl my thumb down along my fingers and push it tight. Then with my left hand I pound the fist, forcing it tighter and tighter.

That knot of a hand is the only thing keeping me on the bull. My hand, my legs, my balance, and my wits, but right now I'm focused on that fist.

I step down one rail and lower my butt onto the bull's back. I can feel the heat of his body through the butt of my jeans. I can feel his ribs hard against my thighs and the sharp bony backbone up the crack of my ass. He snuffles and shifts his weight. I stand up again, bending where I'm tethered by my fist. It's nothing, just him going from one foot to the other. I settle down again, this time curling my butt down and my crotch up against my hand. I lean back. With my left hand I pull my hat tight down onto my head and then grab the metal bars of the gate. My right hand's melded to the rope and feels like one piece. My weight's centered and back. My legs are cocked forward and up. Now's the time.

Here's that moment. Dead silence. Everyone's focused on you. The bull and the guys standing beside you, the clown and the pickup men, the announcer and the crowd. You are the center of their world for just that second. Then you nod your head and the world splits apart.

But I don't want to do it. I realize that it's not worth it. A lot of the guys do it for the adrenalin or for their pride or whatever. The only reason I'm doing it is for this moment. But in this moment, it's not enough, not worth dying for.

But what can you do? Thousands of eyes are on you, pushing you forward. It's like gravity, that roadrunner moment when his body falls but his head stays in the frame and he goes *Beep! Beep!* Even in the laws of cartoons, the head's got to follow. That's what it feels like now. The body's gone and the head's got to follow.

I bob my chin down once, twice. The air opens up beside me where there used to be a gate. The bull pushes off but I'm ready for him and my balance is shifted to the left. He spins in a quarter circle out of the chute. My whole body is yanked by the tether of my right arm. The first impulse is to curl up and hold on with both hands, to bring the feet down and together and clutch with the legs, but that's all wrong. You've got to stay loose, stay back, stay balanced, anticipate. I let my left hand crack back like a whip to keep me centered.

The bull pulls his hindquarters up to his front feet and squares himself down and low. It's a soft landing. I'm almost tricked into relaxing, letting my body fall forward just a little too far. But I know what's going to happen next. He springs up with the force of a rocket and arches his back. The bell on the bull rope clangs repeatedly. Now there's nothing but air between my butt and the bull's back. The only thing holding me on is my right hand and the heels of my boots with the spurs hooked underneath his shoulders. This time when he comes down it's a jackhammer and he reverse pile-drives me. My spine shortens and my arm whips forward and I curl up like a baby. I'm still on, though, still centered.

With all that spring energy he pushes off again, this time bending his body to the right, his hindquarters whipping around to follow. He starts to spin like a top. If he spun to the left, it'd be easier because your arm's across your body like a tie-down helping keep your balance. But when he spins to the right, he's pushing against your arm and you're all loose. It's like trying to push a rope. Rather than letting the extent of your arm pull you around, you have to push off with your muscles to keep yourself back.

This is what's going to do it. I can feel my body getting behind. My butt's sliding sideways and my body's twisted out of sync with his. He can tell, too, because he pushes it harder, twisting his body like he's trying to snap his spine and mine. Each time he spins, those horns scrape back and try to find my right leg. Like the teeth on a saw, they keep revolving back and back and getting closer and closer as I fall farther and farther behind. I'm coming off. The right way—into my hand—but I'm falling instead of jumping.

Do I let go of the rope, unclench that knot of flesh and bone and come in range of the horrible horns? Or do I hang on till he's leveled out, not spinning but pushing forward, and take my chances that he won't smash me against the boards or stop and turn to get me when I let go?

I hang on for all I'm worth. My body rolls in midair. I don't know which way is up. I'm falling directly into those horns. My body uncurls. I hit the end of my twisted arm and I don't think about the horns anymore. My arm stretches out and out and then I feel a pop in my shoulder and pain shoots down my arm and across my body and my head fills with cotton. The sounds go away. The bull becomes nothing more than a hard surface I'm bumping against. With each jump, white hot pain radiates from my shoulder. I'm not even trying to hold on, but the twist of my arm and the rope have me fast. This goes on and on and on and on, and all I am is pain.

Then, all of a sudden, I'm free. My arm releases. I'm floating like a feather on the air, away from that horrible white heat. *Wham!* My body slams into the ground and all the air goes out of me. I can't breathe. I try to suck air in but it's like someone's sitting on my chest and I can't get it to rise. I pull and pull and pull. Finally, a little air leaks in and I feel it and then I try one more time and *gasp!* there's air coming in. Then I remember the bull, the horns. I try to push myself up but white hot pain shoots through my shoulder. I'm down, clods pushing into my back, hazy roar all around me. All I can do is hope the clown has the bull's full attention.

Maggie

I show up at Golddiggers at two in the afternoon when CJ gets off shift. She asked me to stop by, I'm not sure why. I'm not of age—I haven't stopped by her work before because I didn't want to get her in trouble—but CJ knows that.

From what CJ says, Golddiggers calls itself a family place. The same people have been coming here for twenty, thirty years, old people who drink all day like it was their job. Clock in at 8, clock out at 5. It'd be funny if it wasn't so sad. Do they look forward to it? Do they get any satisfaction from it? Or is it despair that drives them? Maybe they don't have any family and they think of the people here as their family. Or, if they do have family, how sad is that? What gets them started when they're twenty-five, thirty? Why do they keep on?

My breath billowing in the air, I walk across the cement stoop and pull open the heavy wooden door and step inside. The blast of heat from the heater hanging above the door feels good. At first it's like a cave and I can't see a thing. The room's quiet with only a few murmurs here and there. It smells of musty cigarette smoke, and underneath there's something sour, yeasty beer maybe, but also like somebody threw up or maybe even peed. My eyes get used to the dark and then I can tell the layout. There's a bar against the wall to my right, which

CJ's behind. To my left, there's a few booths. In the middle of the room, there's a small pool table. At the back are the restrooms, a juke box, and a big screen TV.

Glancing around, I see shapes of people here and there. It's kind of like one of those scenes out of a movie. I step in and everybody turns to look at me. Everything gets quiet. The TV's flickering sports over their heads, but the volume is turned way down. These people, they all look sort of sub-human, but less like the *Star Wars* bar scene than a ghoul-like horror movie. It's because they're not moving and they have these blank looks on their faces. Like they're animals in cages. Bored but desperate.

"Maggie!" CJ calls from behind the bar. Peter's at the other end of the bar. He lifts a hand. I walk up and climb onto a bar stool. I take off my coat and lay my purse down. Without asking, CJ pours me a 7-up and sets it on a napkin in front of me. "You came," she said.

"Yeah." I smile.

"What do you think?"

I'm not sure what she's asking, but the way she sort of stands back makes me think she's asking about the bar. "It's nice," I say, without looking around.

She nods. After a minute she says, "So, you decided what you're going to be yet?"

"My major?"

She nods.

"I don't know. I'm thinking teacher, or—"

"Like Tibs."

"Or maybe a nurse. Something like that where I get to work with people."

CJ smiles on one corner of her mouth. "People service, eh?"

"Helping people, yeah."

She looks around the room. "Maybe you're cut out for it." She nods. "Yeah, it's your thing. Not me. The thought of wiping up after puking people, whether they're five or fifty—not so compelling. Since I've done it a time or two."

"I'm sorry." CJ's take on the world is a little cynical sometimes.

She shrugs. "So, teacher or nurse. Why not a doctor?"

"Mmm. I don't know." I shrug and sip my 7-up.

The relief bartender, a small wiry guy, comes in, and CJ pours herself a beer and a shot and comes out from behind the bar, slapping Peter on the back of the head as she walks by. He smiles at her.

"Want to grab a booth?" she says.

"Sure," I say and pick up my drink. We walk over to the empty corner booth and sit down. It's a round table with a three-quarters circular seat of green vinyl. We enter at opposite ends but both scoot around to meet on the other side.

The relief bartender comes out from behind the bar with another couple of drinks. "Bob bought these for you," he says and sets them in front of us.

CJ looks at a guy sitting at the bar and calls out, "Thanks, Bob." I lift my glass. Bob waves and nods. In one smooth motion, CJ picks up her shot, flips her head back, and swallows the contents. She doesn't even make a face as she swallows, just a small tightening in her jaw. Then she takes a sip of her drink.

"So, what's up?" I say.

"Do you think I'd make a good mother?"

"Well," I say, trying to think how to put it. "You took care of me. You did a ... a good job." It doesn't sound right leaving it that way, so I add, "Yes. I think you'd make a great mom."

"I think I would too," she says.

CJ takes a deep breath and drinks another shot. The lids on her eyes have started to sag just a little. Her voice has slowed down too. The alcohol is taking effect. I've never seen CJ drink like this before, and it's weird. It's like I'm seeing a new side of her that makes you step back and say, "Do I know this person?" I get an image of her ten, twenty years down the road, slumped on a barstool, her arm propped on the bar, her fingers curled around a glass, and her head wobbling on her neck. The image is so sad I swallow involuntarily. I reach out with my hand but then pull it back. We're not the kind of family who touches.

I glance at her drinks. "You aren't pregnant."

She doesn't notice my look. "No, no."

I nod. Good, I think to myself.

The bartender comes over with more drinks. "Peter," he says.

CJ nods to him. "Get everyone one," she says.

The bartender nods and collects our empties, including my first 7-up. "I think I'm ok," I say, as he glances at the two in front of me. He goes back to the bar.

Her face seems to be sliding. It's like her face muscles relax their grip on her skull, and the whole thing sags.

"No, and I'm never going to be." She says and downs a shot.

What? "You don't want to be a mom?"

CJ shakes her head. "Not *want to be*. Can't. I can't have kids. The doctor says I'll never be able to." Then she doesn't say anything. She sits slumped over her drinks and stares down at them. Her head sways a little from side to side. It's like she's melted into a tall puddle.

This is why she asked me to come, to tell me this. I reach out and put my arms around her. "Oh, CJ."

CJ

It's a dark day—overcast, with a bit of wind, probably going to snow in the afternoon. Even smells like snow. It's so cold gloves aren't enough. We're moving this guy, Jack—Jackdaw, I guess—into Tibs's place, a little rundown two-bedroom house.

There's something about this guy I don't like. He's just dislocated his shoulder on a bull, the idiot. What possesses men to do these things I'll never know. Course, I see it all the time in the bar. Testosterone is an evil drug. It makes men do stupid shit. This guy's a bit of a candy ass, even if he did ride a bull once. I mean, granted, his shoulder's dislocated, so he can't help, but even as we're moving him he has to be the center of attention. He talks a blue streak, really loud, and he pauses as he talks, like he expects applause or canned laughter.

And there's something else about him I can't quite place. Call it bartender's intuition. You know the guys, the ones that come in and order a drink and you just know they're going to be trouble later. They start out really quiet, maybe even good natured, but after a couple of beers, their whole personalities change. Jekyll and Hyde. It's like they were hiding their real self the whole time, but the beer dissolved all that niceness. You can't trust them. I get the feeling Jackdaw's that way. Like he's got a whole nother self under there that he's careful not to show, but put a little beer in him, or put him under stress, and he's going to show his true colors.

"CJ," Tibs says. "Could you help me with the mattress?" We've got all the little shit moved, and now we're down to the furniture at the front of the horse trailer. Not much, and what there is is a step down from Salvation Army, more found-it-on-the-street kind of stuff. A stained mattress. Cinder blocks and boards for bookshelves. A beaten-up blonde side table.

"What *is* this guy?" I say, gesturing toward the furniture.

"CJ," Tibs says.

It's that tone, a tone I get a lot, that I'm stepping over a line. But I don't want to let it go. Tibs is going to room with this guy. He should at least know what he's getting into. "What? He's a friend of yours?"

I can tell from Tibs's expression that he is. Well, that changes things. He's already weaseled himself into Tibs's life. What to do? But I can't just let it go.

"Tibs. I'm only going to say this once because I know it's going to piss you off. This Jackdaw is bad news. He's … He's …" How can I get Tibs to realize? "He's the type to leave you high and dry. He'll skip out on the rent, or steal your girlfriend, or something. I'm just telling you."

Tibs doesn't say anything. He's got his hands on his hips, and he tips his head sharply toward the mattress—*come on*, he's saying. He picks up one end and I pick up the other end. As we haul it down the sidewalk, Tibs slips on the ice and drops it but catches himself on his knee. The mattress bounces and folds and almost takes me down before I stabilize it. Tibs crouches over his knees, his shoulders around his ears. "Ow," he says.

"Watch your step," I say. "Dangerous terrain."

After he breathes a bit, he stands up and grabs mattress again. Despite his limp, we haul it up the front steps and through the screen door that Maggie's holding and up the stairs into the small second bedroom. When we come back downstairs we go into the living room where Jackdaw sits in the tan recliner, backrest back and legs up, arm in a sling, a king on his throne. I glance over and there's Maggie sitting on the old southwest-print futon couch. She's perched on the edge catty-corner to Jackdaw. Her elbows are on her knees and her whole body is bent forward. Her head extends from her neck toward Jackdaw, and her eyes are wide and smiling. It's like Jackdaw is a magnet pulling Maggie forward out of her seat. Jackdaw's eating it up. He's all laid back, but you can see his ego bulging in his pants.

I get a chill and it's not from the cold. This isn't good, not good at all. This man, this piece of shit I didn't know before today, has insinuated himself into our family.

Maggie

I'm over at Tibs's. Tibs's and Jackdaw's now. The second time this week. No, the third. Tibs asked me to stop by and check on Jackdaw. And I don't mind.

Jackdaw's in the recliner when I shut the door on big fluffy snowflakes. I stomp my feet and shake my hair. The place smells of Pine Sol. Tibs likes things clean. Jackdaw's in navy blue sweats and a t-shirt that's been washed so many times you can almost see through it. He's got the TV on a basketball game with the volume down. A laptop is in his lap and his legs cross at the ankles. He pecks at the keys with his left hand, and his right arm is in a sling. He glances up and then back down. Then he looks up again.

"I'm sorry," I say.

"Maggie," he says. "I was just thinking about you."

I don't know what to say to that, so I smile. Maybe I blush a little.

"What would you do if a guy you liked was your roommate?" he says.

"I brought Arby's," I say, waving the bags. How do you answer a question like that?

"Mmmm, protein," he says and folds down the foot rest on the recliner with a kick of his heels and sets the laptop on the glass coffee table with his left hand. He winces just a little.

"Help you heal," I say and sit down on the couch and put the bags on the coffee table. I rummage through one and put a beef and cheddar sandwich in front of him. I pull out some potato bites and hold them up to offer them to him, but he shakes his head. I put them in front of me and rip open a squishy catsup packet and squirt it onto the potatoes.

Jackdaw makes a face. "That counts for two vegetables, doesn't it?"

"I'm sorry," I say, "but potatoes have to have catsup. It's a rule." I pick up one that's buried in catsup and pop it into my mouth. The salt of the potato and the sweet of the catsup are perfect together. "Mmmm," I say.

He raises his eyebrows. "First of all, the only way to make potatoes is to fry them in bacon grease until they're brown and crispy." He smiles at the thought, and he looks three years old. With short flipping motions, he unwraps the sandwich with his left hand, and then he rips open a packet of Horsey Sauce with his teeth and squirts it on. I want to offer to help, but he's got it done while I hesitate. "Then you add the onions, not too early so they don't get black but early enough that they just start to brown when the potatoes are done so they're soft and sweet." He gathers the sandwich in his hand, lifts it, and takes a big bite.

We eat in silence for a minute. Then he says, "If this guy was your roommate, so you'd be around him all the time, what would you do? Would you flirt? Or would you play it cool?"

The whole time he's talking I'm intensely aware of Jackdaw's body in relation to mine. When he gestures my way, my body leans toward him a little. When I scoot forward on the couch to eat my potatoes, I also scoot sideways toward him. But all this is careful. I know I'm doing it, but I don't want him to know it.

It makes me think of my sixteenth birthday party. You know, BD, as opposed to AD. Before death, as opposed to after death, as in Mom and Dad. Just right before. I fell head over heels for Justin Donovan. I had a party and invited a bunch of friends from school and Justin was a cousin of one of them. We had music going and a few of the kids were drinking but it wasn't out of control and everyone was having a great time. I'd just got out more food and come back into the living room and flopped down on the couch. Justin was sitting on the other end. He had gray eyes and dark brown hair and this cute thing where he shrugged his shoulders and looked at you under his eyebrows and smiled. Oh, and his hands. He had these incredibly long fingers that seemed so capable. My hand just disappeared in his. I noticed him and he noticed me and it was like there was a magnet pulling us together, a supermagnet and it was all we could do to keep apart. Well, I felt that way, and I'm pretty sure he too. We just seemed to understand each other. God, what a great night. We talked and held hands and kissed. I was so happy I could've screamed, and he ignored everybody else, even though there were girls trying to get his attention. He told me I was beautiful, and he wrote his number on my hand before he left. He was perfect for me. Perfect. But then Mom and Dad died, and how could I possibly be happy then? He called and even wrote a letter—he was from Colorado

Springs. But there was no way. I couldn't muster enough of anything for anything—everything seemed senseless. Then he quit calling. If I have any regrets in life, it's him.

Now, here with Jackdaw, he's asking what I'd do if I was attracted to a guy. It makes me uncomfortable. Is he saying it because he likes me?

"I bet you'd play it cool," he says. "He wouldn't even know it."

I take a deep breath. There's nothing I can say.

He looks away into space. "So how am I going to get them together? They can't just sit in the same room not talking."

"What?"

"I'm writing a story." His face reddens a little. "I'm going to be Billy Boulder. My pen name, I mean."

"Billy Boulder?"

"Cause it's a western. It's about this guy who gets hired on at this ranch … Well, you know. He and the girl like each other."

"Oh." I take a deep breath. "For a story." I'm not sure what he's asking. It sounds like he wants my help. I'm not sure what I think, but he's waiting there, so I say, "Well, you could have them accidentally touch. Their hands or something."

"Yeah, yeah."

"Or you could have them alone together somewhere, and maybe she—or he, it could be either of them—he could say something that makes her realize he likes her. Or do something, I don't know." I feel like I'm blathering.

He puts down his sandwich, wipes his hand on his sweats, picks up the laptop, and slides back in his chair. "Ok. Like, say, they're in a room. He's just come in with, say, some firewood and he's putting it in the woodbox next to the fireplace. What happens then?"

"Well, she has to clean the fireplace, right? Sweep the floors and stuff? So maybe he drops some bark on the floor. She could say something about that. Or pick up the broom and dustpan."

"Yeah, ok." He starts typing. He pecks at the keys with his left hand. Tap. Tap, tap. It must take him forever just to type a sentence. I look at the computer and then at him. Should I offer to type?

"Would she wait till he's out of the room to clean up?" he says.

"No, because she has to do this every time someone brings in wood, and she gets tired of it."

"So she picks it up and starts sweeping so he'll see it and maybe not make such a mess," he says. He types, tap, tap, tap.

"Can I help you with that?" I say.

He glances up and then back down and taps a few more keys. "Can you type?"

I nod and wipe my hands on a napkin. "Fast as you can talk."

"That sounds like a challenge."

"Well, maybe not that fast." I take the computer from him and sit back down on the couch. He's written, *She swept the floor like she would beat a dog, with quick hard strokes, to get it done, to show me.*

"Would she really be that violent about it?" I ask. Maybe I shouldn't say anything—it's his story—but it doesn't sound right. If she's beating dogs, people aren't going to like her very much.

"Well, if she was mad at him."

"Maybe she'd be really gentle about it because she feels guilty about feeling that way. She's supposed to do these things without complaining, isn't she?"

He's quiet for a minute. "I hadn't thought about it that way," he says. "Ok. Read it back to me." I do. He nods and says, "Maybe, 'She swept the floor carefully, softly, deliberately. She swept right up to my shoes on the hearth and then stopped. Then she looked at me'—"

"Wait. I'm sorry," I say, trying to keep up with his words. After a minute, I say, "Ok. Go on."

"'Then she looked at me and smiled. It was a sweet smile that said I was wrong and she was right and she was really sorry about it.'"

"Yes," I say. "She's like that. She's sweet."

We go on. He says a line and I type. I read things back to him. Sometimes I suggest things, but mostly I just type. I like the story, and I like sitting by him and typing. It's like we're touching, only it's our minds that are touching, not our bodies. Like he's working through me. Jackdaw gets up from the recliner and starts to pace as he talks. He's moving and his words are moving in a stream and I'm not even thinking as the words flow through my fingers onto the page. I feel like I'm no longer a separate person—I'm part of Jackdaw and part of the couch I'm sitting on and the computer and the air around us. We're all one and there is no separation and it's the most beautiful thing. And we're creating this beautiful thing on the page.

Jackdaw walks around the couch and sits next to me, still talking. He smells pleasantly of sweat. The couch sinks as he sits, and because I'm cross-legged with the computer in my lap, I tip over onto his lap. Then the connection's broken. I'm me and Jackdaw's Jackdaw and the couch is a dead thing underneath us. Something's lost.

I'm laying sideways across Jackdaw's lap trying to decide how to push myself up when I feel something on my hair, a soft pressure. I stop moving. Then I realize it's Jackdaw's hand. He's petting my hair. Then he touches my cheek and traces my jawbone all the way down to my chin. Gently, with two fingers, he turns my head sideways. He pushes my chin over my shoulder, almost to the point where it's going to hurt. I tense a little, but he stops and leans over and presses his lips onto mine. It's not a wet kiss. It's more like a kiss from an old black and white movie, close-mouthed but all the more moving for it. I relax back into him and my upper body twists toward him. He continues kissing me, but he's not like some guys. Some guys are all tongue and slobber and immediately try to put their hands up your shirt. No, Jackdaw kisses me carefully, respectfully even.

I feel like all my nerve endings, my whole soul, is in my mouth and I want to give it to him.

But after a bit, he pulls back, puts his hands on my shoulders, and tips me back up to sitting. It's not a rejection. It's more like, *now we understand each other*. Then he stands and starts talking. I start typing again. But now when he walks behind me he palms the back of my head or traces my shoulder, and I lean back just a little.

We've just turned on the lamps when Tibs lets himself in. It's snowing harder, and Tibs drops his book bag by the door and shrugs off his coat and hangs it on the coat tree. Jackdaw still paces, and I've moved from the couch to the recliner. Tibs sees us there and says, "What're you guys doing? You look guilty."

We laugh. "I'm writing," Jackdaw says and makes a can-you-believe-it face, eyes wide and teeth showing. "Really writing."

"And I'm typing," I say.

Tibs frowns. "That's great," he says. Then he says, "No, really, that's great."

Jackdaw

Every time I'm around Maggie, I feel like I'm in the presence of a myth. She is so great. Everything she does is just right. Every move she makes is perfect. I want to touch her so bad, but then I don't want to touch her, to soil that perfection that she is. I want to take her away where the world can't touch her. I want—well, I don't quite know what I want.

I invite her over to my house for dinner on a night Tibs is going to be out. The extent of my cooking is fried eggs, so I can't cook for her, plus there's my arm, and I'm as broke as a Model T so I can't go and buy takeout or order pizza. What I end up doing is, Tibs makes a pot roast on the weekend, and so I reheat it in the gravy.

"I didn't know you cooked," Maggie says when she comes in and smells it.

"Well, I don't, not really," I say as I take her coat. I leave it at that.

She turns around to face me, hesitates, and then quickly stands on her tippy toes and kisses my cheek. I have the urge to wrap my arms around her and hug her so hard. It's so strong I back away to keep from doing it. But then I see the look on her face so I take her hand and hold it up and kiss it.

We're silent for a minute, and then she says, "I wish spring would get here."

"Yeah," I say, "it's been a long one." Still holding her hand, I lead her to the kitchen. "You want something to drink? We've got beer and—" I try to think. "And water." I smile and shrug. I should've gotten Kool-Aid or something.

"Oh, just water's fine."

I pull out her chair so she can sit down and I get a glass of water. I have the table all set and the food on the table. We make small talk and eat. She doesn't hardly eat anything, but Tibs's pot roast is really good so I eat a lot. When we're done, I put the plates in the sink and we go into the living room. She sits on the couch to one side and looks up at me, inviting me to sit beside her. It makes me feel weird. Her eyes are wide open and she looks like she's opening herself up, like she's getting naked but she's not. Then, rapid-fire, a series of things shoot through me. First, I have the strong desire to kiss her, but then out of nowhere this anger boils up and I want to hit her.

There's an image in my mind of my mother. My dad has just cleaned her clock, and she's lying sprawled against the wall. Her brown frizzy hair covers her face and sticks to it where she's been crying. She's trying to pull her soft mom body up, scrambling with her arms and pushing with her legs, but there's nothing to grab so she looks like a turtle on its back. Dad is still standing there, and I want to rush in to protect her but I'm afraid he'll turn on me. Then I feel guilty that I can't protect her, and then a wildfire of rage flashes through me. I am royally pissed at her for putting me in this position. How dare she? *She* should be protecting *me*, not the other way around. I shouldn't have to feel this way. It doesn't occur to me to be mad at my dad, though.

I squash the feeling down where it should be, down with all the other stuff from my past. I sit down next to Maggie, still holding her hand.

"I feel like we should be writing," she says and laughs.

"Me, too," I say and laugh too. Suddenly, holding her hand is not enough. I lean in to kiss her. She closes her eyes and tilts her head. When my face is close to hers, I stop for just a second to look at her. She looks like the Virgin Mary, so beautiful, so perfect, so pristine. I want to stop but then I don't. I lean in and close my eyes and feel the softness of her lips on mine. It shoots electricity through me and we're connected, she and I, connected deep and forever in a way I hadn't expected.

I want her. I want her to be mine. I don't want anyone else to have any piece of her. An emotion rises in me that I can't name.

Maggie

When I'm not over at Jackdaw and Tibs's, I'm going to school. In addition to college classes, I've started CNA training. That's Certified Nurse's Assistant. I'm taking a two-month course to see if I like it. Then maybe I'll become an LPN—or maybe even an RN. In the meantime, if I get the certification, I can get a job to help put me through school. My scholarships only cover part of it, and Mom and Dad's money only goes so far. Up till now, the training's mostly been reading books, but we've just started the practicum. It makes me a little nervous. Today I'm at Bethlehem Hospital assisting the nurses, and I'm learning about catheterization, or using a plastic tube to help someone go to the bathroom.

I go from the hall noisy with people into this old guy's room carrying a cath tray. He's in the dark bed nearest the door. A sickly sweet smell hits me. It's a huge arrangement of aging carnations at the bedside. I try to look confident and efficient—like I do this every day, like I know what I'm doing. I've only read about it in our CNA training manual. I place the tray on the rolling stand beside the bed.

"Good morning, Mr. Spanakopa," I say.

Mr. Spanakopa is eighty-nine, and his body is tiny in the hospital bed. His skin is papery and his arms are thin and dotted with brown splotches where they lay above the blankets on either side of his body. He's got a hump on his back. He's been sitting up with the head of his bed lifted watching TV, but he picks up the remote and switches it off when I come in. He smiles and says, "Well, good morning, child."

I smile back. I make small talk as I get the cath and everything ready. But then it's time. "Okay, I'm going to help you go to the bathroom," I say. "Is that okay?"

He fumbles with the covers, trying to throw them back. "Such a bother, being a useless old man," he says. "Can't even pee anymore."

Where's that RN, a Humpty Dumpty of a woman, who's supposed to be showing me how to do this? I glance toward the door, but she's not at the nurses' station. I fidget and then decide to go ahead without her. I can do this. I push back his gown so that I can remove his diaper and he helps me as much as he can. Now I can see his penis. It's small and shriveled nestled there in the hair. It has lots of skin like a shar pei dog— great, he's uncircumcised. There's the musky smell of a man's crotch. I try not to wonder if Mr. Spanakopa was married.

"You'll feel me down here," I say.

This is going to hurt him, I know it is, and I don't want to hurt this old man, but it has to be done in order for him to pee. So here goes. I take the tip of the catheter and try to push it into the urinary meatus. Mr. Spanakopa groans. There's supposed to be some resistance but I manage to slip it in just a little bit before I stop. "You doing okay?"

"Uh, yeah," he says.

I start to push the catheter in and it slides nicely. No urine yet, so I keep pushing. Then it stops and will not move. Mr.

Spanakopa groans and squirms. I stop. "I'm sorry, Mr. Spanakopa."

"It's that damn prostrate, big as a baseball," he says.

I'm not sure what to do. It either has to go in or come out but it's going to have to go in, one way or the other, even if it comes out first. "I'm going to try again," I say. I try to push some more. This time Mr. Spanakopa lets out a screech of a pain. I'm so startled I almost drop everything.

"Woman!" Mr. Spanakopa says in a different voice, ragged, deeper. "You've been wanting to get even with me for years." He looks at me with hate in his eyes. "You just leave him alone."

I don't understand what he's saying. I try to calm him. "Mr. Spanakopa? Mr. Spanakopa. It's me, the CNA? I'm trying to help you go to the bathroom?"

"Dottie, I don't care what you say, if you do that again, I'll wallop you into next week."

What can I do? I can't leave it to go get help.

Just then, in comes a nurse with short dark hair in bright pink scrubs. It's not my RN but someone I haven't seen before. She looks pretty and fresh, her cheeks have a glow, and her name tag says *Bo Hansen*. She leans in and looks over what I'm doing. I get a whiff of Ivory soap.

"Mr. Spanakopa, what have I told you about flirting with the young nurses?" the nurse says.

"What?" Mr. Spanakopa says. He stops looking wildly around the room and focuses on her.

"Are you giving us trouble? He's a trouble-maker, aren't you, Mr. Spanakopa."

"I'm sorry," I say. "I should've waited."

The nurse looks at my name tag and then nods. "You're okay. The only way to learn is to do it." Her voice is soft, but then she says loudly, "Isn't that right, Mr. Spanakopa?"

It's like he's shrunk, so small and helpless in the bed. "I'm sorry, Miss Hansen. I don't know what happened."

"We're just trying to help you go to the bathroom. Remember how this works?" She puts her hand on my shoulder. "Remember? You've got to relax and push a little like you're peeing. Help us out." She looks at me and nods. "Go ahead," she says softly.

I push and it's smooth as silk, slides right in. Urine runs down the tube and begins filling the bag. I take a shaky breath.

After we're done and all cleaned up, the nurse pats Mr. Spanakopa on the shoulder and then takes me down to the coffee shop in the lobby. I order hot chocolate, which she pays for, and she gets a black coffee.

When we sit, I say, "I … Is it always this hard?"

She smiles. "You get used to it. Sometimes it's a matter of getting the patient to relax." She pauses and then says, "But sometimes it's a matter of doing what has to be done. Healing is a painful process."

We're quiet for a minute, and then she says, "And it's not every day you get to touch a strange man's uncircumcised penis," and laughs. That makes me laugh.

"It does get easier, though, right?" I say.

She shakes her head and sighs. It doesn't mean that she disagrees. It just means she's thinking about it. "In some ways it does. It becomes more like any other job. You put in long hours on your feet, but you get to work with some great gals— and some not-so-great doctors. Oh, and some good ones too."

She makes a face. "But you have to separate yourself from the patients. It sounds mean to say it, but you have to depersonalize it a bit or it'll eat you up."

I nod and don't say anything, hoping she'll go on.

She does. "My first night on the job, we had an old lady patient who came in with a serious pain in her stomach. She wasn't making it up—you could tell. Her heart rate was high and her skin was clammy and pale. The doctor ran a series of tests but couldn't find anything wrong with her. He didn't go so far as to say it was all in her head, but you could tell he'd already dismissed her as crazy. Still, he admitted her and kept her overnight for observation. We took care of her, and the pain slowly subsided over the next couple of days, no thanks to the doctor." She pauses and looks out across the lobby. Her cheeks flush as she leans forward and puts her hand on my arm. "You know what made her better? Being cared for by a group of women, plain and simple. And I've seen a lot of cases since. Being a nurse, a caretaker—doing what women do naturally—does more good in these situations than a surgeon's scalpel ever did."

She pulls back her hand and stands up. "Listen to me. You'd think I was running for governor."

Jackdaw

The light is almost gone from the windows. One lamp illuminates the side of Maggie's face. The other side is dark. She's sitting cross-legged on my unmade bed. She's in jeans and one of my old sweatshirts, the computer on her lap. We've been at it for an hour. She frowns. "But he can't take that money," she says.

Outside, the wind shoves against the windows. It's been at it for three days, always there, always pushing. I'm ready for some calm.

"Sure he can," I say. "It's for a higher purpose. He needs it to pay off the sheriff. If he doesn't pay off the sheriff, he'll go to jail, and that'll be that."

"But he's the good guy," she says. She holds her hand outstretched, shaking it, like she's trying to show me something.

"Look, he has to have the money in order to stay free so he can save the ranch. Don't you see that?" I'm trying not to show my irritation, but my jaw's working.

Maggie frowns. "But he's the good guy." She says this quietly, like a child.

I'm writing this story. It's irritating to have to justify yourself when it's your story. I consider dropping the writing for a couple of weeks till I can type myself.

In fact, there's been a couple of things about Maggie that have been bothering me. She doesn't come out and say I'm wrong about things, but she hesitates in the middle of a sentence. We'll be writing, or even just doing something, and she'll start to say something and then stop. On one hand, I want her to tell whatever it is that's bugging her, but on the other maybe she should just keep it to herself. She also has this way of leaving things around. Instead of picking them up or folding them or putting them back in her backpack, she'll just leave them lying there, and when it's time for her to go home, she'll have to hunt everywhere for them.

But it's stupid that this stuff bothers me. Maggie is so cool and so beautiful and so great. She always smells like heaven, even when she's sweaty. I want to spend every waking hour with her, and writing is an excuse to have her here. And I want Maggie here.

But, in the meantime, I need to get Rick, my hero, off the hook. Sure, I don't like having him steal money. That compromises his ideals. But how else is he going to get the money? He has to have it. I don't feel like arguing about it, though.

"Let's forget it for today," I say.

Maggie slowly shakes her head. "But we just got started."

"You don't have to go," I say.

Maggie looks relieved. She smiles. "Okay." She pushes the computer closed, puts it beside her. She tilts her head and puts her chin in her hand. "You know, you could have him borrow the money from her. That would get him out of the jam and give him even more reason to save the ranch. If he's a good man, he'll stand by his commitments."

It might work. But I still don't like it. It feels dirtier than just stealing the money—taking money from a woman. "I don't know …" I say. I hold my hand out to her to help her up. "Want to watch a movie?"

"Sure. What you got?"

"How about *Unforgiven*?"

Tibs

It's the anniversary of Jackdaw's birth, and he and I decide to ditch classes in order to take a road trip to virgin territory, the Big Horn Mountains up in the state of Wyoming. "I hear they have mountains up north," Jackdaw says, quirky half-grin on his face. Maggie can't miss classes, so it's just Jackdaw and I. It's early—March—but the weatherman predicts a warm spell.

We don't have enough funds to stock up on groceries, so we scrounge some beans and rice and then buy a week's supply of burritos from Taco Johns. We arrange our poles and gear in the back of Jackdaw's beat-up Chevy pickup, a jacked-up short box that at one time was red. In bright sunlight, we merge onto the north-bound lane of Interstate 25, weaving through sparse traffic, up through Cheyenne and Casper, through the Hole in the Wall country, to Sheridan. It's hours and hours but it goes by in no time. Then we head west on two-lane blacktop toward the mountains. As we drive, we drink cold Pabst and toss the empties into the truck bed. All around us, the land is covered with plush green carpet. Through the window wafts the smell of warm grass and wet places. We reach the switchbacks that crosscut for miles and miles, erratic Zorro slashes on the steep mountain face. We thread our way up and up, grinding the gears, slowing for the one hundred and sixty-degree corners.

The smell of pines. Powdery mountain soil mounding up one side, air—miles of drop off—on the other. In the vast distance, we perceive the smudgy curved earth as it fades into hazy blue sky.

"So, I've been thinking," Jackdaw says, putting his right hand on the crown of his cowboy hat, lifting it, and sliding it back on, a scooping motion. He's driving with his left hand resting on the top of the wheel, his elbow on the door frame.

My right arm hangs out the open window, and I wave my hand up and down to ride the wind. "When you're thinking, you're stinking," I say, ashamed of the silly rhyme, but the sun shines and we're in the mountains so all's right with the world.

"There's this guy. He seems like a good guy. When he comes to town, he smiles and talks nice, but at home he's a real asshole. But nobody knows it because he's got his ranch and it's doing well."

"Someone you know?"

"No. No." Jackdaw glances at me, his brow wrinkled. "I'm talking about the book, the one I'm writing."

I nod.

"Remember how we said Trollope sucks? Dickens is all right, really knows how to pull you along?" Jackdaw says.

"Yeah, and neither of us read that one—what was it? By the woman."

"Why couldn't we write a Dickens set in the West? A real page-turner. You've read Louis L'Amour?"

"Not really. Hemingway, though."

"Hemingway, sure. But better."

"Fucking better?" I say.

He glances at me and sees the look on my face and shrugs. "With a plot." He waves his hand at me. "I mean, more like Dickens, so it'll be read by everybody, not just English classes."

"Hemingway was read by everybody in his time. He was a reporter."

"Fucking let it go," he says. "What I mean is, we should write something that everybody'll read. We should. You should, too."

I don't reply. I'd already been thinking about this. It occurs to me that all you have to do, really, is sit down and put words on paper. That's it at its most elemental. I do know that there's more to it than that, but it's amazing that *For Whom the Bell Tolls* began just as ink in a pen. Or was it ink in a ribbon? No, in a pen—I believe Hemingway wrote long-hand before he typed. Possibly lead in a pencil? Steinbeck used pencils.

Whatever the case, I have attempted it. It was agony, and the results were disappointing to say the least. No, not disappointing. Abysmal. The worst garbage. But now that Jackdaw's said it, the fact that I tried sounds ridiculous. It feels as if he took a secret that I hadn't even mentioned and he divulged it to a third party. He stole it and then ruined it. That sucks. To top it off, he's been busy tapping away at the keys.

He glances over at me and laughs. "Oh, Grandma, don't go there. The Tibs Brood gets a little old." He tips the beer can and sucks down the dregs and tosses it into the back. "Beer me," he says.

I reach down to the floorboards and pop the top on the cooler and submerge my hand in the water, ice bumping me like frigid marbles. I fish one out and pull the top with a *click-*

psshh. It foams up and over and I jerk myself up and away from the seat as foam spills between my legs and runs down to my crotch.

"All right," I say and hand him the beer with my left, swiping at the seat with my right. "What about this man, an archaeologist? He's an Indiana Jones character, only not so close to a cartoon. His job brings him to the Middle East, say Egypt, and he makes a major discovery. He excavates a pharaoh's tomb or maybe a temple, something that has been secret for centuries. Yes, and maybe there is a sect that still practices there today. Secret rites, secret entrances."

"Yeah, yeah," Jackdaw says.

"Maybe one of his employees, a translator maybe or a liaison, is part of the sect."

"And then the liaison kidnaps the archaeologist and holds him hostage," Jackdaw says.

"Or, or, there's a girl, the liaison's sister maybe, and she and the archaeologist are attracted romantically, but this dig is so important to the archaeologist he can't choose the girl over the dig. It's the girl's desire, but he can't. He's torn."

Jackdaw nods.

"I don't know, though," I say. "I don't want it to be too, too ..." I can't think of the word. I don't want to imitate Dickens. I want it to approach real life, represent two people in a room and all their desires and tensions and intentions.

"Damn, Tibs," he says, "you ought to write some of this shit down."

"Yes, I should."

"No, really, you should. It's like your dad when he was in Egypt, only more exciting."

I shrug.

"You're a great man, Tibs," he says. He really means it.

We continue driving. We reach national forest on the top of the mountain. There are remnant patches of snow under the pine stands on the lee sides of hills and the breeze through the windows has a chill but the sun blazes and is warm through the windshield. The highway winds among forests of deep green pine and open parks of bright green grass ablaze with flowers. Hillsides abound with purple lupine and clumps of orange Indian paintbrush. The borrow ditch is awash with yellow clover, and a few white-purple pasque flowers line the pavement. There are also tiny hot pink shooting stars, singularly and in pairs.

After a period of time, we pull off the blacktop onto a gravel road, which morphs into a humpy two-track. We follow it up a valley that contains a stream and eventually find a camping spot, a fire-ring under the pines on a short faint side road. There's no other campers, no cars. We leave all our gear in the truck and grab our fishing poles and walk up the creek. It's choked with willows at the mouth, so it's tough going at first. Once we push past the impediment, though, it's prime fish habitat, rapids interspersed with deep pools and overhangs, rocks, and brush. Perfect. We fish the lower pools and catch three fingerlings and a nice-sized cutthroat.

Dark descends by the time we push back into camp. With freezing fingers, we clean the fish by feel as the light dies. We gather a few twigs and spark a fire but eat cold burritos washed down with ice-cold Pabst. We don't bother pitching the cheap K-Mart tent—we just throw our sleeping bags out under the stars. There's the snapping of the dying fire and the murmur of the wind in the trees and the tinkling of the creek. The pungence of smoke and pines and mud. The air's clear and cold on my cheeks, but I lie there warm and snug in my sleeping bag and watch the satellites and meteors until my eyes close.

The next day, we're up in the early chill hours, goose-bumped as we slip on cold jeans and tuck our hands into our armpits. Thin patches of ice line the creek. Jackdaw kindles a campfire while I dice onions for the fish, encase them in tinfoil, and place them on the fire. Jackdaw makes coffee. Then we pitch the tent as the food cooks. When it's done, the fire warms us as we eat the steaming fish with our fingers, extracting the bones, and drink coffee so strong it makes your teeth clench.

We decide to hike up and fish down. It's midmorning by the time we reach a constriction—where the valley turns into a canyon that cuts in so close to the stream that you can't go any farther without wading. Here we turn around and start fishing our way back. I take a hole and Jackdaw takes the next, leapfrogging. We are fly-fishing, and Renegades work well for me. I finesse two big rainbows, and Jackdaw catches a monster cutthroat.

It's warm when we make it back to camp. I lay basking in the sun for a nap, while Jackdaw spends the afternoon fashioning a willow case with handles, two light snowshoes stuck together, to roast the fish over the open fire. The aroma wakes me. The fishes' skins are crispy brown, and the meat is orange-white and feather-flakes off the bone. We eat them with crunchy cattail roots like celery stalks that I harvest from the stream.

The next day we fish again, this time up a feeder stream. It's one of those unseasonable days that makes you realize that summer is approaching. By midday the temperature rises. We tie our jackets around our waists, and we've begun to sweat. Climbing along a ridge, we descend through bushes onto a flat-topped boulder jutting from the hill that overlooks a deep pool.

"Downright hot," Jackdaw says, propping his rod against the bushes.

"Hotter than Marilyn Monroe in a bikini," I say.

"Daisy Duke."

"Pamela Anderson."

"Pamela Anderson package check," Jackdaw says and smiles. We both grab our crotches.

I crouch down and look over the edge to the pool below. The water pours over a half-submerged log just upstream, below there's a good rapid, and right below me a deep pool. The sandy bottom disappears into shadow under the rock. "Perfect," I whisper. "I bet there's a big one right there under that edge. And I believe it's my hole." I let the gloat come through my voice. I unhook my fly from the cork handle and start to strip line.

I'm just about to cast, standing with my pole raised high, when Jackdaw streaks by me and over the edge of the boulder. He's shucked his clothes and his skin is as white as creek gravel. "Not if I get to it first," he yells as he goes over the edge. *Sploosh!* He enters the water feet first. The water is not that deep so he stands and his head and shoulders are above the water. He staggers to the shallows, water pouring off him, and he sucks lungfuls of air and then little gulps, his body reacting violently to the cold water.

"Shit! Damn cold! And I fucking hit bottom," he says. He stands in the shallows. He looks at me and yells, "Get your ass down here." It echoes off the canyon walls above us.

I resist. It's a fair jump and the water is obviously damn cold, but the air is hot and Jackdaw stands there and the sun and the cottonwoods glow in green light. The fish are gone now, anyway, so what the hell—I toss my pole back on the rock, struggle out of my clothes, and jump. The cold hits me and my lungs seize up. I push the bottom with my feet, stand, and stagger, my arms held up like chicken wings. I'm nothing but sensation. I'm cut in half—waist down the water's cold pressure and my legs in goose bumps. My nads suck up into my stomach. My top half feels the warmth of the sun and the air like a soft blanket caressing my skin. I open my eyes and wade to the shallows where Jackdaw stands. I totter as I step on a rock and he reaches out and playfully pushes me backwards. I'm tipping, but then Jackdaw relents and pulls me back to center.

From the creek, the rock is insurmountable, and the bushes are so thick along the bank that there's no place to crawl through to get back to our clothes. We limp up the creek for quite a distance, the sun warming our shoulders, before we find an overgrown winding game trail that leads up the side of the ridge. We scramble, pulling ourselves up with the bushes scratching at our skin, and thread our way back to the top of the boulder. Then we spread out our clothes and lie down on them and let the sun shine upon us.

I lay face down and close my eyes and feel the cloth of my shirt against my chest and where my thigh touches the roughness of the rock and its warmth and the even pressure of the sun and every once in a while a breeze blows and the hairs on my body prickle. I can hear Jackdaw whittling a piece of wood.

We don't talk. We just be. The creek tinkles; time slips by.

When I sit up, Jackdaw's carved the perfect bare butt. He places it on the lip of the rock and flips his knife closed. "Bare-Ass Rock," he says.

"Tibs's Bare-Ass Rock," I say. "I *am* the model."

"Naw. Too skinny."

I laugh. We put on our clothes and fish our way back to camp.

We fish and laze about for three more days before we retrace our route south. As we're leaving, Jackdaw says, "This place is fucked up."

"Yeah," I say. "Fucked."

I wish my skills would allow me to describe this feeling. If I could, I guess then I could label myself a writer. Hemingway could do it. I can't. Being there with Jackdaw is both the most exciting yet the most comfortable feeling, like it all holds so much possibility you want to offer your barbaric yawp to the world. Like you felt in your dad's arms when you were a kid and he tossed you up and caught you, excited and free but safe at the same time.

Maggie

Jackdaw's just picked me up for a Saturday date, and we stand next to his truck outside my house.

"Here, turn around," Jackdaw says. "I've got a surprise for you." He places his hands on my shoulders and turns me so that my back is toward him. I feel his warm palms and smell his cologne—something musky, not too strong. It smells really good.

I am surprised as he flips a black silk scarf over my eyes. "What—" I say.

"Shshshshsh," he says as he ties it.

I can't see anything. The scarf covers the upper half of my face and falls just over the tip of my nose. It's tied tightly—not so tight I'll get a headache but tight enough I'll have a hard time getting it off.

I hear him open the truck door with a *scrape*, followed by the *clunk* of the latch as he releases it. He scoops me up into his arms and cradles me like a baby. My arms are pinned to my sides, but I feel safe. He puts me into the truck, tipping me forward so I don't bang my head, and then shuts the door with a strong *thunk*. Half a minute and he gets in his side and starts the engine and drives. I scoot across the seat to be closer to him.

We reach the blacktop at the end of my long bumpy drive, and instead of taking a left toward town, he turns right up the canyon toward the mountains. There's the *whiz* of the tires on blacktop and the pulling right and left as the truck rounds the curves.

"Where are we going?" I ask.

"Uh-uh," he says in a sing-song voice.

Trying to fill the silence, I say, "Did your dad really make you run behind the car?"

He doesn't say anything, and then he says, "Ah, you missed it. There was a deer just jumped across the road."

"Not either. You would've slowed down."

He laughs. "You're right. It was actually a llama."

"A what? A llama?"

"Yeah, there's this sheep rancher that runs them with his herd. It must've gotten out. It's one of those white ones with the big brown splotches and black ears."

I've seen this llama, but I say, "Huh-uh. You are so lying."

"You just don't know, do you?" he says, the humor in his voice.

Smiling, I turn toward his voice. "Do you always blindfold your dates before you kidnap them?"

"Only the likely wenches." He takes my left hand that's resting in my lap and interlaces his fingers with mine. We ride in silence for a while. Then he withdraws his hand, downshifts, and pulls off the blacktop. The truck moves up and down and bumps—we must've pulled onto a two-track. The grade gets steeper and steeper, until Jackdaw says, "Hold on." He bumps my knee as he downshifts, and I'm pushed back against the backrest as we hump, bump, and grind our way up a steep incline. On a really steep part, I can hear the rasp of the tires as they slip on the dirt and grind against the ground, and I can feel the truck slide and balk. My heart beats faster.

But then we reach the top, the two-track levels, and we come to a halt. With a ratcheting sound, Jackdaw pushes in the emergency brake. He gets out his side, comes around, and opens my door. Wind gusts in, and I hear the rustle of papers on the floorboards. I try to pull the scarf from my eyes but he takes my hands in his. "Not yet," he whispers in my ear. He helps me out of the truck and from behind guides me across uneven rocky ground, bracing me against the current of air. I hear the eerie twang of wind through powerlines, and it feels like I'm floating as my body senses a vast space around me.

Jackdaw unties the scarf, yanking loose some strands of my hair tied into the knot. He pulls the cloth away. My first impression is that I'm standing on air, hundreds of feet above the ground. In front of me is a vast openness, and in the far distance the earth not so much ends as fades into the haze. Closer in are fields and roads and towns. The sun is low behind us and vast shadows splay out across the foothills below. I am standing at the very edge of a cliff, my toes inches away from open air. I involuntarily take a step backwards into Jackdaw's body. He wraps his arms around me, and I feel both safe and scared out of my wits. He doesn't move back from the edge, though.

"It gives you perspective," Jackdaw says.

"I'm, I," I say, pressing back against him, trying to find words. Maybe I'm the one who's being a scaredy cat. Kids do crazy stuff all the time, things I think are dangerous. Jackdaw wants me to be brave—Doesn't he? Is that it?—and I want to be brave for Jackdaw. I take a deep breath and try not to push back too hard.

"I used to come here when I was in high school. When things were particularly bad," he says.

"Because you can see so much?"

"Yeah, that and …"

I glance down at the drop. "And?"

"I don't know. It could get pretty bad. Family pretty much sucks."

"Can we?" I say and pull his arms from around me. I want to please him, but this is scaring me to death. I lead him over to a boulder and sit down, and the rock under my butt is solid, good. "Sit?" I say, trying to keep the high kid-like note out of my voice.

He glances back over his shoulder and then eases himself down beside me.

I take his left hand in both of mine. "I don't think that's true," I say. "Your family might not've been, well, the best. But, generally, for most people, family is what life's about. Family is the reason we're here. I lost my mom and dad when I was sixteen, and what I wouldn't give to have them back again, you know? I mean, what do you have if you don't have family?" I glance at his face but can't read the expression.

"A life," he says with emphasis.

He had family but then didn't want them? What did his family do that made him like this? I've been wanting my mom and dad for so long that it's hard to think of something so bad that you wouldn't want them at all. It makes me sad and feel really sorry for Jackdaw. I want to fix it, whatever it is.

"I'm sorry," I say and pull his hand up to my chest and hold it close. "I'm so sorry."

He lets me hold his hand as he stares out over the cliff.

"That would never happen," I say, "with Tibs and I. I mean if you and I were …" I feel the blood rising in my face. I realize what I'm saying.

"Don't make promises you don't know anything about," Jackdaw says. His voice is deep as he says this, and he pulls his hand out of mine. There's silence.

But then Jackdaw turns to me, takes my hand again, tilts his head, and says in a bright voice, "Cause I'm going to be the rock star of novelists, so you'll have to be my groupie." He stands and pulls me up. "Think you can handle it?"

I laugh with relief and say, "Does that mean I need to get a tattoo?"

"Only if it involves a certain black bird."

We get into the truck and carefully turn and then slide our way back down the rutted two-track. Right before we pull onto the blacktop, he answers a text from Tibs, and we drive home as it gets dark. It's fully dark as we turn off the highway, but then the road to my house is lined with small dim lights, the kind people put along their driveways. It wasn't before. Jackdaw pulls over and stops. We get out, and there's something in the darkness. I hear the *pb-pb-pb* blowing of a horse and see its shape in the darkness.

"You thought the surprise was over," he says as he leads me over to it.

A smaller shape detaches from the horse, and a voice says, "Your carriage awaits." A flashlight flicks on and points to the step, and Jackdaw helps me in and then follows. The carriage slants to one side as the driver climbs into the front seat. He urges the horse forward.

"Wow," is all I can say.

"What can I say," Jackdaw says. "I'm a romantic."

We drive up to the stone porch of my house, and the driver gets down to help us out. By the yard light, I can see the driver is a guy about our age in a tuxedo coat and levis and boots.

"Thanks, man," Jackdaw says as we walk up the steps.

"No problem," the guy says. "You Casanova, you."

The door opens as we cross the porch, and there's Tibs with a grin on his face. "Gentleman, madame," he says with a bow.

"What?" I say, looking at Jackdaw.

All the lights are out in the house, but the place is filled with candles. The couch and chairs have been pushed back, and kitchen table has been moved into the living room. There's a fire in the fireplace and a bouquet of roses on the table. Jackdaw makes a big deal about bowing and pulling out my chair as I sit, and Tibs serves us dinner. He and Jackdaw joke a lot about servants these days, you just can't find a good one. There's another guy in the kitchen cooking, a friend from school, Jackdaw says. We eat steak and crab legs and rice pilaf and drink red wine. We have a key lime cheesecake for dessert. The guy who cooked goes home, and then Tibs goes home, giving Jackdaw a high five. Then Jackdaw and I sit on the couch in front of the fire, me snuggled into his arms. Jackdaw's like a purring cat, very happy and lovey.

CJ

I hear Peter walk in the door. I got off work earlier and came over to his place. "Hey, I'm home," he says as he closes the door. He comes down the hall and into the living room, where I'm laid out on the couch drinking sour tom collins and watching bad sitcom TV. I've made him a gin and tonic, which sits sweating in its short tumbler on a coaster. He leans down to put the styrofoam containers of teriyaki chicken and yakidori on the coffee table. They squeak as he lets them go. He stands, shrugs out of his coat, and tosses it onto one of the chairs.

The stench of the bar drifts off him. It's smoke and beer and people odor all swirled together, with an undercurrent of the aged sweat like a locker room. You can't smell it on yourself when you come home, but the next morning, you can't stand to be in the same room with last night's clothes.

Peter scoops up his gin and tonic and flops down beside me on the couch. "Thanks, C," he says. He takes a long pull on his drink.

"Welcome," I say and raise my glass. "You got some catching up to do."

"You so sure?" he says and fakes a drunk head bob and then smiles. He takes another drink. We ignore the food. After a minute he says, "You want to?"

"Sure," I say. I roll toward him and we start kissing. His breath smells of gin and coffee. We put our tongues in each other's mouths. My nose bumps his, and then I spill my drink. "Shit," I say and pull away. "Sorry."

He shrugs and stands up. "Another collins? Vodka?"

"We're out. I'll have a Tom."

He goes to the bar. "Not a Peter?"

"Well, I'll have one of them too. Let's make it a threesome," I say, trying to sound less drunk and more flirty.

"I was thinking more along the lines of two of the three being female," Peter says, filling our glasses. "Peters are like herd stallions, two's too many."

"Peters are definitely like stallions. Peter—I mean *Hoss*." I finish off my first drink and set the empty on the coffee table. He walks back over and hands me another.

"Where were we?" he says as he sits back down.

I take a drink of my collins, and he takes a drink of his gin and tonic. I set my drink on the coffee table next to the empty, and he sets his next to mine. I lean over and kiss him, and he kisses me back. He rubs my breasts, being careful with the nipples because he knows they're kind of sensitive. I reach down and rub his crotch aggressively, like he likes.

"Fuck me," I say, since he mentioned the other day he thought we should try some dirty talk. "Oh, yes, that's right." I lay back and he pulls off my pants.

"Where are those rubbers?" he asks, fumbling with his zipper.

"Don't need them," I say.

"Don't need them?" He glances up at me as he totters on one leg.

"Oh, I went on the pill," I say and keep my eyes wide and on his face.

"When did this happen?"

"Oh, I've been thinking about it." Arching my body sideways, I reach over and take a drink and then arch back to set the glass back on the table.

He finishes pulling off his pants and then says, "Anything I should know?"

For a split second, I think, I should tell him. It's way past where we are in this relationship, but maybe this relationship needs a push.

Then I think, *naw.*

"Anything you should know?" I say. "Like I'm fucking One-ball Paul?" I lift one corner of my mouth.

"Yeah, something like that." He lays down on top of me.

"Yep, I have a honey on the side that I see, say, the fifteen minutes every week that we aren't together."

He tilts his head and raises his eyebrows.

I shrug. "I get tired of fumbling for rubbers," I say and pull him toward me.

I arch my pelvis, and he enters me. I fuck him, and he fucks me, and there we are. Something else to check off the list.

Who knows, maybe the doctor's wrong.

Maggie

"There was one," I say, adjusting my head on Jackdaw's warm chest and tucking the quilt over my exposed shoulder. "Over toward the mountains." Jackdaw's arms wrap around my body. We lay out in my backyard watching for shooting stars.

It's been warmer, but the nights are still cold. Things are thawing, though. You can sense the sap rising in the trees and the animals getting restless. The birds warble loudly and continuously in the morning. You see more people outside, cleaning up their yards and eyeing the flower beds.

"That was not," Jackdaw says, his voice rumbling through his chest and into my ear. "That's a satellite."

"No," I say, rising a little and pointing. "The satellite's to the south. The shooting star was farther north."

"You didn't see a shooting star."

"Yes I did, and I made a wish on it," I say and then regret saying it because then he's got to ask.

"What'd you wish?"

"I want it to come true," I say.

"That's an old wives' tale," Jackdaw says, "that it won't come true. You can tell me."

I laugh. "The whole thing's an old wives' tale."

"Still, you can tell me."

I don't say anything and he lets it drop.

What I wished was for time to stop. I know it sounds silly, but this moment is so perfect, just him and me and the warmth and the stars. I know there will be good times in the future, but I also know there will be bad times, maybe really bad times, and right here and right now everything is perfect. It feels so good to be wrapped in quilts and to feel the heat of Jackdaw's body tendril through me. The bones in his shoulder and chest are against my ear and my hand presses against his stomach, which is soft to the touch but hard and ripply underneath.

I remember when he rode the bull, how he swept off his hat and opened his belly to the crowd, how exposed he seemed, how he was the center of everyone's attention. I want him. He's not like the other guys I've dated. He's got this place deep inside him that I can't touch. I want to be in that place, to fill that place.

"My father hates the stars," Jackdaw says, his voice getting quieter. "He says they remind him of how cold the world is. How most everything doesn't mean shit."

"Mmm," I say. Something about the combination of not being able to see him, only hear him, smell him, feel his warmth, drives me crazy. I want to have sex, now.

I lift my head and kiss Jackdaw's mouth. I want to eat his lips, and I put my tongue deep in his mouth and then pull it out, then flick-tickle his lips and tongue with my tongue. I start rubbing his chest and his nipples. I feel my wanting rise within me like some animal rushing up a dark burrow toward the surface. It's different this time than it was before, with other guys. I've always wanted to make them happy, so I do my best to act passionate. Sure, they've been sexy—and I've felt it some—but this time the feeling grabs me and there's no acting. I want it, I want him now, screw the condoms.

But Jackdaw turns his head and pushes me away. I sit up, unsure, trying to see his face in the dark. He puts his hands on my shoulders and lays me back where I was, my head on his shoulder, and he kisses the top of my head. It's like I'm his sister all of a sudden.

I lay still for a minute, the need oozing inside me. I don't understand. Guys just don't say no to sex, not ever. They just don't. It's like I've discovered a new animal. But his pushing me away makes me want him more, and I feel myself go liquid with it.

I try to kiss him again, but I feel him shake his head. "Mellow out," he says. "We got time, the rest of our lives maybe."

"But I want you."

"I want you too. Don't think that I don't."

"Then …" I lick his ear.

He jerks his head away. "We've got this perfect thing, and it's going so well, just how it ought to be."

"Ought to be?"

"You're … We're …" He doesn't finish the thought.

I'm frustrated and so I decide that's it. Let's see if he's really made of stone. I settle back against his shoulder but this time I rest my head so that my breath caresses his ear. He relaxes again.

"I love you," I say softly. "I love you so much." I want him so badly.

He doesn't say anything.

I move and pretend like I'm getting comfortable, but I put my hand on his upper thigh and just let it rest, not moving it at all. After a minute, he squirms a little so that my hand moves. He means to have it slip off, but instead I drop it to the inside of his thigh right next to his groin. He squirms again, so I start kissing him. At first, he doesn't kiss me back, but then he does slowly and then more firmly and then we're kissing hard. We kiss and rub bodies and nibble necks and chests. Soon we're pulling off clothes and I'm nothing but sensation. He enters me with a hard thrust. Then he starts thrusting harder and harder, all gentleness gone. It sends me up and over and over in waves, and I'm tumbling and writhing and I've never had an orgasm like this in my life. I'm him and he's me and we're this other creature made of fireworks and nerve endings.

After it's over, I think, he's the one. He's going to be my life for the rest of my life.

We settle back, both breathing hard. But he doesn't relax. He just lays there, stiff. I curl next to his body, willing him to let go. I softly rub the skin of his arms. He's still tense, unmoving.

"Oh, babe," I say.

He doesn't say anything, just lays there. But he doesn't move away. He's still there, the warmth of his body all around me.

I fall asleep and dream about my mother. She's wearing khaki capri pants and a turquoise sleeveless shirt and her brown hair is tied back with a long white scarf in that old style with the ends fluttering down her back. Mom was always a little heavy, but this outfit looks really good on her. I don't remember ever seeing her wear it, but it's like we're in a movie and she's the star. She's eating sunflower seeds and putting the shells in a little pile between us. She offers me some, so I take them and put them in my mouth. I eat them for a while but there never seems to be less of them in my mouth. I try to spit them out but no matter how hard I try I can't get them out of my mouth. I try to hide it from Mom, but she puts her hand on the side of my cheek and I can feel how warm it is and I know that everything is all right. She says the word, "Jes." I don't know what it means.

I wake up. It's dark except for the sliver of a moon just above the mountains. Jackdaw snores just a little as he sleeps beside me. And then I know that I'm pregnant. You may not credit it but I just wake up and I know it as if an angel whispered in my ear.

CJ

Big Brenda—a regular from the bar, an acquaintance, kind of a friend, you know how it is—she's putting on a garage sale because her mom passed away. I offer to help because, like I said, I see her every day and she's kind of a friend.

We've had a good morning. Saturday turned out to have good weather, and we're one of the first yard sales of the season. A lot of people stop by.

"How much should I tell them you want for this, Brenda?" I ask, holding up a pastel porcelain figurine of a blonde girl in a swishing blue gown. Her mom had shelves of this kind of stuff that we're selling.

"I always hated that thing," Brenda says. "Tell them I'll pay them to take it away." She laughs but she isn't smiling.

"Fifty cents, then?"

She nods.

I go back to the customer and get eight fifty for it.

It's then I spot Maggie and that idiot she's been seeing. They're standing by the side of the house in the shade where the pictures are propped up against the siding. Maggie and the guy are leaning together, heads bent, and she has a framed picture in her hands.

"It's just a motel print," Jackdaw says.

"But I love it," Maggie says. "The expression on the woman's face. It's love and grief and ..."

"Hey, kids," I say as I walk up.

"CJ!" Maggie says. "Just who I wanted to see today." She lets the picture hang at her side as she gives me a one-armed hug.

Jackdaw just stands there with his arms crossed.

"Look at this," Maggie says. She holds up the picture. It's of a man and a woman standing on the open prairie. They're pioneers or something because he's in suspenders and has a beard and she's got on a white bonnet and a long dress. Their heads are bowed. The man is leaning on a shovel, and the woman has her hands held close to her chest like they'll fly away. She might be praying. In front of them is a small pile of dirt. That's when I notice the small cross. It's the grave of a child.

"Oh! I'm sorry," Maggie says, holding the print to her chest, her eyes on my face. She's remembered I can't have kids.

I shake my head a couple of quick jerks, saying *that's okay*. She didn't mean anything by it. "You want it?" I ask.

"Yeah, I'm going to get it."

"Well, you can have it for free. The owner"—I nod over toward Brenda—"would give it all away if she thought her mother wouldn't haunt her for it."

"The tag says three dollars," Jackdaw says.

"That's okay," I say, not looking at him.

"I'll buy it," Jackdaw says and pulls it from Maggie's arms. "I'll get it."

I reach across Maggie and take it away from him with one hand. "No. I said it's no problem. She can just have it."

He grabs the frame again, pushing Maggie aside. I have one corner and he has the other. "Listen. I said I'd get it."

The frame is cheap, and I can feel it pulling from the print. But I'll be damned if that cheapskate asshole of a boyfriend is going to stroke his own ego with it. "Let the fuck go," I say.

We're staring at each other, each holding a corner of the print. It's pulling apart between us, but neither of us will let go. He doesn't say anything but you can see that he'd hit me and just take the damn thing if Maggie wasn't here. Like a dog in a yard it thinks it owns, it'll bite you soon as look at you.

Then I glance at Maggie. Her eyes are on my face and her eyebrows are up. She's saying, *please, just let him buy it for me*. She's choosing his side. Of course. She's in love. I think, no, I'm not going to let this bastard win, but then I think, it's not about him. It's about Maggie, and I let go. Fucking love.

Then I tilt my head and look at Jackdaw and say, "It's mislabeled. It's really ten bucks."

Just cause I know he'll have to pay it.

Tibs

It's evening, and Jackdaw, Maggie, and I watch the movie *Dogma*. Quite a complex movie, but hilarious also. Do you remember the part about the Buddy Christ? A statue of Christ with a comic-book grin on his face and two gargantuan thumbs-up. George Carlin as Reverend Glick. Hilarious. Maggie isn't enjoying it—she crosses her arms and tucks in her chin—but Jackdaw loves it. He's drawn to the two avenging angels played by Matt Damon and Ben Affleck. We've finished off two bowls of popcorn, which Maggie produced from the stove top, rather than microwave, because Jackdaw prefers it that way.

The sun has set. It's dark outside, and inside the house we haven't bothered to turn on the lamps. There's just the illumination from the TV. Jackdaw and Maggie nestle on the couch, and I'm flopped on the red beanbag on the floor. Jackdaw sits with his back against the backrest, and Maggie's on her back with her head in his lap. At one point during the show, I glance over at them. It's hard to sense things in the flickering light as my eyes adjust from the glare of the TV to the dark of the room, but then I see Maggie looking up at Jackdaw's face while he watches TV. There's an expression on her face—I don't know if I can describe it. It's pure worship, like Jackdaw is her whole world, like he's cocaine or amphetamine or something similar, and Maggie tries to draw him in with her gaze.

When the movie credits roll, Jackdaw says, "Ah, a feel-good ending. Not in my movie. In my movie, the two avenging angels would've won." He's in an odd mood, restless, as if he's looking for something.

Maggie taps his chest with her fingers. "No you wouldn't," she says.

"Yes I would. More realistic that way."

Maggie shakes her head. "You're saying taking everyone out with machine guns is more realistic than believing in a kind and good God?"

"Heck yeah," he says. "Help me out here, Tibs ol' boy."

"Hey," I say, "if you think I'm getting in the middle of this one, you're mistaken."

"So you think having faith in this kind God is where it's at?" Jackdaw says.

Maggie pushes herself up and then shrugs.

"What are you, two years old?" Jackdaw says. "You think faith is where it's at?"

Maggie shrugs again.

"Do you have faith in me?" he says.

Maggie doesn't hesitate: "Yes."

The television screen has returned to the DVD's main menu. The same quirky music repeats in an infinite loop, and the same series of lights and colors flash into the room.

"If you have faith in me, lay down on the floor and close your eyes." Maggie glances at me. I'm sure she can't see it, but I raise my eyebrows. I'm not sure either. Here is my best friend and here is my sister; I'm not getting in the middle of it. So she lays down on the floor.

Jackdaw walks to the kitchen and returns with a knife. It's only a paring knife, but it's sharp.

I reach over and turn on the lamp.

"Ok, Maggie," Jackdaw says. "You can open your eyes."

Maggie opens them and blinks and then stiffens, but she remains still.

"If you have faith in me, lie really still and don't move a muscle."

Slowly she nods.

He stands over her with one foot on either side of her waist and aims the knife toward the floor. Then, casually, with the smallest of motions, he lets it drop. *Thunk!* It lands between Maggie's shoulder and her ear and sticks into the wood. Maggie hasn't moved, but you can see relief flood her face.

If I had been the one on the floor, I would have found some way out of it. Seriously, I would not be there in the first place. There's no way I'd let anyone drop knives at me, even if he is my best friend. But imagine the strength, the courage, the love, the trust it takes just to lay there. To just let it happen and not move. I'm telling you.

Jackdaw

I'm so glad to be writing again—writing again alone. Maggie, well, I couldn't really write with her. It's a wonder I wrote anything at all. I'd've done better to hunt and peck. She was always there, like those annoying good angels sitting on your shoulder. She was always pulling the story this way and that, making it do things it shouldn't. She tried to make it this sappy sweet thing—shit, really—instead of what it is. Maggie's like that, always pushing. You think she's one thing, so sweet and innocent, pure as the driven snow. She really has this look, this glow about her. But the wool's over your eyes—she's really not so pure. I would know.

But I think the story's good. Really good, I think. It'll grab people's imagination. I can picture myself, up on a podium, all these people in the audience wanting to hear what I have to say. The women wanting to have me and the men wanting to be me. I'll drawl a little bit as I talk, break out the cowboy hat, maybe. Maybe I'll do something like Chuck Palahniuk does—have my own club. They'd come to my readings and we'd have some sort of way of identifying ourselves. Instead of fistfighting, we'll do things like gunfights or I guess we could just do fighting. I'd make them do this stupid shit before they could join, too, and I'd have my own groupies.

Rick O'Shea is the title of the novel and name of the hero. Well, antihero, really. In the end, he's the one who's behind it all. He won't just rape the girl and steal the ranch, he'll kill men for pleasure. He's a sociopath. He's psycho charismatic crazy. As I'm writing it, I just keep thinking, I'm not writing it, he is. They all think he's the good guy, he's the white hat, he's Christ on a cracker, but he's not. He's shamming.

In real life, people don't want to believe that someone can do things like that. That fathers can beat their sons and wives and make them work when they're so sick they're seeing things and lock them in the granary for days at a time with no food and little water. When a guy does bad things, people want to believe it's because it's beyond his control. He had to do it or face something worse. What people don't want to admit is that some guys are just bad. They like doing rotten things, and they get a lot out of it. A wife beater doesn't feel bad about beating his wife. He may say he does but he doesn't. Don't be fooled. And especially when people know someone, they don't want to think bad about him. They tell themselves, he couldn't possibly have murdered anyone—he looks like my Uncle Fred and good ol' Fred would never do something like that. Well, what does a murderer look like? I'm here to tell you, he looks like your Uncle Fred and like your Aunt Tillie. Some people are just monsters. They can't be rehabilitated because they don't have an illness. That's just the way they are. They desire little boys, or they desire killing girls, or they desire beating their wives. They don't see it as a bad thing. It's just the way they are.

Art's supposed to help. Something about the creative act gets all the bad gunky out. What if that's not true? What if it's just another way to make the straights feel better about themselves? If it's true that people are the way they are, that psychopaths are the way they are because they want to be, then why would putting a few paints on a canvas change that? Sure, art reflects the inner monster. Maybe that's why I'm writing *Rick O'Shea*. Maybe I do take after my old man.

Maybe, but I don't think so. I'm not my old man—I'm not. I do the right thing. There are basic standards in this world, and I am going to go above them, even though some people don't. Decency. Honesty. Integrity. Doing the right thing, like I said. I can choose not to be like my dad. This is America, for Christ's sake. The American Dream. Anybody can make good.

Maggie

Tibs asks if I want to go on a double-date. It's Jackdaw and I and Tibs and this girl named Jenny. We decide to go into Denver on a Saturday and catch a preseason baseball game. Jackdaw's been a little weird lately, so I think, just the thing. He doesn't seem to want to spend as much time with me. When we sit on the couch, he doesn't like me to sit close. He says it makes him too hot. He's still sweet and kind, though. I think it's all because he's working on this novel. The main character is kind of a meany, and it gets him down. A baseball game will be good. Get away, have a little fun, maybe he'll relax.

We stop at Jenny's house to pick her up at about nine in the morning. We're in Tibs's Ford Fiesta, Tibs driving and Jackdaw and me in the back. Jenny comes out. I've seen her before on campus—she's a quiet girl who looks either granola or religious. She has pale skin and brown calf eyes and shoulder-length dark hair with bangs. She never wears makeup and is a little heavy but pretty anyway. Today, though, she has on some makeup. I feel sorry for her because it looks like she doesn't know how to put it on. Her eye shadow is a little too seventies blue and her cheeks are a bar of pink. She's wearing a low-cut blouse, a pair of really tight jeans, and tall clunky sandals. She's trying really hard. It makes my heart hurt just a little.

When she gets into the car, she said, "Hi, Tibs," in a breathy way that's full of meaning.

"Hey, Jenny," Tibs says.

She smiles at Jackdaw and me.

"Hi. I'm Maggie, Tibs's sister," I say. "This is Jackdaw."

"I know you," she says, looking at Jackdaw. "I saw you at a poetry slam in the Union. You did that improv piece about coffee and cigarettes. Something about coffee and cigarettes, that's as good as it gets."

"Mmmm," Jackdaw says.

Jackdaw's arm's been out of the sling for a while. He types by himself now, and I miss our sessions. I really feel like I contributed something to what he was working on. But now we hang out when he's not writing.

Funny thing. He's quit wearing cowboy clothes altogether. Just one day, he started wearing other things. Now he tends to wear a lot of black. Black t-shirts and even a black turtleneck, which he looks really good in. His black-framed glasses—he puts them on during the day now. Black Chuckie Taylor high tops. He's started growing a soul patch. He's thinking about getting his ear pierced. Really, I'm relieved that he doesn't ride bulls anymore—that was scary—but it's a little weird. He seemed like he loved it. Well, maybe not loved it but like he had to do it, like in order to be a man he had to be a bull rider. But now that's all gone, like the flip of a switch.

"I think I had a class with you," I say to Jenny. "What was it?"

"I don't know," she says, looking at me and then at Tibs. "You two're brother and sister?"

"Yeah," I say.

"You don't look much alike."

"What with the penis and all," Jackdaw says.

Jenny looks puzzled a minute and then laughs. "Oh, I get it."

I don't think Jenny is dumb. I just think she really likes Tibs and she really wants him to like her and she's a little socially awkward. She's just trying to fit in, like the rest of us.

We head off to Denver. Puffy clouds dot the sky, but the sun shines. It should be a nice day, and maybe a cloud or two will give us some shade. Over the seat, Tibs and Jackdaw start talking about graduating and what they'll do. I try to get Jackdaw to hold my hand. His hand either lays like a dead fish, or he forgets and pulls it away to gesture while he talks. I try once or twice to get Jenny to talk, but she doesn't say much, just looks at Tibs and laughs at his comments. Then we're in Denver. We go to the ball park and buy tickets and find our seats way up in the Rock Pile. They are only five dollars, and they are nose-bleed seats. We don't mind because it's a beautiful day, and none of us are real baseball fans. Tibs and Jackdaw go and get us hot dogs and nachos and beers and we sit and eat and watch the game. They think to get soda cups to pour our beers into—they're old enough, but I don't think Jenny is of age, like me.

I only sip mine, though, just in case I'm pregnant.

"So," Jackdaw says. "There's this nut doctor and he takes a bunch of patients to a baseball game. When they go they're all combed and buttoned up and look like normal people. The doctor's all dressed up in shirt and tie."

"I think I've heard this one," Tibs says, nodding.

"They go and come back. The patients are all bedraggled, and half of them don't have on pants. The doctor's tie is gone, and his hair is all messed up. Another doctor asks him, 'What happened?'"

Jenny looks at Jackdaw sideways with a little bit of a smile on her lips, like she's not sure what's coming next and not sure if she wants to know. She glances at me. I smile and nod my head.

"He tells the other doctor, 'We started out having a great time. When everyone cheered, I said, 'Up, Nuts.' They stood up. When they were done, I said, 'Down, Nuts.' They sat down. It was going really well.' 'It was?' the other doctor said. 'Yeah, until the guy walked by yelling 'Peanuts!'" Jackdaw took swallow of beer.

I laugh. Jenny laughs just a little. But Tibs really laughs. "I hadn't heard that one," he says. "Good one." Then Jenny laughs a lot.

We sit and watch the game. After a while, Jenny stands and says, "I've got to go to the bathroom. You want to go?" She looks at me.

"Sure," I say. I want this to work. Jenny seems nice, and Tibs really needs a girlfriend. It's like he wants one but can't get out of his head long enough to try.

After we've climbed down the steps onto the concourse, Jenny says, "Your brother is pretty smart, isn't he?"

"Yeah. He's going to be a really good teacher."

"Do you think he likes me?" She doesn't look at me as she says this.

"Yeah. Yes. He asked you out. He's just a little shy. Always has been."

"Oh." She doesn't look convinced.

"The thing about Tibs is he … Well, he may like things but he doesn't do anything about it. So, for instance, if he needs a bed, say, for his apartment, he'll sleep in his sleeping bag for six months before he goes out and gets one. Usually CJ or I figure it out for him or he happens on a solution." We're at the bathroom now and there's a line so we wait.

"He's … lazy?" she says.

"No, no. That's not it. It's like he's afraid to make a decision, in case it'll be the wrong one."

She nods, still a little unsure.

I smile and lean toward her. She smells like strawberry lip gloss. "So what you have to do is help him along. Nudge him, you know? I don't think you want to come on too strong, cause he might run away, but a good push wouldn't hurt."

"So, like, what?" She's nodding now. "Like, I could, I don't know, let my knee rest against his. Or, or, I could lean over and reach for some nachos or something and touch him?"

I nod. "Yeah. Or you know what? You could say you want a t-shirt or hat or something and you'd like him to help you pick it out. Something to get him up and walking. And while you're walking you could slip your hand into his arm. Just something so that that first touch is out of the way."

She's nodding and smiling. "Yeah. Ok! Yeah."

We go to the bathroom and then back to the stands. We sit for a while and then Jenny says, "Hey Tibs, I'd like to get a

Rockies shirt for my cousin. He's about your size. Could you come and help me?"

Tibs shrugs and nods. "Sure," he says.

They get up and walk down the steps. As they disappear from sight, I see her lean toward him and laugh.

"I sure hope they get together," I say.

Jackdaw shakes his head. "I think Tibs does better worshipping from afar."

"I don't know about better," I say. "You think he's happy like that?"

"Happy?"

"It's like this bike he wanted when we were kids. It was me who told Mom and Dad he wanted it because he wouldn't. And when he got it for Christmas, he was so happy. It's like he won't let himself do things he wants."

"Maybe he's afraid when he gets it it won't be like what he imagined it would be."

I laugh. "Am I like that? Are you disappointed?"

"What? Of course not." He puts his arm around me. "Of course not. Really. You're my Em."

When Tibs and Jenny come back from the concessions stand, they're holding hands and smiling. I nod and smile as Jenny sits down next to me. She smiles back.

During the second half, Jenny's nervous so she gets pretty drunk. Toward the end, she says she has a headache. I don't have any aspirin or anything in my purse. The game finishes, and as we're going down the concrete bleacher steps to leave, she trips on those ridiculous sandals and falls, tearing her jeans and cutting her knee. She's pretty upset. I offer her a clean napkin, which she dabs at the blood on her jeans. Tibs and

Jackdaw make a show of holding their hands together and carrying her to the first aid station, where they put on iodine and a bandage and give her some aspirin. Tibs puts his arm around her to help her to the car.

On the way back to Loveland, Jenny and I ride in the back and Tibs and Jackdaw are up front. Poor Jenny. She's just wrung out—you can tell. When we drop her off, Tibs smiles at her and says, "Feel better."

But the next day Jenny calls and leaves a message on the answering machine, Tibs tells me. Later, when I'm there, Jackdaw says something to Tibs about what he calls her fuck-me shoes, and then Tibs never calls her back. She keeps calling and calling and he screens his calls and won't pick up. I feel so bad for her—and for him.

Tibs

Jackdaw and I reach a milestone. We're passing through the gate to adulthood. We're putting away childish things. It's graduation.

He and I sit in the huge arena that hosts basketball games and rock concerts. Arts and Sciences, of which English is a part, is one of the largest colleges on campus, so we get the big venue. Us graduates fidget on folding chairs in the middle, and the families sit on the cement concourses encircling us. The administration is reading off names and handing out diplomas, the voice echoing through the big open space and reverberating its unintelligibility. The ceremony takes all day, which is too long for everyone to stay focused, so there's a carnival atmosphere—people coming and going, texting or talking on cell phones, intermittent clapping as the names are read, flash bulbs strobing. It's unseasonably warm—people sweat—so the place has the odor of human bodies and perfumes and coffee.

We're supposed to be sitting alphabetically by last name, but Jackdaw's sitting next to me in the Js. I locate CJ and Maggie where they said they'd be in the stands and wave. CJ's turned toward Maggie talking, but Maggie sees me and waves. Then CJ turns and waves too.

I turn to Jackdaw. "You see the girls?"

"Huh?" he says. He's been slouching—sitting with his butt slid forward and his shoulders curled, his head down. Every once in a while, he scans the concourses.

"Over there. There's Maggie and CJ." I point and wave again. They're talking and don't see me.

"Where?" He squints. He's not wearing his glasses. I point. He fishes under his robe and retrieves his glasses and puts them on. With his palms on his seat, he pushes himself up and then forward and then rests his elbows on his knees. He scans the crowd, without moving his head at first and then more openly.

"Right there." I point again. "Near that railing. See?"

He's not looking in their direction.

"Over there," I point and wait. He sees where I'm pointing and looks.

"Oh, yeah," he says and nods his head, facing halfway between the girls and me, like he doesn't want to commit to either. Then he focuses forward. For the rest of the ceremony, he retains his glasses, and when he thinks I'm not looking, he glances up into the seats but generally not in the direction of the girls.

When they start on the Ds, Jackdaw joins the line beside the podium. When his name is called, Jackdaw ambles across the podium to the man holding out diplomas. He receives the diploma and grasps the hand that is offered and then looks out across the crowd. He doesn't seem to be searching anymore; his face is blank, granite. He doesn't celebrate. He just walks off the podium, and then I lose sight of him. When the Ds file back to their seats, he isn't with them.

I line up at the podium with the Js. Time blurs as my nerves get to me. When my name is called, I walk across the podium, receive my diploma, shake hands, and smile in the direction of CJ and Maggie. I clutch the diploma to my chest as I cross the podium and go down the stairs and through the equipment that is masked from the audience by a paper-draped metal frame.

I've had my time with great authors and great minds. Now is the time to shuffle out the back and start a new life, a "real life." No more discussing great authors. No more dreaming about my life after college. No more kidding myself that I'm just getting the degree as a fallback position and what I'm really going to do is write, that that book will be published before I graduate. I won't be the next Hemingway. I've graduated. Deadline passed.

I guess I'll be a teacher.

Maybe it'll be okay if I find a nice girl to spend my life with. Maybe if I can figure out a way to find a girl, the perfect girl, and then screw up the courage, go all Hemingway, and just ask her out. Maybe, despite my flaws, she might find me attractive. Just maybe, though I can't see it, but I'm hoping. I want her to be beautiful and funny and smart and maybe a little smart ass to make up for my lack of smart ass. Someone strong and caring but not so strong that she's overbearing. The yin to my yang. I will just have to focus on it and try a little harder. There is someone out there for me.

So, a) find the perfect girl, b) screw up the courage to ask her out, c) get her to marry me, d) live happily ever after. Then, the writing won't matter, right?

Maggie

Jackdaw's at my place, and we're sitting out on the stone front porch in plastic lawn chairs. The sun is low, and the breeze cools the warmth of the day and tinkles the wind chimes. We've just finished dinner. I made a big meal, grilled some steaks, mashed some potatoes, made some homemade gravy, baked some refrigerator rolls—all his favorites. I want him in a good mood, relaxed.

I have to tell Jackdaw that I'm pregnant, we're pregnant. My body's been changing. It's different, and so I know. This is going to be harder than I thought, though. At first I was so excited I couldn't wait to tell him and I had to stop myself just to be sure. But now I'm not sure how he's going to take it. He's been acting weird lately. He's always busy and gets annoyed with me a lot.

Can you believe it? I'm actually pregnant. I know I should be upset, worried about the future, and I am, but I'm going to have a family! That outweighs it all. I've been thinking about it nonstop, and it's really the solution to everything. It'll make it all right, you know? And I really can't tell you what that means to me. Like I'm gaining something I never knew I was missing. It's like I won the lotto. There aren't enough exclamation points for that.

"What's wrong?" he says. "What now?"

"Nothing's wrong," I say. "Everything's wonderful."

He reaches for my hand, something he hasn't done in while, and smiles.

"I'm pregnant," I say. I didn't mean to say it. It just comes out.

He looks at me, the smile still on his face. Then you can see him register what I said. The smile flattens and his eyes widen. I can't stand it that his face changes, his hand stiffens, so I look away and take my hand away. When I look back, his smile is gone.

"What did the doctor say?" he says.

I don't need a doctor to tell me. I know. "He didn't," I say. "I mean, I haven't been to a doctor."

"You took one of those home tests?"

He wants proof, but we don't need proof. My body is proof enough. It's been loosening up, quickening, and my pants are starting to get tight. I've missed my period. But he's not going to believe me—I can tell. But I say, "I'm pregnant."

Relief floods his eyes, and his shoulders relax as he takes a big breath. "We'll take a test. It'll be fine. You're not pregnant. You're imagining things."

I don't say anything.

"You'll take a test," he says.

"You don't have faith in me," I say.

"What? No. Yes I do."

"If you believed me, you'd take my word for it."

"It's just a test. Scientific, you know. To confirm. The doctor'll make you do the same thing." He sits forward in his chair. "Tell you what. I'll go get it. Right now. Then we'll know for sure." He stands up, goes in, and gets his keys and leaves in his truck.

I go inside and sit on the couch and cross my arms. I flip on the TV and surf the few channels and then turn it off. I sit there as the sun goes down and the room darkens.

He's so sure, I start to doubt. What do I have to go on? My body. A dream. But it all seemed so real, and I want it to be true, I really do. If we have this baby, we'll be doing something bigger than ourselves. We'll be ensuring our future. There's going to be an *us* to us, and he'll come back to me.

When he gets back 25 minutes later, he's in a good mood. "These puppies are accurate," he says. "I was reading the package. In no time flat, you know. You know for sure, ninety-nine percent."

I look at him. I'm not sure I want to take this test. If it comes up positive, what's he going to do? I think he would do the right thing because he's that kind of a guy, but he's been acting weird lately. What else is he capable of? And if it comes up negative, what's he going to do? What am I going to do? I've been so sure—I've just known—and it's like I've adjusted my whole life to include this little person. I tell myself twenty, thirty times an hour, there's a little person inside me. I'm going to be a mom.

"You going to do it?" he says.

"Yeah." I shrug and push myself off the couch. I take the package from him and go to the bathroom. I unbutton my jeans and peal them down to my knees and sit on the toilet. I pull the box out of the bag he handed me and use my teeth to tear the plastic wrapper. I pull open the box and pull out the pink plastic stick and the paper directions. I put the directions on the bathroom counter next to me.

I'm supposed to pull off the end of the plastic thing and pee onto the white wickie thing. So I do. I pull the plastic thing off but my pants keep my legs together so I put it on the counter and push my jeans down to my ankles. I pick up the pink thing again and spread my legs and put it down there, trying to get it positioned. It's awkward.

Then I can't pee. I had to a minute ago and now nothing comes out. It's like my body went on strike. I reach over and turn on the sink. Maybe the running water will help. It does, but I almost miss the stream that comes out. I catch a little and hope it's enough.

Then I cap it and put it on the counter and stand and pull up and button my jeans and wait. I can see as the liquid starts to pull into view, a ragged line of color that races across the little pane. I watch the color move in streaks in the liquid. You're supposed to see a cross if you're pregnant. I look. The horizontal line shows like it's supposed to but there's no vertical line. It's not a cross.

I can't believe it. I was so sure. It's like all Jackdaw's weirdness has affected this. It's like he's wishing so hard it's made it so. Well, if that's the case, maybe I can make it happen. Maybe if I wish hard enough it'll come true, if I wish harder than Jackdaw.

"Em?" Jackdaw says through the door. "See anything yet?"

I don't answer. I focus on the little pink window and stare at it and say to myself, "I am pregnant, I am pregnant." The muscles in my body tense as I push everything I have toward that little window, trying to make a cross. "I am, I am." I take a deep breath and close my eyes. I start chanting under my breath, "I-am-preg-nant, I-am-preg-nant." Then I hold my breath. At first my body relaxes a little and then, starved for air, my lungs try to expand, to push against my chest, and with all my will I hold my breath. When it seems like my lungs are going to burst, I stutter-breathe—I let a little out and then gasp to fill my lungs and open my eyes.

There it is, a cross. It wasn't there when I closed my eyes, but now it is, unmistakably a cross. A burst of laughter like a sob pushes up from my chest.

"Maggie?" Jackdaw says. Then he pushes open the door. He glances at my face and I'm not sure what he sees. He looks down at the pink plastic and sees the cross. He looks up at the wall. Then it's like he slides a little on his bones. His face relaxes and his eyes go blank and shiny and his arms fall to his sides. He doesn't say anything for a long time. Then he says, "I suppose I'll marry you then." He doesn't reach out to touch me and he doesn't even look at me. He turns and walks out of the bathroom.

He's just surprised, that's all. He'll get used to the idea and—you'll see—he'll be as excited as I am. This is a chance for him to give someone else what he didn't have. I don't know all the particulars of his childhood, but I know it wasn't good. With this baby, he can make it all right. He loves me, and he'll love this baby too. We're going to be a family!

CJ

It's the anniversary of our parents' plane crash, and Tibs, Maggie, and I sit in Maggie's living room. We always try to be together on this day. We never mention why beforehand—we just make plans. Outside there's a cold misty rain, the kind that brings up the fog. The damp is heavy in the air, making it chillier. I brought some pizza, which we've eaten, and we're making noise about breaking out the cribbage board, but for now, we're just sitting.

"How do you think things would be different if they hadn't died?" I say.

"I don't know," Tibs says. "Maybe the world would seem like a safer place."

Maggie doesn't say anything. She's only half listening.

"Do you really think it was bad weather?" I say. "That report. They said something about *a convergence of events*."

"Yeah," Tibs says. "I wondered about that too. What events? What do they mean, *convergence*?"

"Yeah," I say. "Just weather, or something else?" Their flight was from London to Egypt, and I had read about surface-to-air missiles bringing down airliners. Rain or no rain. I mean, how much rain do you have in a desert country like Egypt?

Tibs says, "What I wonder is, were they afraid there at the end?"

"Of course they were afraid," I say. "Who wouldn't be? What I wonder is, did they think of us?"

Maggie has been sitting there watching the rain on the window. Now she says, "Of course they thought of us, CJ. I'm sorry, but what are you thinking?"

Where did that come from? She always defends them, but there's a new anger in her voice.

Maggie continues, "Most parents, normal parents, worry all the time about their kids."

"Quit fucking defending them," I say to Maggie.

"CJ, I just mean that all parents think all the time about their kids. I guess you have to be a parent to really understand."

Maggie's being a bitch, which is unlike her. What right does she have to rub my nose in it? "Fuck you."

"CJ," she says.

I raise my hand.

"I don't mean that," Maggie says.

"What?" Tibs says. "Don't mean what?"

Maggie glances at Tibs and then back to me.

I turn to Tibs, "What she's talking about is I told her I'm fucking sterile." I turn back to Maggie. "Get down off your high horse, Sis. Since when do you know what most parents think?"

"You're …" Tibs says.

"Turns out," I say, "ol' CJ's just as crusty on the inside as she is on the outside. I can't have kids."

Tibs doesn't say anything.

Maggie says, quietly, "We were talking about our parents. I do know them."

"You were too fucking young, so you don't know them, not like we do."

Maggie's face turns red. "I'm sick and tired of you telling me I don't know things, just because I'm younger. Well, CJ, I know things you don't know, things you'll never know, because I am pregnant." She's trying to hurt me with her words.

"You don't know …" I say and then realize the last thing she said.

"You're …" Tibs says. You can see things clicking in Tibs's brain. "That means … Unless …"

Oh God.

"CJ," Maggie says. "I'm sorry. I didn't mean to say those things. But I'm pregnant. We're pregnant, Jackdaw and I." She holds out her hand to me, but I ignore it. "You're going to be an auntie."

Tibs smiles broadly. "That's great, Maggie. So great."

"Jackdaw?" I say. That bastard is now related to me. He has license to really fuck things up.

I turn to Tibs. "This is your fault. I warned you what an asshole he is. At least maybe now he'll act true to form and skip out. At least there's that."

Maggie's face blushes red again, and Tibs sits up and forward, his shoulders up around his ears.

"You're wrong about him, way wrong," Maggie says. "He's going to marry me, and we're going to have this baby, and it's all going to be all right. You're wrong."

Tibs nods. "CJ, Jackdaw's great. You've been around the losers at the bar too long. Not everybody treats everybody like shit."

"I didn't used to think so," I say, "but ever since Jackdaw's been around, things have been fucked up. Mark my words—he's going to screw us all."

Tibs says, "CJ, you're the one who's wrong here. I think you need to apologize to Maggie. She's marrying Jackdaw, and I think you need to be supportive."

"If you want to fuck up your life, Maggie," I say, "You can do it without me. I can't stand by and watch." I turn to Tibs. "I wish I was wrong, but I'm not, Little Brother." I walk out into the rain.

Jackdaw

A gray day, no differentiation in space or time. As I drive out to my ol' man's farm, time slips backwards. I'm nineteen, fifteen, eight. By the time I pull into the graveled yard I'm wearing high-water denims and a snap western shirt and the weight of the world.

Maybe it'll be different this time.

The farm looks the same. Everything in its place, nothing daring to grow out of line. I go to the barn, where everything's clean but there's little light. One lamp casts a circle on the workbench and light filters in from the open door. When I walk through the door, the ol' man's working on a tractor. His back is to me as he bends into the engine. He's wearing his tan Carhart bib overalls and a white t-shirt and a pair of steel-toed boots.

He always wore a white t-shirt. Always. White white. On him, it looks like military dress blues. I remember the time he and Mom and I went to some barbeque. We hardly ever went anywhere, so this time really stuck in my mind. I was so proud to be walking next to my dad. He looked bigger and stronger than any other man there, with his rock-hard arms from working the farm. It was late summer, but not too hot that day, and I trailed him up and down as he talked to this guy and that guy, his voice gruff. Mom was right there, too, following him around like he liked, so he was in a good mood. They'd closed down a whole street and all the people in the houses had pulled out their lawn chairs and their grills and were talking with drinks in their hands. Somebody put on some music and put the speakers on their porch and turned it up loud. People from other streets must've been there too, and it was crowded. The little kids were running through sprinklers, and us bigger kids went to the baseball diamond in the small park across the way. I was the pitcher for our team, and there was this guy on the other team. He was a big fat kid twice my size, I swear, and had on a *Star Wars* t-shirt and girly gym shorts. He was pretty good at bat, but when he wasn't batting he yelled things at me. "You throw like a girl" and "Do I have to put hair around it?" and "Pitcher, pitcher, he's got an itcher." I told him to shut up, but he didn't. I told him to shut up again, and this time he pushed me. We got into this big fight, and he got me good but then I had him down on the ground beating the piss out of him when the adults came running over. They pulled us apart, and then on the way home, my dad said, "You're one tough little motherfucker." Boy, I was so proud I made a point of trying to get in fights every day at school to see if he would tell me that again. He didn't though.

I look at my dad's back. "I graduated," I say, trying to keep accusation out of my voice.

He stiffens and grunts.

I think about asking him if he got the invitation, why he wasn't there, even though I know better. Naw, why bring it up? Bigger fish to fry.

He bends over to retrieve a wrench from the toolbox, and I see the side of his face. I haven't seen him since the day after high school graduation. He looks the same, exactly the same. Broad shoulders, broad cheekbones, a stub nose, dark eyes, and dark spikey hair closely cut. His broad hands are oil-dark, though later they'll be scrubbed raw-clean. When I was a kid, I thought that if I could just chop off those hands, everything would be all right. I've always paid close attention to those hands. They're like weather vanes. They tell you what's coming, and then they're what comes.

The ol' man's Butch Donner. Jackdaw really stands for Jack Donner. We're descended from the Donners of the Donner Party. One of my great-greats was Uriah Blue Donner, son of Jacob Donner who was the brother of the head of the Donner Party. Uriah didn't go to California, though. He stayed in Illinois while the rest of the family took their fateful journey. It was well-publicized at the time, so he must have read about it in the papers before he even got a letter from his cousins. Could you imagine? It'd be like hearing on the evening news that your family was in that plane crash in the Andes or something, and then they ate each other.

"I'm getting married, sir," I say.

This time he looks at me, disgust making his back straighten. Most people wouldn't notice. "You didn't have enough of that institution?"

Something way down deep inside makes me want to fling words back at him, but I keep my temper in check. It doesn't do any good to lose your temper. You have to be smarter than that.

He turns his back on me like the conversation's over.

"I'm getting married," I say, "and that's not all." Why am I dragging this out? Did I think it would get any easier? I fold my hands in front of me. "We're having a kid." I watch his back closely.

He stops and then slowly turns all the way around. He narrows his eyes. "It's yours?" he says.

I have the impulse to say, hell, maybe not. But this is more because I want him to be on my side. I know from experience a good way to soften up the old man is to talk about how shitty women are. But I've already given my word to marry Maggie, and besides, why should I give him the satisfaction? I don't say anything.

He shrugs like, hey, we're just guys here. I take a step back.

"Did I ever tell you about Buckeye Mulligan?" he says. He has, over and over, but I let him go on. "Buckeye joined up after this girl said he'd knocked her up. He was the best damn sniper, out of Texas, I think. Used to shoot jackrabbits out of moving pickup trucks. They still tell Buckeye stories down at the VFW. I was there and saw him shoot this raghead up in this mosque thing. A tiny window, shelling all around us. Buckeye stepped out from behind the wall into broad daylight, aimed like a son-of-a-bitch with the whole world shooting down on him. One shot—Bam! One less raghead." He's getting to his favorite part, so his face takes on a grin like those plastic kid teeth you stuck between your lips. He continues, "Ended up, a shell took ol' Buckeye so hard it blew his heart clean out of his chest." He eats this shit up.

"What's your point?" I say.

"He's a fucking hero, that's my point."

"You want me to join up to get out of marrying Maggie?"

126

"Do you a helluva lot of good."

"You wanted me to join ever since I could lift a rifle," I say, watching his hands. Then it comes to me. "No. I don't think that's it."

"What're you talking about?" His hands curl into fists.

Now I know why this story has bothered me for so long. "The only way I'll ever amount to anything is if I *pull a Buckeye*. I ain't shit unless I been shot by some foreigner. Ain't that right, *Dad*? That's the only reason you've wanted me to join up all these years."

I decide right then and there that he's right. It's better if we pretend the other's dead. Live and let live.

Or, better yet, live and kill the fucker off. If only I had the guts.

Tibs

The temperature is high, and the doldrums, air unmoving, have paralyzed the city for three days. Jackdaw, Maggie, and I are in the county offices, an old building of blonde limestone. The air conditioning can't surmount the heat. We're sweating in this woman's office, a justice of the peace. She's a lawyer in both name and appearance—short gray hair and a gray business suit.

I'm standing next to Jackdaw, acting as his best man. He's in his western attire—suit coat over pressed jeans and cowboy boots. Maggie's dressed in a simple navy skirt and a white shirt with no sleeves. Her red-gold hair loops in big floppy curls. She has this girl I've never met before as her bridesmaid. The nondescript girl is pleasant enough, but I don't think Maggie knows her that well. CJ should've been in attendance, instead of this girl, but CJ's being her charming pig-headed self, as usual.

I had phoned CJ: "Maggie really wants you to come."

"Then she shouldn't be marrying that asshole." She said it evenly, as if she were being reasonable.

"CJ."

"You're the fucking asshole." This, again, without raising her voice.

"Why am I the asshole?"

"Because you brought that bastard into our lives, into her life." An edge crept in.

I was trying to make peace, but this made me angry. "CJ, Maggie needs you right now. Can't you quit being a self-centered chickenshit hard-ass and just come?"

"Chickenshit? That's more your territory."

I should've just hung up on her, but I tried one more time. "Remember Maggie's birthday?" I said.

There was silence on the line.

Of course she remembered Maggie's birthday. Three years ago, it was Maggie's sweet 16. Mom and Dad had had to fly out the day before to go to Egypt. Dad's work, of course. We generally didn't do much on birthdays, but this year Mom suggested she have some friends over. They were going to give her a sensible Ford Taurus when they got back, and it was a surprise. All CJ and I had to do was to attend to make sure the kids didn't destroy the house. Chaperones, I guess. I assumed that CJ was going to be there and CJ assumed I was going to be there, so neither of us were. The house came through fine, but something else happened, to Maggie—we never knew quite what. Maggie wouldn't speak about it. It must've been horrible, whatever it was. But, subsequently, we found out about Mom and Dad, and the incident was lost to the chaos. CJ and I did not remember to give Maggie her car for a couple of weeks. All three of us walked around in cocoons of self-pity for the next year. Maggie dutifully attended school as she was supposed to, the good girl. CJ acquired her bartending job and started drinking. I attended college and wasn't around much anyway. Busy, you know.

"This is different. This is you, Tibs, screwing up your life and everyone else's."

CJ always brings out the best in me. I said, "So CJ's concern is with other people all of a sudden. And she's cutting her sister purely out of family feeling. How sweet."

"Oh, go fuck yourself," she said and hung up.

So now we're standing in this steaming office, sans CJ. Jackdaw hasn't said two words, and Maggie's face is rapt like the sky just opened up and she's gone to heaven.

Could this happen to me one day? Standing at the alter with a woman so in love I can see her heart beat? Ready to give her whole life to be with me? God, I hope so. Not very likely, as there are no prospects in sight and even if there were, how in the world would we connect? I'd have to, to, to—I don't know. I don't know what I'm going to have to do, but—damn it to hell—I'm going to give it my all. If it's at all possible, I'm going to do my best. If some of the dregs of our society can do it, I certainly can. Certainly. Certainly?

The Justice of the Peace focuses on Jackdaw and then Maggie. "Ready?" she says.

"Yes," Maggie says and takes Jackdaw's hand. Jackdaw nods.

"Okay, Jack, you're first. Repeat after me: I, Jack Joseph Donner, take you, Magdalene Jane Jordan, to be my wife."

Jackdaw pulls in a deep breath. "I, Jack Joseph Donner, take you, Magdalene Jane Jordan, to be my wife."

"And these things I promise you." The woman's voice lowers, as if what she's saying touches her emotionally.

Jackdaw looks at Maggie, and without moving Maggie melts toward him. "And these things I promise you," he says.

130

"I will be faithful and honest with you."

Jackdaw looks into Maggie's face. "I will be faithful and honest with you," he says earnestly.

"I will share my life with you."

"I will share my life with you." His emphasis is on the first two words.

"I will help and care for you."

"I will help and care for you." He nods as he says this.

"I will respect and trust you."

Jackdaw hesitates. Then he says, "I trust ... respect and trust you."

"Through the best and worst of what is to come, as long as we live."

"Through the best and worst of what is to come, as long as we live." When he's done, he takes a deep breath.

The woman turns to Maggie. Maggie repeats each word carefully and slowly after her, as seriously, earnestly, as if her life depended on it. Then she leans forward and whispers to him, "I will."

"Now I pronounce you man and wife," the woman says.

That's that. Now Jackdaw is my brother-in-law, a member of the family. Suddenly I feel buoyed, hopeful, like I am the one who's been married.

Part 2
December

CJ

I bartend Christmas eve—we stay open 365 days a year. A few lonely people hang out. Jack Flash, who owns a repair shop, George who we call Jetson, and Anthony Scarlotti play pool. Joanie, also known as the Bag Lady, passes out with her head on the bar. It's cold, the kind of cold that makes the snow squeak under your feet, and the heaters work double-time to keep up.

My cell rings. I mute *The Grinch Who Stole Christmas* on the big screen and glance at the phone. I see it's Maggie, so I let it ring and turn the sound on the TV back on. But then it rings again right away. I'm not going to answer it, but then it's Christmas and Joanie raises her head off the bar and rasps, "You going to get that?"

"Maggie," I say as I pick up.

"Don't hang up," she says. "Please don't hang up."

"Yeah," I say, "okay, what's up?" It's so good to hear her voice but I try to keep it out of my tone. I'm not ready to forgive her yet.

"Can you help me? Can you come? Tibs isn't answering his phone." There's an edge, a panic, I don't remember ever hearing.

"It's Christmas. I'm working. Shouldn't you be all happy and shit?"

"It's time," she says. "I'm in labor."

So where's Jackdaw? I almost say it, but if she's calling me, he's pulled a stunt. True to form, though she won't admit it. Throwing it in her face now, even to me, seems harsh.

"Please, CJ, please?"

I have the impulse to tell her to stick it. She was so sanctimonious last time we talked. But the desperation in her tone stops me. "Sure," I say. "Of course. Just let me call Peter."

Peter's drunk at home by this time but not so far gone he can't come in. I drive the twelve miles out to Maggie's. On the way, I call Tibs. No answer.

The stars are really bright. You can't see them very well in Loveland because of all the lights and because of Denver, but once you get a little ways out of town you can, especially up in the canyons. When I get to Maggie's, I step out of my car, and there's the whole Milky Way soaring above me, sprinkled like bits of broken glass on black pavement. I think: I don't know much about the stars. I can make out the Big Dipper and the Little Dipper and Orion. Why don't I know more about the stars? People for hundreds of years have been led by the stars, navigators and astrologers, lovers and wanderers. Maybe that's why I don't have any direction, because I don't know the stars.

When I let myself in, I'm shocked. Maggie is huge. Her face is puffy and she looks like one of those fertility goddesses, with her wide hips and her belly huge and round and her little belly button sticking out under her draped shirt like a little plastic turkey timer. She even smells fertile. She's wearing loose cotton clothes, almost a kid's sleeper, and her face looks so young. Her hair isn't washed, just pulled back in a band, and her eyes are a little wild, a little lonely, a lot scared. I immediately feel like a shit-heel.

She's packed a bag with stuff for her and a little green diaper bag of stuff for the baby. I hesitate and then say, "Should I get ... call Jackdaw?"

Maggie looks away as she says, "I'm early, and he's on the road."

We drive, pedal to the floor, to Bethlehem Hospital in Loveland, Maggie panting in the passenger seat. We get checked in. It smells like all hospitals—like it's trying to cover something up. They have Maggie change into one of those funky robes that I have to figure out how to tie for her and the little white socks with rubber grips on the soles. The OB on call, a woman, comes in and checks her and decides it's the real deal so we move to a birthing room. This room is all pale pinks and greens. Cheery wallpaper borders of hippos and elephants skirt the ceiling. There's a window seat that you can sleep in if you want. Maggie lays on a bed on rollers in the center of the room, with an IV and other equipment all around. The room's big—too big and too empty.

When the doctor leaves, Maggie says to me, "It's a boy. We're naming him Jes."

"Jes? Like Jesse James?" That ought to make Jackdaw happy.

"No," she says. "Just Jes."

They have Maggie's belly hooked up to a heart monitor so we can hear the baby's heartbeat. The baby does all right early in the labor, but as it progresses his heartbeat starts to go down. They give Maggie some meds to speed everything up, and when the meds take, Maggie's in a lot of pain. She lies in bed, her knees propped up with pillows under the sheet, the freckles on her brow merging into one huge brown blotch. Her breathing goes *whoo-hoo whoo-hoo*, and the baby's heart monitor goes *beep-beep beep-beep* and the IV machine clicks as it drips liquid into Maggie's veins. The huge dark room stretches out around us, and the pool of light and heat is a spotlight.

Then the nurse comes in and checks Maggie's cervix. It's time. She goes out to get the doctor. I look at Maggie and she tries to smile. I say, "Ready to pass a watermelon through the eye of a needle?"

Maggie snorts through her breathing.

The OB and the nurses come in. I grip Maggie's hand and they tell me to hold one of Maggie's knees while a nurse holds the other. The doctor checks the baby's position by putting her hand inside Maggie and then says, "He's going to be able to give me a high five in just a minute. I'm going to count to ten, Maggie, and as I'm counting, push for all you're worth."

She starts counting, and Maggie pushes. I've never seen such effort. It makes me tired just looking at it. She pushes and pushes and her face turns beat red. She grunts.

"There we are, Maggie," the doctor says. "There's his head. Don't push for a minute." The doctor adjusts the baby and then says, "All right, Maggie, one more time and this baby will be out."

Maggie takes two deep breaths and then pushes again. She's drenched in sweat and so tired at this point. I feel all motherly toward her, like when she was little and we were at Grandma's and I'd helped tuck her in. Protective. I want to tell the doctor to stop for a minute so she can rest, but of course there's no stopping. So Maggie pushes and out comes the baby. The doctor cheers and the nurses cheer and I cheer and kiss Maggie. You can hear the baby starting to tune up, that choked cry of a newborn, as the nurses suctioned out his mouth. Maggie pushes herself up on her elbows to try to see him as the doctor holds him between Maggie's legs wrapped in a blanket. The doctor puts the baby on Maggie's belly, rubs him a bit, and then pulls the blanket away.

He's lying on his side. He's such a scrawny thing. He's this little wrinkly blue-green-white creature, dark hair plastered to his head, just like they're supposed to look. Those mobile little hands with perfect little fingers and fingernails. Thin shoulders that scrunch up to his ears. His head is out of shape, scrunched up longways. His knees curled up to his chest where they've fit just right for months. At first he's blue but then he turns red as he breathes and cries. He looks bedraggled but also more perfect than anything, I don't know, like he's an alien from a superior race or, say, a god. How can it be that nine months ago he didn't exist but now here he is, with all the organs he needs, and one day he'll be a man, probably taller than me. It's beyond knowing.

The OB rolls him onto his stomach, and the sound of voices dies away, and I glance at the doctor. Nothing overt, just a stiffening of her body, almost unnoticeable. I don't know why, but adrenaline shoots through me.

"What?" I say. "What!"

Maggie looks at me and then the doctor and her face slides.

I glance back at the baby, at Jes. On his back is this maroon-purple lump, like someone balanced a bulge-ugly peeled fruit on his spine.

The doctor snatches the baby up and the cord is clamped and cut. She takes him over to the work area. A nurse takes over with Maggie. Another nurse runs from the room and we hear a page directly after calling for another doctor.

Maggie's hands hover in midair, reaching over where Jes just lay. A huge sob escapes her throat. It's a bottomless sound. She looks at me with holes for eyes.

"Tell us what's going on," I say to the room.

"He has myelomeningocele," the doctor says over her shoulder. "We're taking him to the NICU."

They bundle him up and sweep out the door as we sit there dumbstruck. "What's myel—" I don't know how to say it. Maggie starts bawling with huge gulps of air. Poor kid. It's a sucker punch.

The nurse helps deliver the afterbirth and then Maggie's OB comes in to check but she won't say anything about it. "The neonatologist is running tests," she says.

We wait. It's two in the morning in the recovery room when Tibs joins us. He finally got our messages. Maggie sleeps. We wait some more. It isn't until 6:30 that another doctor comes in to tell us what happened. This doctor looks like she shouldn't even be out of college yet. Her tag says she's Dr. Melanie Bontemps. She wears a doctor's lab coat and shoes with really high soles, like she's trying to be taller.

She comes in and says in a cheery voice, "Good morning! How are we today?"

Maggie wakes up and Tibs and I stand. I say, "What's wrong with Jes? What's going on?"

Dr. Melanie Bontemps comes over and props one leg on the bed and says, "Well, it looks like your baby has myelomeningocele. It's what's called spina bifida, or SB."

"What does that mean?" Maggie says. "Is he all right?"

The doctor smiles really wide and crosses her arms over her chest and says, "Well, he'll have to have surgery or he may not make it." She takes a deep breath and puffs back her shoulders and says, "In cases like this, it's a good idea not to get too attached because there's a good chance that the baby won't live. Could even be brain dead." She's still smiling as she says this.

The baby that was just crying and wiggling and opening his eyes? Brain dead? I grab Maggie's hand.

She continues, "He'll probably never walk and might not be able to go to the bathroom by himself."

We're in shock, speechless. I have a wild out-of-control feeling rising inside me.

Dr. Melanie Bontemps continues, "So it's a good idea to start getting used to it all."

When she says it, I think, get used to it? Just like that? That's like telling a post-surgery amputee, oh by the way, we just lopped off your arm.

"Get used to it? Get USED to it?" I say. It's all I can do not to grab her by the shirt and shake her till her teeth rattle. "What the FUCK are you talking about? You turn your skinny little ass around and go get someone for us to talk to, RIGHT NOW!" I take a step toward her and she takes a step backwards. Then she turns and, back straight, not too quickly, leaves. I turn to Maggie and say, "Don't worry, Maggie honey, we'll get to the bottom of this. I don't think she knows what she's talking about."

Maggie's crying again, poor kid. It's amazing she doesn't go into shock or something.

I go in search of a doctor. I finally track down the pediatric neurosurgeon, who comes in to talk with us. When we tell him what Dr. Melanie Bontemps had said, his jaw clenches. "I'm sorry," he says. "You have every reason to be hopeful. With modern medicine, spina bifida is very manageable."

Then he goes on to explain what it is. It's like having a spinal cord injury. It's not something that can be healed. A person will always have it. It affects the lower legs—all or partially paralyzed with little or no feeling. People with SB may or may not walk. They may have a hard time with bowel and bladder control. The good news, though, is that it's not a progressive disease. It is what it is at birth. Unless there's complications. Fluid can build up in the brain and cause brain damage. Secondary infections from surgery can cause problems. Other things. The key is: no complications.

The doctor says, "But there's no reason to think that your baby," he glances at the chart, "Jes is his name?—that Jes can't grow up to walk and lead a relatively normal life."

A normal life. We could all hope for that.

Jackdaw

My cell phone rings and breaks through the fuzziness of sleep. I try to remember where I am. I was hauling a load of cherries from Loveland to Rapid City, then canned goods on to Chicago, then a refrigerator truck back to Kansas City, then, I don't remember. Oh, yeah, Texas. I'm in Texas. I fumble to find my wristwatch. The red numbers read *2:17 a.m.* I've only been asleep an hour, maybe two—I drove extra because the dispatcher was on my ass.

I drive truck now. I'd operated some heavy equipment during the summers in high school—you know, driving tractor for my old man—and then in college I worked construction during the summers so that I wouldn't have to work so much during the school year. Good money, especially for this broke-ass no-scholarship boy. So it was only natural to take one of those truck driving courses to get my CDL license. Construction's generally just in the summer, and truck driving is year-round, plus with the baby coming we need the insurance package. Maggie has some money from the settlement when her parents died, but it's not enough, and what sort of man would I be to sponge off her?

That's what guys do. You do what you got to do to support your family. When you're a man, you step up the plate and give it your all, even if it's for something you aren't quite sure you want. But if you make a promise, you stick by it. Don't matter if the other parties involved don't keep up their part of the bargain.

Being on the road also gets me out of the house. With Maggie all pregnant, it's like she's turned selfish all of a sudden. I try all I can to make her comfortable, and she doesn't complain much, but I can tell. It's that quiet thing again. She doesn't finish her damn sentences. She's always there, and the only time I can really breathe is out on the road.

Plus, driving truck gives me lots of time to think about what I'm going to write, though there's not much time to get it down. I've got everything figured out and then some. But when you get done for the day, you're just so wiped that there isn't enough left to get it down, even if you bring a laptop into the diner or hook it up to the cigarette lighter in your truck. It just drains it all out of you, especially when the company is pushing you to put in all the hours allowed and then some. I'm not getting nearly as much done as I'd hoped. Then, the little bit I'm home, I either sleep or try to get something done at a coffee shop in town. It's not working very well, though.

Before my cell rang, I was dreaming that I was standing at a podium in front of a crowd of people dressed for the holidays. They're looking at me. At *me*. Sexy people. People who matter. They're hanging on my every word. I can do no wrong. They're laughing and clapping at all the right places. I could've written the worst book in the world, but it doesn't matter because here I am, *The Author*. There's this woman in the front row with boobs the size of basketballs mounding up the front of her shirt. She's looking at me in that way, you know, the I've-got-to-have-you look. She knows what she wants. She waits and waits until the line for autographs is down to just a few and then she thrusts out her chest and smiles and gets in line. She comes up and has a book signed and asks if she can get her picture taken with me. Which is all an excuse for her to come around and put her hand on my ass. I am drowned in her perfume, but then I'm jerked out of it by the phone.

I see it's Tibs on the line. I open it.

"Hello?" I say.

"Congrats, man," comes Tibs's voice. "Merry Christmas. You're a dad."

"That wasn't supposed to happen for another couple of weeks. Everybody all right?" I rub my eyes, sit up in the bunk and bump my head on the cab of the truck. I wobble and shake my head, trying to rattle the sleep loose.

"Maggie's doing great. It's a boy, like we expected. Named him Jes, just like you guys decided."

"Right, right."

"He's seven pounds, two ounces. And he's hung like a pony."

I laugh. I imagine this little boy baby with a huge dick. He's got dark hair and little round cheeks and pudgy fingers and he's sitting up and laughing, his big dick between his legs. Then, all of a sudden, he gets real for me. Before, when Maggie got fat, it was sort like she was just sick. It was hard to believe that there was a baby in there. Now, I realize, really realize, that there's a baby. That's he's my son. I wonder if my dad ever felt that way. A new person that's part of me. Suddenly, now, I want to see him.

"Well, I think I can get out of my next run. I'll come home," I say.

"Um, there one more thing."

"Yeah?"

He hesitates before he says anything, which makes me sit forward on the bed.

"Yeah?" I say again.

"Something's not right. With him, with Jes."

"What?"

"The doctors haven't told us yet. All I know is what CJ told me. He was looking fine, but then there's some kind of growth on his back. But he was breathing and hollering just fine."

My vision of this perfect little boy morphs. His skin turns sickly yellow. Hair grows all over his body. His limbs bow and deform. It's Maggie all over again. She was this perfect thing, perfect in body and mind, and then she changed. She became an animal. Baseness took over. And then I had to bind myself to her, or I would be an animal too.

"I'll call you this afternoon," I say.

But then I don't. All of a sudden I can't face it. I pick up the next load—auto parts this time—and head out to Nevada. I try not to think about it, but I do. I think and think. It grinds round in my brain. I need time. I need space. I need to figure this out, damn it. There must be a way to be a man, to do the right thing, that doesn't feel so fucking awful and doesn't feel like I'm breaking into a thousand pieces. This wouldn't have happened if Maggie hadn't turned out to be so different from what I thought she was. It's really her fault, really. If only she hadn't seduced me. She put me in a situation where I had to marry her. I had to or I'd be just as bad as she is. She probably planned it all along, knowing the only thing I could do and still live with myself is to marry her. Fuck that. How dare she. Hell, she and Tibs could've been in on it together, for all I know. He's always had a weird thing for me. It's fucking wrong, is all I got to say. All of it. I don't know how I'm going to do it, but there must be a way. Fuck it all.

Maggie

Jes is scheduled to have his first surgery as soon as possible at Denver Children's. I have to stay in the hospital in Loveland, so CJ stays with me and Tibs goes with Jes in the ambulance. Tibs takes a video with his phone on the way. Later, I'm released and CJ drives me to Denver. It's one of those nondescript winter days, the sun shines, cool but not too cold, no snow on the ground, no wind. A day like any other day, only it isn't. A thought occurs to me. Maybe they told us wrong. Maybe, you never know. Maybe he's really all right. Maybe it's all a lie. Maybe he hasn't even been born yet. I feel my belly just to make sure. No, he isn't in there anymore. The flicker of hope fades.

Tibs meets us in the waiting room, square chairs in square arrangements on a purple-patterned carpet, and I watch Tibs's video while we wait to see Jes. I stare at the small screen, trying to make things out. As I watch, my hand makes its way to my belly.

At first, the video is blurry as it adjusts to the light but then it clears. Jes lays on his stomach with his butt in the air and a bandage on his back. They've got straps tightly across him and an IV in the little veins in his scalp. It looks like a really bad hat, only you wince at how painful it must be. He's got a monitor that shines bright red on his finger that measures his heart beat and his blood oxygen level, ET's heart light. He's got a blood pressure cuff strapped to his leg. He's really quiet, not crying or anything. His eyes are really big and wide and he's craning his neck and looking around like he's saying, "What the heck's going on? Someone get me out of here!" His eyes just take up his whole face, a deep navy blue, these pools you could fall into. He's just so scared, you can see it. Oh, how I wish I could've been there. I ache for him.

But what makes me feel better is Tibs's big warm hand cupping the side of Jes's head. It's so big that if Tibs made a fist, it would be larger than Jes's head. I glance over at Tibs. You've got to think that Jes knew he was there and was comforted by that. A wave of gratitude washes over me.

We start the second video, and there's Jes hollering at the top of his lungs as they unload him from the ambulance into the hospital. Everything is shaky and blurry. Jes's voice is so strong. You can tell he's a fighter. That makes me feel better. It makes me smile. I don't like to hear him in pain, but it doesn't sound like pain. It sounds like he's decided he's had enough and he's giving it all he's worth. That's our little fighter.

The camera follows the gurney down the hall. They come to a set of double doors and the nurse holds out her arm and stops the camera, which angles down to the floor. You can hear the nurse say, "I'm sorry, sir. You'll have to wait over there." Tibs's voice says, "Oh, oh, okay." And then the camera clicks off.

Then, next is in the recovery room. The view is from above, and little Jes lays on his stomach again and his face is twisted around to the side. His little arms and legs sprawl out around him like little crab limbs. On his back is this huge bandage. He starts to come out of the anesthesia and tries to lift his head. Boy, he's strong, too. It's bobbling up and down and then he lets it rest on the bed. His eyes are all scrunched from being under. Tibs talks to him. "Jes, how are you doing, little guy? We're right here." Then Tibs takes his hand and gently strokes Jes's arm. "You're doing fine, Jes. You did great," he says. The video clicks off and that's all.

I want so bad to hold him in my arms.

The nurse comes and gets us to take us to the NICU. That's the neonatal intensive care unit, an ICU for babies. She gives me an orange wristband with lettering like Tibs's. At the NICU, she talks into a box on the wall and then they buzz us in. The nurse stops us and tells us one person at a time. CJ pats my arm as I walk through the door. The nurse shows me how to scrub up at the sink, just like when I was training to be a nurse—you use a special brush for the fingernails and lots of soap and scrub for three minutes.

Once my hands are dry, the nurse takes me into the room, which is well-lit with fluorescent lights. It's weird to see wooden rocking chairs next to blocky metal machines and curvy plastic hospital furniture. Babies are scattered throughout the room in clear plastic cribs that look like little horse troughs. They're all hooked up to monitors, and the room is pretty noisy with the *ping* and *bong* of machines and alarms going off and the nurses talking. Some babies are down to their diapers in what look like little tanning beds. They've got little eye-patch sunglasses so the light doesn't reach their eyes, and they're surrounded by blue light. It's like they're in an egg of light and warmth. Other babies are wrapped up in blankets like burritos.

Some mothers or fathers sit in rocking chairs and feed and rock their babies.

As I walk through the room, I feel so bad, so bad for these babies—especially the ones off by themselves with no nurses or family around.

Then they show me Jes. I can't see him very well at first because he's pulled the IV out of his head, and the nurse is in the process of putting it back in. I crane my neck. All I want to do is touch him, but I can't. *He's mine, mine,* I want to say. I stand there helplessly as the nurse pushes in the IV. "Hey, baby, hey, Jes," I say. I tense for his crying but he doesn't cry. He just squirms. Has he had so much trauma in his life already—the surgery and everything—that he's learned to accept it? Already? This thought breaks my heart and I stand there, arms crossed in front of me and tears streaming down my face. I want to take him up in my arms and hold him. Just squeeze him and make him feel safe. The nurse finishes.

I settle for putting my hands on his shoulder and his calf. It's the only skin that's free of bandages and wires. Then I really get to see him for the first time. He seems skinnier than babies should be, sort of gangly and uncoordinated. He can't really focus on me, but he does turn his head when he hears my voice. He's tiny, so little and helpless. His eyes are really big in his head, and his face has a yellow undertone, like he has a bad fake tan. He has dark spiky hair with his dad's hairline. You can't tell with a baby's nose, what shape it's going to be, but I think his mouth looks like mine. His eyes are a deep blue, large on his face. I can't tell if they're mine or Jackdaw's. He has this barrel chest and skinny little shoulders. His neck is wobbly like all newborns. It's amazing to think he was inside me just a day before.

All of a sudden it seems like he knows me and I know him. He reaches out to me, strains in my direction, without him doing a thing. "Help me," he's saying.

God I wish I could. Something, anything.

The nurse says it's time to feed him and asks me if I'd like to hold him. Boy, would I. I sit down in the rocking chair and the nurse props my elbow with a pillow and puts a pillow on my lap. She gathers him up, being careful with his back and all the wires, and places him in my lap. It feels so so good to hold him but I'm afraid I'll hurt him or cause more damage. The nurse says, "It's ok. Be careful, but his back is protected." They had told me at the other hospital that it's probably best not to breast feed, what with everything, and so my breasts are sore and leaking, but it's all okay with him in my arms. She warms up a bottle in a little green bowl of hot water. Then she hands it to me. She pulls a chair up beside me.

"Give it a try," she says.

I try to put it in his mouth but he won't open it.

"Try tickling his cheek and lips with the nipple," she says. "It prompts the suckling reflex."

I tickle him on the cheek, and he turns and gloms onto it like there's no tomorrow. He takes a couple of really big sucks and then stops. I look at the nurse and she says, "He's trying to figure it out." You can see it, too, his little brow furrows as the gears turn. He sucks a little and then stops and then swallows.

"That's fine," the nurse says. "He's doing great, just what he's supposed to."

He's doing what he's supposed to, she says. How I want to hear that. He's normal. I whisper it to myself and to him: "You're doing great, just what you're supposed to." He eats 20 ml and then pushes the nipple out of his mouth and won't take another sip.

I glance at the nurse. She nods. "His tummy is used to being fed through the umbilical, so it's not very big." I laugh with relief.

After that, the nurse leaves us alone in the rocking chair. I hold him carefully and whisper to him, "How you doing, little guy, my Jes? Mommy sure loves you. She loves you so much. We're going to be all right."

When I say that, he smiles, I swear. His very first smile. Some people say that when babies smile so young it's only gas, but now that I've seen it I know they're wrong. I think babies smile because they know they're loved, they can hear it in your voice and feel it in your body. It's not just an animal response to gas. No, it's a deeply ingrained instinct to love and be loved. It's the reason we go on living. It's the reason we die, sometimes, too.

I stay in the NICU as long as possible. At some point, Tibs and CJ send word by way of the nurse that they're going home to get some sleep and will be back the next day. Early the next morning, they kick me out for a few hours so the doctors can do their rounds. CJ and Tibs haven't made it back yet, and I call and leave a message on Jackdaw's cell phone. I tell him we're doing okay and ask him when he's coming home. The nurses let me back into the NICU. While I'm in, Jackdaw calls back and leaves a message that he can't change his run after all. They need him for a little extra, so it'll be a week, maybe two before he can come home. "I'll call you," he says.

I hold Jes when he's awake and I watch him when he sleeps. I step out and see CJ or Tibs for just a minute before coming back into the NICU. They show me how to change his diaper, how to prepare his formula and feed him, and how to clean his surgical site and umbilical cord.

"Do you want him circumcised?" the doctor asks.

I haven't thought about this. It's really something Jackdaw should decide but he's not here, so I shrug. "Can we have it done later?"

"Yes," the doctor says, "but don't wait too long." He gets up and turns to leave.

"No," I say. "No, I don't think we'll have him circumcised."

The doctor nods. "You sure?"

"Yes." He's already had one surgery, and he may need to have more. Circumcision seems like pure vanity.

Jes's bilirubin goes up, meaning he's jaundiced, so they put him in the warm blue tanning bed with the little shades. The blue light hurts my eyes after a while.

"Maybe you should take a walk, get some air, maybe a bite to eat," the nurse says. As soon as she says it, I realize how tired I am. I roll my shoulders. "Really," she says, "you can't take care of him if you don't take care of you."

Reluctantly, I stand and sway a bit and then stretch. I glance at Jes, who's sleeping, and then make my way out the door and into the hall. The windows are dark. I find a clock and it's eleven at night. I didn't know that.

I go to the vending machines in the basement level and buy a pack of peanut butter crackers and cream soda, salty and sweet. I sit in an empty hall and eat them and sip the soda. The place is deserted this time of night. For a minute, I feel like I'm in a horror movie. It creeps me out. I get up and take the elevator up. I bypass my floor and keep going up to the top floor. When I exit the elevators, there's a room with a cross on the door, so I push through it. It's a chapel.

Everything in the room is designed to be soft, like a padded cell. Colors are muted, tans and slates and roses. It smells like carpet. Sounds are absorbed by the thick floor and wall coverings. A few short polished wooden benches line the center aisle, and a lone wooden cross is illuminated on the front wall. Lights are recessed along the wall and create a halo around the room. Instead of anything overtly religious, alcoves are decorated with plants that have no dead or imperfect leaves.

There's nothing alive in this room.

I'm so tired. I decide to take a nap on one of the benches. I lay down and cradle my head in my arm. The wooden surface is unforgiving. I shift and try to find a comfortable position. I close my eyes.

I feel the waves of tired wash over me. My limbs ache with it. But then there's something else. The ache turns into a pain, a physical twist at my core that makes me want to scrunch up in a little ball. I take deep breathes and feel the hardness of the wood against my hip bone and my shoulder and my elbow. I feel the backrest propping me up. I breathe.

Was it something I did that made Jes this way? Something I should've done but didn't? I didn't drink, especially since I knew I was pregnant from the start. I tried to eat right, get a little exercise. I even took vitamins—not every day but at least most days. No, I really tried the very best I could. Didn't I? It's like my body betrayed me. It didn't do enough, I didn't do enough. Something was lacking and didn't give Jes what he needed. Something early on because that's when it happens. I should've done more, better, something.

I think about the Jes that could've been, Jes-without-SB. He wouldn't have had surgery already. His legs would kick and move like his arms. He wouldn't have to go through whatever else is coming, the surgeries that are in our future. He would eventually be able to walk and then run. He would kiss a girl and fall in love and marry and have kids. I cry, at first with wracking sobs but then tapering off, and I fall asleep.

Then I wake up slowly. I think, I'm awake. But then I think, this is a dream. I'm still lying on the pew in the chapel. The light is different, though—coming from all around instead of just along the wall. Someone is standing over me, so I sit up. It's Jesus. It's the Jesus that looks like a hippy, like in those cheesy watercolor paintings. He's dressed in white and blue draperies, and he's even got the brassy halo thing. It's Jesus, but then I know it's also Jes, and he's all grown up. He morphs. He looks like Jackdaw, gangly but toned with spikey dark hair, but he's got green eyes like me. He's wearing an orange t-shirt over a long-sleeved white t-shirt and tan canvas shorts and tevas. He doesn't have leg braces or anything. He's perfect. "Mom," he says, "I'm all right." I feel a sob rising in my throat. "Really, Mom, I'm okay," he says. I reach out to him. My hands just touch the soft cotton of his shirt, and then my sobbing wakes me up. I sit up on the bench (again?) but there's no one there. I lay back down. I want to go to sleep again so I can see him, touch him. Please, come back. But I can't sleep because I'm crying too hard.

Tibs

I'm trying to assist with Jes as much as possible, but I've got student teaching too. Luckily, I scored a placement close to home, maybe because I opted for the spring semester. I've been observing and assisting for the past weeks, but today is the real McCoy, where I show my stuff.

Mr. Ahmed, my mentor, stands beside me at the front of the room. He is short and athletic, dark hair and dark skin, with a Chicago accent. "You ready?"

I nod. "At least you're letting me start with Hemingway."

The school is one of those constructed in the sixties, square red brick building with squared cement walkways and a flagpole out front. The classroom has a bank of tall windows along one side and those ubiquitous pale yellow plastic and metal desks with the pork chop surface like an arm extending on the right side. The classroom itself, though, has been upgraded with a computer for the teacher, a white board, and a projector mounted on the ceiling. We've cracked the windows a little because the heat is up too high, and the cold breeze feels good.

"Remember," Mr. Ahmed says. "It's not what I, the teacher, do for them. It's what they're doing, what they're learning. Passive oral learning has been shown to be much less effective than hands-on, taking it as your own."

"Yeah," I say, nodding. "Yes."

The hall bell rings, and soon students file in in twos and threes and take their seats. My hands shake with adrenalin, so I turn to the whiteboard and take deep breaths so they won't notice. On the board I write, "The Short and Happy Life of Francis Macomber." Soon, the second bell rings and the class quiets. A good sign. They know when they're supposed to pay attention, and they do it without asking.

"All right," Mr. Ahmed says. "You know Mr. Jordan. Today he's going to help us with Hemingway. Over the weekend, you read the assignment." It isn't a question. Mr. Ahmed's in control. Whether they like it or not, students learn better with a teacher who keeps a tight rein. That's something I'll have to prepare for and implement.

Mr. Ahmed looks at me and nods. Then he walks to the back of the room and leans against the wall.

"So, what do you all think?" I ask, raising the book and looking around the room. Some of the guys sit forward with their elbows on their desktops, their books in front of them. A lot of the girls lean way back with their arms crossed. "Isn't Hemingway great?"

This brings a snort from a big blonde girl sitting toward the front. I look at the seating chart. "Yes, Jessica? What did you think?"

"I stopped reading after the first page," she says. This brings bursts of laughter from the girls and a few of the boys. Great. My first day teaching, and I fail.

Mr. Ahmed says from the back, "Jessica, you just got an F for the day. You didn't do your homework." He nods to me. "Mr. Jordan."

Now what? "Okay. I guess … Jessica, why did you only read the first page?"

Jessica shakes her head and refuses to answer, but the girl beside her, a black girl named Sherise, says, "Because the woman in the story is a bitch." She glances to the back of the room. "Sorry, Mr. Ahmed."

A boy sitting toward the back says, "And it was boring." He glances toward Mr. Ahmed. "But I read it all," he says, "all of it." More laughs.

"All right," I say. "Some of you didn't like some of the characters. Some of you thought it was boring. Anybody else?"

"I thought it was cool," a boy with a black crew cut, Danny, says tentatively. Some of the other boys nod. "The way he was a coward and then became brave. Even though his wife took him out in the end."

"She what?" Jessica in the front says.

"If you read it, you'd know," Danny says. The boys laugh.

"Okay, okay," I say. "First, I guess we should make sure we're on the same page. What happens in this story? Danny, since you liked it?"

"This husband and wife are big game hunting in Africa with a guide. The husband chickens out and runs when he's supposed to shoot a lion, and then the wife does the guide instead of the husband and then shoots the husband dead when they're hunting buffalo."

Yes! "Good, Danny. Great. Yes, that's the gist of it. Anything else happen?"

Another boy says, "Well, the guy goes from chickenshit to brave."

"Yes," I say. I feel great because they are getting it, some of them. Some of them read Hemingway and liked him. Maybe I'm getting through—Hemingway's greatness breaking through their shell of self-absorption and technology.

"Yes. Good. Did everyone get that?" I say. A few nods. A few blank stares. "Some of you didn't get that?" More blank stares. "Well, Hemingway says a lot even when he doesn't seem to be saying anything. You have to pay attention. Those of you who were bored by the story, you probably didn't get what was happening." I don't have them convinced, I can tell. So I say, "All kinds of things are happening. The tension's so high you could cut it with a knife."

I try another tack. "Let's say you're walking down the hall, and you say hi to your best friend in the world. Then she or he cuts you, doesn't say hi back. What does that mean?"

"She's mad at me," a girl says.

"Right. Same goes here. Every little detail means something. Read this like you were reading the actions of your best friend, or your boyfriend or girlfriend, or your parents. Or you're in a life-threatening situation. It all means something."

As I say it, I realize it's true, so irrevocably true. Everything, absolutely everything, means something. The world is so full of meaning, it's overwhelming. The fact that I chose a tan shirt today, that means something. It reflects how tentative I feel and how I wish to blend into the walls. The way the building is laid out, large open halls with lots of windows, that means something. This is practical but it also reflects the optimism of its time and a focus on the kids themselves, a new approach to education. It all means something, only a small slice of which I can comprehend and understand. The world is a text and texts are the world. How can one person hope to capture that in words? All of a sudden, I am paralyzed. It's futile, really. Some people approach it, like Hemingway, but some of us no-talents don't stand a chance.

CJ

The nurse lets me in to the NICU for Maggie to teach me how to catheterize Jes. His bladder doesn't work right, something related to his SB.

"Here's what you do," she says. "Make sure you've got everything. You don't want to get partway through and realize you forgot the lube or something." On the tray are the catheter, KY jelly, some cotton balls, and a bowl of water with a few soap suds. "You washed your hands right?"

"Nurse Ratchet would've tackled me before I got past the sink," I say. The one we call Nurse Ratchet looks young but she tells all the other nurses—and the patients—what to do. When she tells you, you do it.

I watch as Maggie lays Jes back, opens his diaper, grabs his penis, pulls back his little foreskin, and cleans in a circular motion with the cotton balls dipped in the water. She explains it as she goes. She feeds the plastic tube into the end and pushes. Jes squirms a little. "Shshshsh-shshsh-shsh," Maggie whispers. She keeps pushing the tube and then stops as piss comes out the end and empties into the bag. Then she slowly pulls it out and does up his diaper.

This is a Maggie I've never seen. She doesn't hesitate. She's confident and competent. It's not that I doubt Maggie's

163

abilities. It's just that she takes charge. Being a mother of poor little Jes, in a weird way, is good for her. It's the role she's been preparing for her whole life.

"Next time, it's your turn," she says.

I shake my head and then nod.

"You want to hold him?" she says.

"Uh, sure. I guess." I hold out my arms and she puts Jes in them. I scoot back and sit in the rocker. "He's heavier than he looks," I say.

"Yeah," she says, smiling. "I think he's got an old soul. It weighs a lot."

I tickle his cheek. He turns his head and mouths my finger. I tickle his chest and he squirms. I tickle his leg, but he doesn't react. I tickle it again.

"He can't feel anything below the waist," Maggie says. "It's like he was in a car accident. His spine was injured. But it's good for him if you to move his legs and massage him. Gently."

"Will he heal?" I say as I move his legs in a careful bicycle motion.

"No. It's not like that. He'll never ..." She doesn't complete the thought and then excuses herself to go to the bathroom.

I look at my nephew. He looks up and then sees my face. His eyes play over mine, over my nose and mouth and then back to my eyes. I tickle the skin on his legs and then move his toes back and forth, first his right and then his left. "This little piggy," I say. I tickle the bottom of his left foot. As I do it, he jerks his arms. Wait a minute. He's not supposed to be able to feel anything. I tickle it again. He shifts his head back and forth, like he's trying to locate something. He does feel it. He does. And then he smiles.

That's it. I'm in love. Totally and completely.

Maggie comes back. "Maggie, look at this," I say. I show her.

She shakes her head, her brow wrinkled, but then says, "Do it again." I do, and Jes becomes a little agitated, waving his arms.

"How?" she says. She reaches out and touches the bottom of his foot with the palm of her hand. He stops and then seems to relax. She sits down but leaves her hand on his foot.

I put my hand over her hand. "I'm sorry, Maggie," I say. "I've been a fucking asshole."

She looks at my face, looks away, shrugs, and then looks back at my face. She nods.

It's that easy, this small miracle of forgiveness.

Maggie

I walk out of the swishing glass doors of Denver Children's carrying Jes in a portable car seat. Tibs goes to install the base and bring the car around. There's no resistance, no fanfare, just me blinking in the unforgiving light. They've taught me how to feed Jes and change his diaper and clean his wounds and all that, but I'm totally unprepared. How can I do everything that's needed, be the total support for another human being, especially one with special needs? His whole life is in my hands, and I feel the weight of that responsibility. The little nursing training I had helps, but it also makes me more aware of all the things that can go wrong, all the ways the human body can fail us. What am I going to do?

Tibs picks us up and we snap the car seat into place. I spend the whole hour and twenty minutes to my house turned around watching Jes.

"Jackdaw coming home soon?" Tibs says.

I glance at him and shrug. "He said he'd be back this week."

"Don't be too hard on him," Tibs says.

I don't say anything.

When we get there, Tibs helps me carry everything in. "You okay, Sis?" he says as he stands in the kitchen.

I nod and shrug.

"Okay, then," he says.

The house looks bigger than it did before, and messier. I hadn't realized how dirty this place had become. You know how a place becomes unconscious? But when you leave and come back, you see all those things you took for granted. What I see looks like a rodent burrow. Dirty dishes piling in the sink, spills on the counter, mail and newspapers on the table. Why had I brought the vacuum onto the kitchen linoleum? The living room has a nest of blankets on the couch and a pile of books and magazines on the coffee table. The rug is filthy.

Right there, I vow a new beginning. Everything's going to be better. I'm going to be a better person, the perfect mother, the perfect wife. Somewhere along the way, I let Jackdaw down, and I don't think it was just the mess, but now I'm going to live up to what he expects of me. I'm not sure what that is, but I'm going to figure it out. And I'm going to be such a good mom, Jes is going to heal and he's going to get better. He's going to grow up happy and healthy. It's going to be all right.

As Jes naps in his car seat, I begin to clean. I make a clean spot in the kitchen that radiates outward. First, I do the dishes and then clean the countertops and table. I move the vacuum to the living room and sweep and mop the kitchen floor. I pick up the living room and vacuum. I wipe down the bathroom, clean the toilet, and wash the floor. I pick up and vacuum the bedrooms. The house is done and I'm wiped out by the time Jes wakes up. So I sit in the chair and feed him and drink a cup of coffee. All's right with the world.

We develop a pattern over the next few days. I sleep when Jes sleeps, and I'm awake when he's awake. My life becomes smaller, a series of very short days, but it's better too. All my concerns have narrowed to this lovely little being and we're doing fine. CJ calls and stops by every day or two to let me have a little extra rest and to bring groceries.

Late in the afternoon of the fourth day, which is cold and overcast, Jackdaw's pickup pulls into the driveway. I see his familiar outline on the driver's side. My stomach flutters like the first time I saw him. I run to the bathroom and splash water on my face and brush my hair. I pick up Jes but then put him down again. It's cold outside, and maybe Jackdaw would like to come in first, but he sure is taking a long time. Jackdaw is so handsome walking up carrying his bags. They must be heavy because he's walking like he has the weight of the world on his shoulders. He's also lost weight, which looks good on him. He's rumpled from travel, a scratch of a beard, clothes wrinkled, but that makes him look even better.

I go to the door, hesitate, and then go through it. I step out onto the porch. I can see my breath in the air and feel the cold through my light jacket. I cross my arms and rub my shoulders as I watch Jackdaw.

He walks heavily up the steps and then stops and lets his bags drop. His face doesn't change as he looks at me. I don't know what he's thinking but I try not to let how disappointed I am show on my face. Something makes me hang back, even though I want to hug him so bad. He looks from my face to my belly and then away to the side. I walk to him.

He looks back at me and then slowly puts his warm palm on my cheek. "You're just as pretty as I remember," he says, his voice low.

Relief goes through me. It's all right! It's all right. He'd been acting so strange before when I was pregnant, and he didn't come home right away. But now all that vanishes into his warm palm. This is what I needed, I wanted. "And you're just as gorgeous," I say and wrap my arms around his body. I hold him so tight I try to pull him into me. His arms wrap around me to but he doesn't hug me exactly. He holds me loosely, like he's afraid I'm going to break.

"Jackdaw?" I say into his shirt. "I missed you."

"Yeah, baby, I know."

We stand for precious minutes like that, and then he pulls back and picks up his bags. I hold the door open for him to walk through. Then he puts his bags down in the entry and walks into the kitchen. He slows as he walks past Jes, but it's like those magnets with the wrong ends together—he steers a wide slow arc around him. He stops but doesn't turn his head and stands for half a minute. Then he goes to the fridge and reaches in for a beer. I pick Jes up and go over to Jackdaw and say. "Here he is, Jackdaw. Jes, meet your daddy."

Jackdaw looks at him, but not really looking at him, and says, "Uh huh."

"Jackdaw?" I hold Jes out again.

"Now, Maggie, let me sit down, at least."

I follow him into the living room. He sits on the couch. I bring Jes and sit next to him. "Doesn't he have the most intelligent eyes?" I say. "He just watches everything. Look, Jackdaw."

"Maggie," Jackdaw warns as he pushes himself up and away and stands with his back to me. I've done something wrong.

"He's your son. Won't you even look at him?"

Jackdaw spins back around. He half-laughs. "He's your son. He came from you."

"What do you mean? He's your son too."

"I mean—" He throws his hand out like he's about to say something and then stops and shakes his head. Then he walks out of the room back to the kitchen. I follow with Jes.

"Jackdaw? Jackdaw? What's the matter? He's yours. He is. He couldn't be anybody else's."

"I don't care if he is. He came from you and what you are. It's your fault." He goes back to the bedroom and shuts the door and the radio is turned up loud.

I stand in the middle of the kitchen, Jes in my arms, staring after him.

Jackdaw

What is that damn noise? For God's sake, it's—what—two in the morning? No, it's only 11. What the fuck?

Oh, yeah, I'm *home*.

I was having the best dream too. I was standing up in front of a crowd, a *big* crowd, and I was talking. They were listening, laughing, saying, "That Jackdaw, he's our man. There's no one like Jackdaw." But you know the best part? There was my dad, front row, smiling. At me. He had his chest all puffed out. He turned to the guy next to him and said, "Yeah, that's my son." Like a fucking TV commercial.

Maggie lays beside me. Stirs. Then she flips the covers over, running a cold breeze up my back. She goes into the other room toward the squawking. I roll over and put a pillow over my head. I fall asleep again, grasping back toward that dream.

Then I'm waking up again, this time out of a sex dream, one of those where the woman is perfect, and willing. I've got a hard on. I turn toward Maggie, wanting to feel her warm tits and continue the dream, but she's not there.

"What the fuck?" I say it out loud as I sit up. Light through the window shows it's broad daylight. I yawn and push off the covers and walk out into the living room. There's Maggie curled in a blanket with the kid on her lap. Curled around him like she used to curl around me. All I can see of the little mutant is a scrap of black hair.

I want to go over to her and shake her awake. Listen, bitch, I want to say. I want to shake her to get her attention. I want her to be there for *me*, to fuck *me*, to make *me* breakfast.

Instead, I turn to the bathroom and turn on the shower. As it's warming up, I piss. Then I step into the shower. It feels good on my shoulders, the prickly hot streams massaging me. I jerk off, but when I come it's like I haven't. I don't get that satisfied feeling. Which leaves me with this urge to pull the cabinets off the walls and throw them through the window.

I throw on some sweats and go back out into the living room. I smell coffee. Maybe that'll help. When I go into the kitchen, Maggie has the little mutant laying on his back on the kitchen table. He's spread-eagle, and she has his pecker in her hand and she's trying to shove a tube up it.

"Good morning, baby," she says to me as I walk by. "How'd you sleep?"

I don't say anything, just go to the cupboard and get a cup and pour myself some coffee.

"I hope Jes didn't wake you," she says. "I tried to be quiet."

Yeah, right, I think.

She finishes what she's doing and wraps it in a diaper and then a blanket and then holds it to her chest. She makes this guttural sound and rocks it. Her attention is totally on it. She's focused on it.

The bitch. Now I know how Dad felt.

Maggie

Ever since Jackdaw came home, he's been acting weird. The transition has been hard on all of us, what with being up all night and getting used to having a baby around. Plus he's having a hard time concentrating to write. Next thing you know, he'll be back out on the road.

But you know what I've decided? It's going to work because I'm going to make it work. Jes is going to get better because I'm going to take such good care of him that he'll be so strong and healthy. And I'm going to make everything perfect for Jackdaw, cause he likes things to be perfect.

So I start right away. Three times a day, I go through the house and make sure everything is picked up. When I take a shower in the morning, I wipe down the bathroom. I make big breakfasts and make sure lunch is on time and plan ahead for dinner. I have Tibs or CJ get things at the store for me, things Jackdaw likes, like cherry Twizzlers and Chunky Monkey ice cream and Coors.

I try my best to keep Jes quiet around him because all Jackdaw does when he looks at him is frown. I don't quite know what to do about that, but he's going to get used to him, and after a while, he'll learn to love him. How could he not, with Jes as adorable as he is? I'll just keep Jes happy but present, you know?

The day that Jackdaw and Tibs decide to drive into Denver, I make big plans. I bake a ham and make mashed potatoes and gravy from scratch. I don't have much besides ice cream for dessert, so I improvise and make homemade chocolate sauce. It turns out a little runny but okay. I stop when I need to and feed Jes and cath him. When he naps in the afternoon and the ham is baking, I take a nap too so I'll be nice and rested. I hum as I take a quick shower and do my hair, Jes lying in his car seat on the floor, waving his hands, and staring up at the ceiling. At the sound of the hair dryer, he wrinkles his forehead and turns his head. When I turn the air on him, he blinks and looks surprised. I laugh.

I'm just setting everything on the table when Jackdaw and Tibs walk through the door. Jes sleeps in his car seat in the corner. Jackdaw shrugs off his coat and hangs it.

"Hmmm? That smells good," Tibs says, making a show of sniffing the air as he's unzipping his coat.

That would ruin everything! I look at Tibs, willing him to look at me. He does. I try to tell him without telling, trying to make him understand.

He does. "Too bad," he says. "I'd love to stay for dinner, but I've got papers to grade." He smiles at me, zipping his coat back up.

"You sure?" Jackdaw says. "There's plenty."

"Nope. Duty calls."

"You should stay," Jackdaw says.

Tibs shakes his head and claps Jackdaw on the shoulder as he makes his way out the door. "Later."

"Hey hon," I say. "Supper's ready."

Jackdaw washes his hands at the sink and sits down.

"I made ham, your favorite," I say.

He doesn't say anything.

"How was your day? What did you do?" I serve myself a small slice of ham.

"Not much." He's cutting off chunks of ham, dipping them in gravy, and putting them in his mouth.

"Do you like it?"

"It's all right."

We eat in silence.

After a while, I say, "Jackdaw?"

He says, "Hm?"

I say it again, "Jackdaw?"

He looks at me, with his face sort of sideways to mine, but he's looking at me.

"Did you have a good day?"

He sighs. "Yes, Maggie. I did."

I push my chair back and walk over to him. He pushes back his chair to let me sit in his lap. I curl my face down into his neck to inhale his smell, deodorant and sweat. I don't move, and he doesn't move, and I try to melt my body into his.

Then I start to kiss his neck. I move to his lips. I kiss him soft at first and then harder, willing him to kiss me back. He does, and after a while, he's kissing me hard, pulling me to him like he wants to pull me inside him. He puts his arms around me and stands, scooping me up and holding me in front of him. He carries me to the bedroom.

I think, Jes? But he'll be all right. If he wakes up and needs me, he'll holler.

Maggie

We're stripping and kissing and before I know, before I'm even ready, Jackdaw spreads my legs and enters me. It hurts a little, but Jackdaw's need is strong. But then he stops. He pushes me over and up on all fours and enters me from behind. Then he's thrusting into me so hard I have push back and bend my neck so I don't hit the wall. He's saying something under his breath, something he's sort of chanting with each thrust. I'm trying to get myself excited, but it hurts so I just hope he comes soon. I hear Jes start to tune up in the other room. Not crying yet but just making crabby sounds. What should I do?

Jackdaw is thrusting harder and harder. He comes, but then he almost immediately pulls out and pushes himself up off the bed.

"Hon?" I say.

"I'm taking a shower." He turns and goes to the bathroom.

I push myself up to go to see to Jes.

I've got to keep trying, keep going. I hope I have the energy.

CJ

I don't know what to do about Peter—really, whether I should do anything at all. We have a convenient relationship. I have someone to have dinner with, and he does too. We've been at this so long, it feels like old socks. But don't socks sometimes start to fray? Get holes in them? That's when you want to throw them out.

For instance, I bartend on a sunny Thursday and Peter sits at the end of the bar. His shift is over, and he's half plowed already. It's lunchtime. In comes a man and wife. She's pretty, wearing one of those fashionable maternity tops under a blue wool coat with dark pants and low heels. He's in a slate blue suit with a yellow tie. Since the wife is obviously pregnant, I think, uh oh, I'm going to have to refuse to serve a pregnant lady. But no, she just orders soda water.

It's funny because the husband does all those things that expectant fathers are supposed to do. He helps her off with her jacket and pulls out her stool and helps her into it. All the things I don't expect Jackdaw did for Maggie. This guy is so, I don't know, protective. For some reason this strikes me as funny, fucking hilarious, so when I'm done serving them I walk down to the end of the bar where Peter is. I lean against the bar with my back to the couple.

"Hey, Peter, get a load of this." I nod backwards toward them.

"What?"

"The pregnant couple. The guy's killing himself for her."

"All a conspiracy for women to dominate the earth," Peter says and laughs. "Get us bound so tight we can't see the world for the diapers."

"Yeah. Women get pregnant to dominate the earth." I shake my head. "They can hardly walk, but, boy, are they controlling things."

"Besides, pregnancy is bad for morale, not to mention business."

I'm in a prickly mood, so I say, "No. Good for business. Bringing up more customers."

"In twenty-one years. Not exactly what you'd call a smart business model."

"So you'd rather see humans die out than lose customers? Alert the press. Local business owner advocates mass sterilization. That ought to draw the crowds."

"Oh, CJ. Are you getting your period?"

"Fuck you, Peter."

"What is it up to now? Every two weeks? Every week?"

I decide to ignore this. "So, what you're saying, Peter, is that you don't want to have kids."

He looks a little shocked. "Where did that come from? CJ has a biological clock."

When he says that, it comes to me. I've been thinking, well, maybe Peter and I will decide to get married one of these days, and then we'll adopt. Kind of the way you think when you're twenty and you have your whole future ahead of you. Yes, you'll get married and have kids—you just take it on faith—but you haven't met the right guy yet. But I'm twenty-seven. Most people my age are married. And Peter isn't just holding back. He really, really doesn't plan on marrying me, or having kids.

And now all of a sudden I'm sad. I realize that it's over between us. Peter and I will never sleep together again. Not only that, but it's been over for a long time, and I just hadn't seen it. I cough because I feel like crying—just because it's over doesn't mean it isn't sad. A part of your life moving into the past.

If they're your favorite socks, you hate to toss them in the garbage, even with the holes.

Maggie

Jackdaw's never home now. He says Jes's noise makes it so he can't concentrate, so he goes into town to write. Other times he's on the road. We don't see much of him. I miss him, you know? Even when he's here, he's still gone. I keep trying to make things better. Make things nice for him. But I get tired. I'm up and down every two or three hours. Jackdaw sleeps through it all. Maybe because he drinks a little to help himself sleep.

But—guess what—Jes is a month old today. Can you believe it? He's doing okay. Not gaining lots of weight, it's true, but doing all right. To celebrate, I give him a bath, lather him up with great-smelling Johnson's baby lotion, and put him in this cute African animal onesie. I'm lying on the couch. Haven't changed out of my pajamas. It's late morning and Jes lays on my chest and blows bubbles. He's just learned how to do it. First he spits a bunch so his chin is covered with slobber, and then he opens his mouth like a guppy. These little spit bubbles poke out and then *pop!* It's the cutest thing. The first time he did it, it surprised him so much he squeaked.

He's awake a lot more now too. He loves to watch things. Whenever I'm near, his eyes never leave my face. He loves things that move. He watches his hand as it waves in front of his face. Sometimes he acts like it's a strange thing, and sometimes he starts to wave it madly like he's figured out it's part of him. I've made a mobile out of some wire clothes hangers, white cardstock, and a black marker. He loves it. There's also a bright red and blue plastic rattle he likes.

He makes this funny noise sometimes though. It's a little scary. When he breathes, it sounds like a high-pitched wheeze. It's sort of like you'd get from pneumonia, but he hasn't had a fever or any other symptoms. It hasn't been bad at all so I haven't taken him to the doctor, but I'm going to mention it next week when we're there.

He's also been doing this thing lately where he'll take the nipple in his mouth but then spit it out again. I'll try to put it back in but he'll turn his head away like he doesn't want it. He's really really hungry, though, you can tell. He turns his head when something touches his cheek, and he gets that pinched hungry look. Sometimes he just leaves the nipple in his mouth. It's like he's afraid to suck or something.

Lying on my chest, he starts to fuss a little. He's hungry, past time for him to eat. I pick up his bottle and put it in his mouth. He's so hungry he sucks hard on it. Then he stops for a bit and sucks hard again. It's like his body is trying to keep up with his sucking. He doesn't take very much before he spits it out and won't take any more. Then he drifts off to sleep. I decide to take a cat nap before it's time to cath him, so I put my head back and close my eyes.

I must've fallen asleep because I come awake and Jes struggles in my lap. He's fighting something, arching his back and rocking his head side to side. His lips are blue, and then rapidly his whole face turns blue. Panic shoots through me. I put him to my shoulder and jump up. I flop him into his car seat and grab my cell phone and purse and run out to my car. I don't even bother clipping him in. I just throw the seat into its base and jump in the front and start the car. As I'm driving, I call 911. The ambulance meets me in 8 minutes, about halfway. I leave my car by the side of the road and get in the ambulance with Jes, who's started to come out of it a little. His color is much better. His O_2 when they hook him up to the monitor is 76. It should be, say, 95, above 90 anyway. I'm sure it was much lower before. They put him on oxygen right away. When we get to Bethlehem Hospital, Jes's O_2 is up to 89, even without oxygen. We are admitted through the emergency room and spend five and a half hours waiting, talking to the pediatrician on duty, not our regular pediatrician, and taking tests. As we're discharged, the pediatrician, an older man who doesn't volunteer much information, says, "Well, keep an eye on him." CJ drives us home.

When I tell Jackdaw about all this, I keep it low key, like Jes's just had a cough. Something tells me he wouldn't take it very well if he knew the truth.

The same thing happens twice more that same week. Each time, my heart races. We go to the emergency room, but by the time we get there, Jes is doing much better. We always seem to get the same pediatrician, and he always makes notes as I describe Jes's symptoms, but each time he sends us home and says, "Well, keep an eye on him." I want to grab this man and shake him. He acts like I'm making it up. Like I just do it for the attention.

The fourth time it happens, my heart doesn't race quite as much. How can a person get used to something like this? But I do. I don't bother calling 911. I strap Jes in and we drive to Denver Children's. Jes has totally recovered by the time we get there, but we're able to get in to see Dr. Erickson, our neurosurgeon. He's a tall thin clean-shaven man with glasses who always wears bright ties with Disney characters. He looks Jes over and asks some questions. Has he been making any noise while breathing? How has he been eating? There's a condition called Chiari II malformation, he says, that can cause problems in kids with SB.

Then, as we're sitting there, Jes does it again. He's struggling to get air, arching his back. His O_2 goes down and down and down. Dr. Erickson hits a code blue, and people rush in. I kiss the air above Jes's head as they whisk him off. But I feel better being here in the hands of a doctor I trust. A while later, Dr. Erickson comes back in. He explains that the harsh breathing is called stridor and is an indication of the Chiari II malformation, and what has been happening is Jes can't swallow like normal so the formula has been draining into his lungs. His lungs fill with fluid, so he's drowning in his own food.

At first I feel self-righteous because I'd been right. I wasn't imagining things. Dr. Erickson took me seriously and I was right. But now, to find out it's my fault. My God. I almost drowned Jes. My God! I should've known something was seriously wrong. I should've sensed it. I feel awful.

Dr. Erickson has me sign a surgery consent form and directs me to the waiting room. I sit there trying not to think: Right this minute, they've got a knife and they're slicing into him. He may be totally out, but the body has to know. It has to be sending pain signals to the brain, even if whatever they're

183

giving him stops the signal. The body knows. Do you suppose the body is like an old glove? An old glove holds the memory of the hand that it held. Its curves stay cupped and show everything about the hand's history. If you shovel dirt, the shovel handle rubs the leather and wears it away. If it's cold and dry, the leather cracks. The body has to be like that, showing little signs as we age of what's happened to us. Little body memories. Poor Jes. His body memories are bad things.

You know what surgery really is? It's the same thing as getting in a car crash, only you're closer to help. As far as the body knows, it's just like you got mangled in some farm equipment.

So, instead of thinking about it, I distract myself by trying to figure out what other people in the waiting room are like. A woman, overweight and wearing black spandex and an old spangled t-shirt, is talking on a cell phone. "Yeah," she says, "he came over like he always does and then expected me to have sex with him, can you believe it?" She reaches over and pushes the shoulder of a younger woman, a larger version of herself. "Sue says I should kick his ass out for good." The younger one gives a throaty laugh. She's obviously a smoker. There are two small girls with pixie faces and long brown hair sitting at their feet playing. The younger larger woman reaches down and slaps the older girl. "What'd I tell you about that?" she says in a loud voice. The poor kid get this expression on her face that just makes me ache for her, head tilted to the side and down and forehead scrunched up. She's trying not to cry. How could that mother be so heartless? It's like she's a kid herself and never learned that you're not supposed to hit, you know? Later, when the woman isn't looking the older girl pulls a toy away from the younger girl, who starts crying.

I have an urge to get up and grab the girls by the hand and walk away with them. How can these women take these little girls for granted like that? Don't they know how precious they are?

Around the corner is a big Hispanic family, at least three generations. There's gray-haired grandparents, parents, sulky teenagers wearing bright colors, and kids who everybody seems to look after. They're talking in Spanish, so I can't understand what they're saying, but everyone seems to listen well. A young couple come out and everyone stands and they talk. They all pay attention and talk and give each other hugs. It makes me happy for the kid who's in surgery right now, to have a family like that.

I wait and wait. I want to call Jackdaw, so I flip open the phone, but then I flip it shut again. Am I protecting Jackdaw from Jes, or am I protecting myself from Jackdaw? I don't know.

The waiting room desk person calls me over and says that the surgery is over and the nurse will come and get me. When he does, he says that everything went fine. I walk to the recovery room, and Jes lays there all bleary-eyed and confused from the anesthesia. He is taped and wired everywhere. His head is bandaged all the way around, there's a tube coming out the front of his throat that's hooked up to a ventilator, and his belly has a bandage on it and a tube coming out of it, plus all the usual monitoring wires and IVs. I look at him and feel really really bad. He's lost under all the equipment, so small and so helpless. I see all the bandages and seeps of blood and I think of all the places he's been cut into, tore apart, all the pain. It makes me feel weak.

I don't want my reaction to come through to him, though. He may be just a baby, but I want him to feel safe, protected, like someone is taking care of him. That it won't happen again. When they have me pick him up and rock him, I try to relax, to let my reactions go. "You're all right," I repeat again and again. "You're going to be all right."

But it has to show through, don't you think, how horrible I feel? He has to look at me looking at him with a scared look in my face, and he has to feel how my body is tense all over and frantic. How tight I hold him. He has to know.

That night is the worst. I can't sleep. I've had too much coffee and not enough water and not enough food and my head pounds and my body aches, but I don't feel anywhere near as bad as Jes. I pray and pray. If we make it through tonight, I promise, I'll do anything, anything.

Early in the evening, I get the type of the nurses I used to dread when I was training. They stand around the nurses' station and gossip. When I push the button for help, they ignore me for a while, and when they do come, they make me feel like it's my fault for pushing the button. But, thankfully, halfway through the night, there's shift change, and our nurse is a good one. She's overworked—because she's pulling other people's weight, I'm sure—but she's really nice, and when I push the button, she's there.

Most of the night, it's just me and Jes in a cold dark room, the *ping* and *puff* of the machines, the heartbreaking cries of the kids down the hall, and every once in a while people walking by and talking in hushed tones. I hold Jes as close as I can. "It's going to be all right," I say. "Jes, it's going to be all right, it's going to be all right, it's going to be all right."

After a day, I go home with Jes on a ventilator and a feeding tube. The ventilator helps him breathe and the feeding tube helps him eat. This becomes normal, part of our daily routine.

He can't cry any more, though tears roll down his cheeks. He can't make sounds because of the ventilator. I have to pay special attention to how he's acting to see if he's in pain.

Mornings, I suction his trach. You have to be careful. Since that's where he breathes, you have to do it quickly and carefully because you have to get his ventilator hooked back up so he doesn't turn blue. You unhook the plastic collar that holds his trach in place and clean and replace the cotton protector. Then you hook him back up.

Jes struggles a little sometimes. I know it hurts. I try to be gentle but to hurry too. It's so hard. I get so tired of hurting him. Every day I have to hurt him. I know it's for his good, and he's really patient with me, as good as he can be. But I dread it. I think, now I've got to go hurt my little boy. But I do it because I have to, because he needs it. How is he going to get well if I don't? So I do it. I hurt him.

Then I feed him. He gets his formula through his gastro tube. Then I wash him and change his diapers. Next, I give him some physical therapy and massage him a little. I move his arms and legs and rub him firmly but gently. I tickle his skin lightly with my fingers, even over the skin where he can't feel. I also stimulate his mouth. Since he can't eat with his mouth, it's good for him. I use these little rubber things that are nubby and have different textures. By the first naptime he's really tired. So am I, but I get to spend time with him, and that makes it all worth it.

When I go into his room and he's awake and he sees me and his whole body changes. It's like a switch. He turns on. I can't really explain it. Words don't work. It's like he creates this beam of energy that washes over me. It's like he makes my devils go away. He hardly moves, but I know just by walking into the room I've caused a miracle. Miracles are like that. They aren't things you plan for months and then make happen. Nobody can make them happen. And lots of times they're so small that nobody even notices. A miracle. I don't know how to explain it any other way. I only have to show up, such a little thing, and without moving he showers me with light.

It's Friday, and we're going through our routine. I can hear Jackdaw and Tibs talking in the living room as I change Jes's diaper. When I open it up, he's got diarrhea and a bad case of diaper rash. It smells awful. Under the tan-brown mucusy mush, there's pink splotches radiating out onto his butt cheeks and under his scrotum. When I wipe him clean, he struggles against it, and his butt starts bleeding.

Tibs comes in. "Hey, I'm going to head out," he says. As he turns to leave, he sees Jes's butt and says, "Maybe you should see the doctor about that."

Quickly, I think, yes, it's Friday, we'd better go before the weekend because if we wait we have to go to the emergency room and it costs a lot more money and it's one big hassle. Then, I sag. I think, I don't want to go to the doctor. I don't want any more doctors. Yes, yes, I do appreciate everything they've done, but I'm so sick of hospitals and doctors and surgeries and machines. I just want to be left alone. I don't want to have to hurt him anymore. I don't want him to be cut open any more. I want all the tubes taken out and all the machines disconnected. I just want my little boy, just my little boy. I'm so sick of this, sick to death of it.

God, why did you do this?

CJ

On one hand, little Jes is so perfect, so wonderful, so right, and watching Maggie with him is a dream. It's like she was meant for this. With everything he's going through, he's still such an angel. You just love him so much. It makes me ache to have a child.

But, then again, maybe not. Maybe I'm thankful that I'm sterile. Watching Maggie, her heart bloody and beating outside her chest for little Jes, it just hurts too much.

Tibs

CJ and I are concerned about Maggie. She always was slight, but now she's approaching too thin. She always has these raccoon circles around her eyes, and she's distracted, like she's thinking about something else or she's simply too tired to think. CJ and I have talked about it, and we're not quite sure what to do, other than go out and help her as much as possible. I don't know how much assistance Jackdaw is, really.

My cell rings as I'm scouring the sink. I glance and see it's Maggie, so I wipe my hands and answer it.

"Hey, Maggie," I say with a cheery note in my voice.

"Tibs, I was hoping you'd be home."

"I don't have to be home to answer my cell," I say and then regret it.

"No, I meant you'd be home so you wouldn't be out with Jackdaw."

"Oh." I try to make amends. "That's not what I … I meant it as a joke."

"I know," she says, neither taking offense nor laughing.

Quickly I say, "Are you doing okay? Is there anything I can do?"

"That's why I was calling. You aren't out with Jackdaw, are you?"

191

"No. He's not out there?"

"No." There's silence on the line. It gets longer and more pregnant.

I say, affecting a John Wayne, "We-all, what can I do you for, little lady?"

"It's, well, could you help me with Jackdaw?"

Alarm bells go off in my head. The quickest way into trouble, with them both hating me. "I don't think I'm—"

"No, wait! Before you say no."

"I'm sorry, Maggie, of course."

"All I need is for you to help me make Jackdaw love Jes."

"What?"

"I mean, maybe if you talked to him, convince him to give him the benefit of the doubt, spend some time with him, then he'll warm up to him, you know?"

"He doesn't spend much time around the house, does he?"

"No, he can't concentrate, he says. Maybe if you talk to him?"

It's the least I can do. I'm not sure exactly what it is I am going to do, but I'll try.

The next day, Maggie tells me Jackdaw's in town, so I drive around till I spot his red truck. I exit my car, and then I see him through the window of the café as I walk up. He's staring off into space, and his closed laptop sits next to him on the table.

The café's one of those hip places with wifi and ficus and tapas platters. It has tables topped with craft tiles in all different shapes and a couch and easy chair with a low dark coffee table. The guy and gal working the counter are young and hip. He's got a three-day growth of beard and is wearing purple t-shirt that says "Save the Ales." She has dirty blonde dreads and a nose ring. I order a latte.

"Hi," I say to Jackdaw as I sit at his table, "that's the way I write too." I unzip my coat.

"Hey Tibs."

"What you doing?"

"Coffee," he says and lifts his mug in an explanatory gesture. "I was just thinking about this time my dad took me target shooting."

"What happened?"

"He didn't bawl me out."

"Hold the phones."

"No, really," he says and looks at me out of the corner of his eye without turning his head. Then he says, almost inaudibly, "At least I'm not …"

"What?"

"Forget it," he says. "Did you want something?"

"Not really." I say and tap the table. "Well, I was thinking, maybe, well, wondering how things were. You know, between you and Maggie."

"Don't go there, man." He pushes up his glasses and pinches the bridge of his nose.

"I just talked to her, and she sounds beat."

He doesn't say anything.

"I was thinking, maybe, between the two of us, we could watch Jes for a night while Maggie stays over to CJ's and sleeps. You know, give her a break? CJ and I are pretty worried about her."

He looks down at his hands and after a pause says, "Hey, did I tell you the book's coming along? I think I've figured out how to end it."

"Yeah? Going well, then?"

"Oh, you know, some days a diamond." Then he doesn't say anything, just keeps looking at his hands.

"Well, got to go." I stand up and grab my coat. "What about it? You and me and the little man?"

"Ah, I don't know." He shakes his head. "Now's not a good time." I can tell from his voice, it's final.

Maggie

Eight in the morning and I lay on a quilt on the floor next to Jes's bed and bawl. I've been bawling for a half hour with no signs of stopping. The crying puffs my eyes closed and presses my sinuses and makes my throat scratchy. I'm just so tired. Beat. Exhausted. Absolutely gone. Being tired wouldn't be so bad, but it's the way it makes you feel emotionally. The worst part is, I feel this huge whirlpool inside that sucks everything down and down and twists me into knots. If I didn't have Jes to need me, I'd be thinking suicide. It's awful. There's no end in sight. It's poor Jes in pain and me giving him pain and not able to make it better. The way he looks at me. He doesn't blame me, but he looks at me like, Mommy, make it go away.

I can't do it. I just can't do it anymore.

The doorbell rings. I sit up and swipe my eyes with my fingers and then pinch the snot off my nose and rub it on my shirt. I glance at Jes, who's sleeping, and at his machines, which are fine. I take a deep breath and go to the door. There's a woman standing there with the rising sun shining across her slantwise. She looks a little familiar. She's slender, wearing a pink coat over scrubs with large pale green and purple flowers on the top with green bottoms. She's carrying a big blue shoulder bag. She has short dark hair, and her face looks fresh-scrubbed, healthy. She's not wearing any makeup or jewelry.

When I open the door, she holds out her hand to shake. She says, "Hello, I'm—" As I quickly wipe my right hand on my shirt and reach to take hers, she glances at my face. "Oh, hon," she says and drops her bag on the stone porch and steps forward and puts her arms around me. I get a whiff of Ivory soap. I stiffen. "Oh, hon," she says. Then it wells up inside me—I'm bawling again, I can't help it. I'm just so tired. "Let's get you some hot chocolate, some tea, something hot. That's just the thing." She let me go, picks up her bag, and then leads me into my own house. She finds the kitchen, puts her bag on the table, and pushes me toward a chair. She opens the fridge. "Got any half and half? Ah, milk'll have to do." She rifles through the cupboards until she finds what she's looking for. She microwaves two mugs of water. She unwraps the tea bags and dips them in and out, in and out. She puts in lots of milk and lots of sugar and stirs. Then she puts one in front of me and sits across from me with the other. This gives me time to recover.

"I'm the nurse. From the agency. Your family set it up?"

"My family? My husband?"

"No. Seems like a woman and a man—your sister and her husband, maybe?"

"Probably CJ and Tibs, my sis-ister and brother." This makes me choke up again—because of their thoughtfulness, but also because it wasn't Jackdaw.

She starts talking, giving me time to recover. "I'm the home health nurse. To help out. Give you a break, let you get some rest." She pauses. "You may not remember me. My name's Bo Hansen. I used to work at Bethlehem where you were training?"

I nod, trying to remember. "Yeah, I think so."

She changes the subject to nursing, how she decided she'd had enough of doctors and hospital swing shifts. Time go home health full time. We finish our tea.

"Now, Maggie, let's check on Jes and then get you to bed," she says. We go into Jes's room. He's awake and when Bo leans over his crib, his eyes fasten on her face and his jaw opens a little and drool slides out of the corner of his mouth. He's taking in this new face. She says, "How's our little man today?" and puts her palm on his forehead. He continues to look at her. Then she just takes charge. She checks his trach and the ventilator and asks me the last time he ate and about his cath schedule. She changes his diaper. Her movements are sure and efficient. I feel a little better.

"Now, you just go on. Take a hot bath if you'd like. Get some rest. I'm only supposed to be here for 12 hours, but I'm not doing anything tonight so you want to sleep a little later, that's okay." She smiles at me again. There it is again, the sob rises just below the surface.

I don't bother taking my clothes off, anything. I just fall into bed, and I'm asleep.

CJ

Tibs and I are in Maggie's warm kitchen. I pull the papery skin off boiled potatoes for potato salad. Tibs forms hamburger patties. He slaps the patty back and forth between his hands and then places it on the plate. There's the heavenly smell of a Sara Lee apple pie in the oven. Maggie is asleep in her room, and Bo the nurse is in Jes's room. The asshole husband is nowhere to be found.

The nurse comes out into the kitchen and opens the fridge. She pulls a bottle of antibiotics out of the door and shakes it.

Bo is a good-looking woman. She works out, you can tell. She doesn't wear makeup, but she's got that beautiful skin that doesn't need it. She keeps her dark hair really short. She never wears boring nurse uniforms. Her clothes always have intricate animal patterns or flowers on them, and she's always color-coordinated. It's funny. She doesn't wear makeup or jewelry or rings, but she always looks so put together, like she's got purpose in her life.

"Something smells good," Bo says.

"Oh, that's just me," Tibs says.

Bo looks at me.

I smile and shrug.

"No, really," Tibs says. "Want to smell me?"

"Oh, I can smell you," she says, "from way over here." She smiles and waves the bottle of antibiotics, as if to say, got to give Jes his medicine, and goes back down the hall.

"See, that right there," Tibs says, "now don't you wish you could capture that? She's indescribable." He's got this look on his face, like he's a kid and there's a marshmallow in front of him and he's not sure he's supposed to have it.

"A nurse. There. Described. What's so hard about that?" I know what he means, but I'm being difficult because he's my brother.

"No. The overall impression of her in that moment."

"She came in to get medicine out of the fridge. What's there to describe?"

Tibs slaps another patty onto the plate. "CJ. Don't be obtuse. You always were a bull in a China shop."

I smile. There's the brother I love. "Better a bull in a China shop than a steer in a feed lot."

"Absolutely." He chuckles. He's got this shoulder shake when he laughs that is so Tibs. "Pull your head out, CJ. You know what I mean."

"Sure." I hold up a peeled potato. "She looks like one of the pictures of potato salad you see in those food magazines."

"What? CJ." He shakes his head.

"No. She does," I say. "You know how those magazines take the most amazing pictures? They can take a picture of an onion and make you want to pick it up and eat it like an apple."

Tibs looks skeptical.

"What I mean is, they can take something everyday and ordinary and it looks wonderful, like you want to go out this minute and buy some or make some. Just from the picture, you can taste the mustard and mayonnaise and feel the hard crunch of the celery and soft crunch of the pickles and the softness of the potato and egg. They make it look good for you, even though you know it's loaded with fat and calories. Bo's like that. She makes you want to go out and try some."

"CJ!" Tibs says. "You're downright poetic. Nurse Bo as potato salad. I like it."

My cheeks get a little hot.

"That's exactly what I mean," Tibs says. "You just did it, right there. You described it. It wasn't a cliché and it was perfect."

"It's just being honest."

"No, it's thinking outside the box," Tibs says, "which is you to a tee. Outside the box."

"Boxes are for Precious Moments," I say.

"Exactly."

We continue to work in silence. I get the potatoes peeled and start chopping them. A thought occurs to me. "Say, Tibs, didn't you write a short story in high school, something about playing football?"

"What? Oh, yeah." He shrugs.

"Didn't the guy in it talk about football like that, like he loved it."

"No, nothing like that."

I can tell he wants to drop it, but I'm nothing if not pig-headed. "Seems to me you did some pretty good describing in that. Something about the yell of the crowd rising from the stadium like a Baptist prayer service."

"A sorry-ass story if there ever was one." Tibs slaps the last patty on the plate with such force half of it tears off onto the table. I'm surprised by how mad he seems.

I'm out of patience too, all of a sudden. "Oh, Tibs, quit feeling candy-ass sorry for yourself. If you want to write, *git 'er done*, as they say."

"What?" he says.

"If you want to write, get a god-damn pen and piece of paper and just do it. You're too much in your head all the time."

"Right." He slaps the plate onto the counter and elbows the handle of the water faucet to wash his hands.

"Quit figuring out reasons not to do it and do it," I say.

As I say it, I realize that it applies to me to. I want to do something, change something, get the hell out of Dodge, so to speak. My life is stuck, and I'm sick of it, but I don't know quite where to go, what to do. I need to change something. Peter? My job? The whole kid thing? Unlike Tibs, I'm not afraid to go for it, only I don't know what *it* is.

He goes still for a minute and then looks at me. He raises his eyebrows. I nod. He tilts his head and gets that blank thinking look in his eyes.

We go back to fixing dinner.

Tibs

I motor to Maggie's to deliver groceries and to check on her and Jes. Spring is nigh—it's warmer, with the odor of mud and something else, plants sprouting maybe. You begin to allow yourself to hope that winter will end.

I enter the kitchen door and spy Bo playing solitaire. I'm sure she heard me, but nonetheless I feel like a voyeur catching her in an unguarded moment. The dark cap of Bo's hair contrasts with her skin so that it appears ivory. No, that's a tired old metaphor. It's new-fallen snow against a dark pine bough. It has that quality of freshness, of wetness, of virginity, but also of iciness. The centers of her cheeks blush, as some people do, with their cheeks perpetually red from their cheekbones to their jawline. I wonder whether she, too, always blushes. Or might it be because of me?

I should just turn and retrace my steps. She's here to do a job, and I shouldn't interfere with that. But that's not what I want.

"Hey," I say.

"Jes's taking a nap," Bo says. "Maggie's sleeping too."

I nod. I really should leave. I can talk with Maggie another time. I rest the bags of groceries on the counter and hurriedly put them away. I place the oatmeal and Jes's formula in the cupboard and the milk and eggs in the fridge. I straighten and glance at Bo and catch sight of the back of her neck. Her hair is cut short like a boy's, and the slender cords of her neck flex and pull as she turns her head to play cards.

I want to say something, anything, but my mind remains blank. Why is it always thus? Why can't I just say, "Would you go out with me?" Why don't I have any slick pickup lines, me, who aces every vocabulary test? Why can't I just relax? Fuck.

Nervously, I start to whistle.

Bo's back is to me, but she says, "*Snow White and the Seven Dwarves.*"

"Huh?" I say, brilliantly.

"'Whistle While You Work,'" she says and turns toward me.

"Oh, yeah. The tune." I nod. She nods and turns back to her cards.

You fool, I tell myself, that was your chance. She's inviting you to talk. You chickenshit bastard, are you going to spend your life jumping at shadows?

Everything's put away. Should I go? I should go. But Bo's here and I don't want to leave. If she'd ignored me, I would've left, but she didn't. I take a deep breath. Do I do it? Can I? Will I?

Bo turns and looks at me expectantly, as if she knows. That look is the tow rope pulling the words from me. If she hadn't looked at me like that, I couldn't've said it: "Want to play some gin?"

She tilts her head sideways in a shrug. "You mean you want to lose miserably to a masterful gin player?"

I breathe. This bolsters me. "No. I mean, do you want to lose by so much I'll be ashamed of myself and lose a few hands just so you won't feel so bad?"

She glances at her watch. "Let me check on Jes. You deal. And if you look at my cards I'll know." She points upwards.

"Got a direct connection to the Man, do you?"

She wiggles her eyebrows and then rises to check on Jes.

I deal. My hands are shaking. I'm relieved I showered today, though I'm sweating now. I almost just threw on a pair of sweats and came. I comb my fingers through my hair, what there is of it. Well, I am what I am, not much to do about it at this moment. Maybe not having shaved will lend me a rugged look. Then I laugh: Would Hemingway think such a thing? The odd thing is, I think he would. He hated being overweight in his waning years. Of course, getting the girl still wouldn't've been a challenge, fat or no fat. I comb my fingers through my hair again.

"Nits?" Bo says, coming back into the room.

"What?"

"Nits? You know, bugs, in your hair?" Her voice trails off. "Sorry. Lame attempt at a joke."

I'm not the only one who's nervous, which allows me to feel better.

Bo sits and sorts the cards in her hand. She arranges three on one side and four on the other. She pulls one card from the right and puts it on the left. Then she pulls it again and puts it back on the right. Then she pulls it again and flicks its edge with her fingertip, *click-click*. Then she places it back into her hand, but in the middle.

She nods toward the discard pile. "I don't want it," she says. The card is the three of clubs, so I retrieve it to match the four and five of clubs in my hand, and I discard.

"So that's the way you're going at it," she says.

We play. On the first hand, I knock with seven, and she plays off so that she wins the points plus ten. On the second hand, she's gin. The third, she knocks with three. I finally win the fourth hand with gin. We only play to fifty, because she has to attend to Jes, and she smokes me.

We're gathering up the cards, me handing them to her as she squares them into a pile. I want to ask her out, to say the words, but I can't. I have never had what it takes, the forcefulness. I decide to let it go. Bo pushes herself away from the table, places her coffee cup in the sink, and again approaches the table. She looks at me. It's that look again, the one that got me to ask her to play gin. It pulls the words out of my mouth.

"Bo, would you go out with me?" I blurt. A stricken look comes over her face, so I panic. Have I misjudged her? "You probably don't want to," I say. "I'm sorry."

She shakes her head. "Sorry, it's just … Of course, of course. I'd love to." She smiles widely. "I'd love to."

We exchange details. "Just tell Maggie I'll stop back by later in the week," I say and leave. My legs are rubbery, as if I've just run a 10K.

This could be it. This really really really could be it. Really.

CJ

The strangest thing happened the other day. This guy came into Golddiggers about three in the afternoon on a weekday. As he came in, the golden sun bounced off the windows across the street. It shone through the door into the bar all around him so I couldn't see him at first. All this light, and then he shut the door, and he was just a bum. Looked like a Vietnam Vet, wearing camos and long grizzled beard. Unwashed, but there was another smell too, sweet, almost like cookies. His hair was in two long braids, and a bullet hole was tattooed on his forehead. He wanted wine, a white zin. As he ordered, he wouldn't meet my eyes.

You know how men often are—very physical. They fling their limbs out and generally seem unaware of other people's personal space. It's like they're trying to claim as large a space as possible. This man wasn't like that. He wasn't effeminate either, but he kept his arms pulled in next to his body and his eyes on the bar. He had this big man-purse, which he pulled out to pay me with nickels and dimes.

It was slow, so I tried to make conversation. It's part of a bartender's job to entertain, not just dispense drinks, so I can be quite the bullshitter.

"Just get to town?" I asked.

"Yes."

"I'm CJ," I said and held out my hand.

He froze and then said, "I'm Larry." He didn't take my hand.

"Well, you came to the right place. Friendliest bar in town."

He shrugged.

I got the message to back off, so I didn't say anything and turned to do the dishes in the sink. But I kept an eye on him.

He sat there for a couple of hours and drank two glasses of wine. He didn't watch TV or try to talk to anyone. He was so inside himself, mumbling, having subdued arguments, fidgeting. There was a drama going on, but it was all inside of him.

As I swiped by with a bar rag, he looked straight at me for the first time and said, "You're a hermit crab." His eyes were blue, with whites shot through with red.

"Yeah?" I kept wiping.

He insisted: "No, a hermit crab."

"Whatever, buddy," I said over my shoulder. I'd wiped down to the end by now. If he was going to be weird, I might have to throw him out.

I glanced at him. His eyes were on my face, and his head was thrust forward. It was urgent, what he was telling me. "Soon you'll get a beautiful new shell, one that fits you better."

I raised my eyebrows. Then he turned his eyes back to the bartop. Conversation over.

The thing is, I'd love a beautiful new shell. Anything would be better than this lonely gin-soaked one I have.

Tibs

For the rest of the week, my mind wanders. The hands on the clock are in a race to be the slowest. My students spend their time freewriting. They think it's cool because it's nothing more than goofing off. For teachers, there's no prep whatsoever. The students think they're getting away with something, and the teacher is definitely getting away with something.

My mind, as it wanders, returns to Bo. I resist the urge to call her. I keep thinking of excuses to phone: "Hey, Bo, I was wondering where you'd like to go Friday?" "Have you seen the show at the Imax?" "I need a nurse's opinion about Jes."

But I don't. Instead I ring CJ and tell her about the date.

"That's great!" she says. "Finally screwed up your courage."

"You don't understand," I say. "She's … She could be …" The words escape me.

"I get it," CJ says. And I'm sure she does. CJ's like that. She understands more than a sister should and forgives me anyway. "Don't do anything I wouldn't do."

"CJ. If I did half of what you'd do, it would scare the poor girl away."

She laughs. "Yeah, I guess you're right."

I decide to take Bo to dinner and a movie in Loveland or possibly Fort Collins. There isn't much going on unless we make the trek to Denver, but that's a long way to go on a first date. Better to play it safe and low key. Within easy dropping-off distance. It's been so long since I've been on a date I wonder if I'll remember what to do. You know, open doors, avoid topics like religion and politics, keep the conversation focused on her.

Friday afternoon, I wash my car and clean the interior, retrieving the old beer cans and McDonald's boxes. My body warms with the exercise, and I have to remove my jacket. I shower, shave, and dress, finally settling on dockers, a polo shirt, and a sweater. I could wear jeans but I don't want her perceive me as taking this too casually. As I drive to pick her up, I stop at Safeway and buy a single long-stemmed red rose. This feels old fashioned and formal, and I don't want her to think I'm uncool, but the more I think about it the more I want her to take me seriously. I hardly know her, but already I think this could be serious. She could be the one. I want to get things right, to use a formula that works.

I arrive at her apartment house, a stylish three-story building of red brick and glass. Even the late winter flowerbeds look like sinuous sculptures of desiccated plants and overreaching evergreens. I walk up the airy stairwell constructed of floating concrete steps. I find her number above the buzzer and ring the doorbell. My stomach grumbles and twitches nervously. I think, should I go through with this? But there she is, and she opens the door to allow me to enter. I've forgotten how much shorter she is than I. She's wearing a sleeveless slinky red dress with a slit up one leg and big fat black shoes. She's applied just a touch of makeup and her jewelry sparkles at her throat and her short hair is spiked. She looks edible and formidable at the same time.

I pull the rose from behind my back. "For you," I say—and immediately feel foolish.

She takes it and makes a show of smelling it. "Mmmmm," she says. "Why, thank you. Let me put it in some water." She turns and disappears around the corner into the kitchen. I survey her apartment. It's small. The kitchen, which I can't see behind the stub wall, and the dining the room and living room all run together in an L. There's a bedroom or two through an open doorway. The walls are painted turquoise and dark yellow, and posters of Betty Page and Marilyn Monroe and Lauren Bacall decorate the walls. One wall is lined with square mirror panels veined with gold.

She has a shelf of movies—*Titanic* and *Orlando* and *Forrest Gump*—but there's no books anywhere. I usually peruse a person's books. It's a Rorschach test. It informs me what interests them. What does it mean if there are no books?

She returns.

"Thanks," I say.

She gives a short laugh and raises her eyebrows. "Thanks for what?"

"Thanks for, for ..." I hesitate. I'm thinking, thanks for opening the door, for the effort, for being so beautiful, but it sounds too desperate, so I say, "For wearing such a beautiful dress."

"Well, thanks," she says.

"No, thank you."

She grins and performs an elaborate bow, right hand outstretched and inscribing circles in the air. "No, kind sir, the thanks is mine to offer to you." She straightens.

I stand, attempting to ascertain what to say.

"Oh, for heaven's sake," she says. She approaches me and stands on tiptoe. She places her hands on my shoulders, pulls me down, and kisses me on the lips. I'm so surprised, my arms rise, but then they settle on her waist. "There, now you can relax," she says. "So relax, for heaven's sake."

"Relax?" I say. "How can I relax with a pounce like that?"

"Oh, that wasn't a pounce. That was a peck. A whisker. Would you like to see a pounce?"

I laugh nervously. "Right now?"

She just looks at me.

"Right. Maybe we should go," I say.

Her laugh is low and relaxed. "Yeah, sure." She takes a long black trenchcoat out of the closet and a small sparkly purse off the side table and we go out to my car. I walk around to her side and open the door and give an elaborate bow. She performs a quick curtsy and pulls herself in.

"Is this how it's supposed to go?" she asks once I'm sitting on the driver's side.

"What? You mean a first date?"

"Yeah, yeah. A first date."

I feel better: she's just as out of practice as I am. I let my breath out and then realize I was holding it in. "What do you think teenagers do nowadays? Do you think they hold doors and go to movies like we did when we were younger?"

"Oh, you mean the kissing in the back seat and fondling under clothes and the breathless first screw? Those kinds of things we did when we were younger?" She pushes my shoulder. She wants to shock me. I like it. It gives the evening the feeling of going downhill on an inner tube, out of control but fun. It helps me relax, not so formal.

"So that's the way you want to play it?" I say. "You had better watch it. Wouldn't want the hospital board to know that their nurses are playing doctor."

"You'd tell tales out of school?" she says in mock horror.

"If only I had the skill, my dear, if only I had the skill."

"Well, if you're going to be telling tales, shouldn't it be a whopper?"

"A fish story?"

"But not a cold fish story."

"Mmmm," I say. "A tepid fish story? A warm fish story?"

She laughs. It's loud and then tapers off into a long chuckle. "What's the limit on tepid fish?" she says.

"I don't know, but I'd like to bag a few," I say and put my hand on hers. She turns her hand over into mine. We both chuckle and then there's silence, but now it's a comfortable silence. I hesitate before pulling back my hand to turn into the restaurant.

We dine at Olive Garden. I order the spaghetti and she orders the butternut squash ravioli. She insists we start with calamari and finish with raspberry truffle cheesecake. We both drink Cabernet. Throughout dinner, I want to touch her, but I don't. For the movie, we choose a blockbuster action flick, something safe. Action hero and feisty love interest, one-liner, one-liner. Afterwards, driving back to her apartment, we argue good-naturedly about whether heroines in action movies resemble real women at all. We agree that no one in action movies resembles real people. That's why they can be described in short phrases like "grieving father defeats evil politician" and "amnesiac woman spy serves justice."

She lets herself out of her side before I can come around to open the door, but then I walk with her up the stairs to her apartment. She unlocks her door and then turns. She places her arms around my neck, pulls me down, and kisses me, her tongue pressing through my lips. This time, I participate. I put my hands on her back and start rubbing it. I relax my mouth. I press against her. My body becomes a mass of nerve endings, and I can feel everywhere she's touching me. It feels so good. God, it feels good. She pulls back and then, holding my arm, she opens her door and pulls me into her apartment.

She sheds her coat and drops her purse and then grabs me again. I put my hands on her shoulders and hold her at arms' length. I want her, I really really want her, but I hesitate.

"What?" she says.

"Will you respect me in the morning?" I say, my voice high. I'm only half joking.

She laughs. "I hope I'll respect you more," she says and puts her hand on my crotch. I can feel the hand's warmth through my pants.

We make love on the couch. I'm fumbling my way. Of course I've had sex before, but not a lot, and it's been a while. But, being the avid bookworm that I am, I take pointers from *Playboy*. I'm as gentle as I can be. I kiss her and fondle and suck her breasts and tickle her thighs. She kisses me back and trails down my neck to my chest and licks my nipples. When I take off my shorts, she pushes me over on my back and takes my dick in her hand. She looks at it for a minute, sort of thoughtfully playing with it.

"What?" I say.

"Tell me if this feels good," she says and gently strokes it.

"Harder," I say. "Like you mean it."

"Like this?" she says, squeezing more.

"Ah!" I flinch. "Well, ah, maybe a little lubrication?"

She works her cheeks and then spits on my dick and then strokes it again, working the liquid around the shaft.

"Don't be afraid to put your elbow into it," I say. Then she's got it and I'm lost in the burn in my groin. It's feeling good, oh, yeah. But then I'm closer, way to close. "Stop," I tell her. "You'd better stop." But she pushes my hands away and I give in and she works till I come all over the place.

I wipe up with my shirt and then I go down on her till she's writhing all over the bed and then she comes. It gets me hard again. She opens her legs as I push myself to my knees. I enter her in a rush, but I must've been a little rough because she arches sideways and away. "Sorry," I say and slow down, teasing her a bit. She smiles lopsided and then moves her hips, encouraging me. The first time I came, it was animal need, but this time I feel like I'm inside her and she's inside me and I'm ashamed as tears come to my eyes, I feel so much.

CJ

I bartend on a warm and lazy Sunday afternoon and who should push through the door but Bo, Jes's nurse. She lets in the beautiful smell of rain. She's in tight jeans and a v-neck maroon sweater that sets off the paleness of her skin. A tall woman with a whiskery chin is with her. The woman wears mom jeans—you know, tight around the high waist and hanging loose in the butt. She has on a tan long-sleeved t-shirt and gold studs in her ears. They're talking and laughing as they sit in the corner booth. It's slow, as it usually is on Sunday, just two regulars sitting at the end of the bar.

I walk over to the booth to ask Bo and her friend what they'll have.

"Oh!" Bo says and blushes to her hairline. She's got this natural color in her cheeks, but she turns even redder. I attribute it to seeing someone she knows in a bar. Some people have this weird thing about coming to bars. They're embarrassed to mix the two crowds. They'll come and drink and be everybody's best friend, but then you meet them on the street the next day and they ignore you, like you're some hooker they took home and want to forget about. Or they meet someone in the bar they know from outside the bar and they act like they don't know them.

My estimation of Bo goes down a couple notches.

"What can I get for you two ladies?" I say, face blank, not acknowledging that I know Bo.

"Tory, are you doing a scotch, or something lighter?" Bo says to the woman.

"I've got to be home in"—the woman glances at her watch—"damn, forty-five minutes. I'll just have a beer." She looks at me. "What you got?"

"Light. Dark. You name it."

"I'll have a Bud Light. Bo?"

Bo looks at me. "Um. I'm sorry. Where are my manners?" She turns to the woman. "Tory, this is CJ. CJ, Tory." She gives me a wide smile. It looks genuine. I nod.

Tory raises her eyebrows and says, "Is this …"

Bo shakes her head quickly. "No. This is Maggie's sister. A client."

"Oh," Tory says.

"I'll have a Bud Light, too. And a shot of bourbon," Bo says.

I know better than to react to anything a patron says, so I nod and go to the bar and get their drinks. Bo pays me and nods. I turn back to doing other things. They sit and talk. After about an hour, the other woman leaves and Bo picks up her jacket and purse and moves to the bar.

"Hey, CJ, could I have another round?"

I pour her a shot and pop the top on her beer and set them on a napkin in front of her. I pour myself a shot too. "Here's to your liver," I say and down half of it. The kick of the whiskey shoots up into my nose and makes me want to sneeze.

"Pickled," she says.

"I thought a nurse'd be all health conscious. Drink tea or fruit juice or something."

Bo laughs. It's the first time I heard it. It's deep and ends in a long loud chuckle. "Do as I say, not as I do."

"I'll drink to that," I say and down the rest of the shot.

"Here, here," she says and downs hers.

"Hey, did you hear about the guy who got hit by the car down toward Boulder?" I say, making conversation. "You're a nurse. This'll interest you."

"Someone got hit?"

"Yeah. This guy. He came in here once, actually. His name's Larry. A bum. Looked like a vet, a war veteran? He was down on Highway 287 at night, drunk, they say, and this Ford Explorer driven by a doctor, of all things, popped up over the hill and pegged him."

"Killed him?" Bo takes a drink of her beer.

"No. That's the funny part. The doctor said that the guy was a bloody mess. The doctor called the ambulance, and they came and took him in. On the way, though, he died, so they took him to morgue. A couple of hours later, someone found him halfway off the gurney trying to get up."

"Really? I bet some doctors got in trouble over that one," Bo says, shaking her head and chuckling. She stands up to go. After a pause, she says, "Oh, hey, I'm having a few friends over on Saturday. Would you like to stop by? I make the world's best spaghetti. What you say?"

I shrug. I feel sheepish—I've totally misjudged her.

"Really, CJ, you should," she says. "Sparkling conversation. A whole new groove."

I tilt my head, still not sure.

"Tell you what. If you show up, great. If not, another time." She scribbles the address on a napkin. "About five or six …"

You know what? I just might. I very well might.

Jackdaw

I try my ritual. I refill my cup of coffee. I sit down and turn on my computer. Once it comes up, I open the file. I take a sip of coffee. I close my eyes and shut out the world and transport my body physically to that world, the one I'm going to write about. I smell the sagebrush on the hot wind. I hear the creak and rattle of the wagon, its motion as it lurches over the humps in the road. I feel the vast openness above me and look up to see the deep blue of the sky fading to white along the horizon. I see the few feathering clouds. The wood plank of the wagon seat is hard against my butt bones, and the heavy thick leather reins lay stiff and taut in my palms. They're warm where my hands are but cool on either side when I pull to get a better grip. Small puffs of dust rise from the hooves of my team of horses, a blue roan named Lincoln and a big sorrel named Red. Red lifts his tail, long and shiny like the tresses of a girl. As he's walking he shits, and the earthy smell reaches me. It's a good smell. I come up over a rise, and ahead I see a town in a sea of sagebrush. I see the false fronts rising along the main road. I see a small herd of horses in a corral out behind the stable. I see a crowd of people gathered in front of a man who's standing on a gallows orating. I shake the reins and urge the horses on, "Hah, let's go."

That's the world of the book, but I haven't written another sentence. It's all in my head. I try and try. Nothing comes. I surf the web. I write a sentence and erase it. I argue with myself, tell myself what a shit writer I am. Then I surf some more.

But I've been thinking about another book, maybe the next one, if I can ever get this one written. All that time on the road gives you lots of time to think things through. It'd be called *John Gaunt*. It would be about a peddler named John Gaunt who could sell a three-legged dog to an Eskimo. It's basically the story of the guy who comes back to a frontier town to get revenge, only at the beginning you think he's just a good guy trying to find a place to settle down. Deep down, he's hungry for power. He'd like nothing better than to be a corrupt mayor.

John Gaunt changes how he acts with different people, changes how he talks, so that he can sell things better. He also has this knack for knowing the exact things people want. So as soon as he finds out, he gets it and sells it to them for a really good price, or trades it for something they don't want but at a loss, so they're in his debt. Pretty soon everybody in town owes him favors, and he starts calling them in.

It's always something small. He asks a boy who he sold an ivory-handled pocket knife to to put a burr under the storekeeper's saddle. Because of that, the storekeeper gets bucked off and breaks his leg. Because he has a broken leg, it takes him twice as long to walk from the back of the store to the front. In exchange for an ostrich egg from Africa, the storekeeper's daughter steals a brass monkey from the front counter while her father stumps up from the back. After selling the storekeeper a harmonica from Hapsburg, John Gaunt asks him to nip Madame Lafontaine's favorite handkerchief from where it's drying on the line. In exchange for a copy of *Don Quixote*, John Gaunt has the wife of the mayor drop Madame Lafontaine's handkerchief into the carriage of Preacher Sonnenberg. And so on.

It all comes to a finely orchestrated climax at the election where the votes are so split that John Gaunt is elected mayor.

I still don't know how it would come out though. It seems right that my guy should end up as governor of the territory. It's all there in the logic of the story. He's good at what he does, not to mention ruthless, and he'll make it. But that's predictable. I need something different.

I did think of another ending. It could just work—I don't know. Suppose John Gaunt was cursed by an old woman he sold something to, an old woman who knew what he was really up to. She cursed him so that everything he did came out backwards. Suppose every time he tried to twist the knife a little deeper, the opposite happened. It did something good. And ironically he gets elected mayor because all of his good deeds. Then maybe he has an epiphany about goodness and evil.

Is it just possible for someone who's black as a well-digger's ass, self-serving and manipulative, motives as unsavory as a two-day-dead cat in the noonday sun—is it possible for him to turn his life around? Can he do good? I can almost see it in this story.

Only I sit here at this damn computer. Can't get a word out. Nothing. And it's killing me.

Maggie

For once I've had enough sleep. You can't believe what a luxury that is. To wake up with your legs all relaxed, no headache. It's as good as that first drink of sweet cold water when you're really thirsty. As good as cozying up to a crackling blaze when your toes and fingers are like ice. It's just the best.

I poke my head in Jes's room and Bo smiles at me. Jes naps, so I take a shower. I don't have to be anywhere, so I take a really long hot one. The warm needles of water feel so good—I shut my eyes and just stand under it. I know I'm going to be all itchy, so then I put lotion on. I put on my most comfortable pair of jeans and a sweatshirt and pull my hair back into a ponytail. I feel unusually, well, good.

Then I go in to see Jes. He rubs his eyes and then holds his arms out, which means he wants to be close. I pick him up and sit down in the rocking chair and snuggle down with him. I curl around him so my face is right next to his head. I don't have anywhere to be, nothing to do. I don't think about anything. I just sit there and feel the warmth and weight of Jes's small body on mine. I smell his hair. It always smells the same, warm and fresh and clean like grass in the sunshine. I breathe deeply. I play with his hand, slapping his fist against my palm. He's relaxed and just lets me do it. It may sound like nothing special, but I've got to tell you—it is. He's not in pain. His breathing is fine. He's not hungry. Bo has just cathed him. We just lay there, him looking at me and playing with my nose and my hair and my hand.

Then he starts to get restless, so I pull down the book *Barnyard Dance* and read, "Stomp your feet! Clap your hands! Everybody ready for a barnyard dance!" It's got these wonderful illustrations of cows and pigs and chickens dancing together. I read it and put a lot into it. We dance along with the words, me rocking and bobbing my head and waving his hands in mine. "Turn with the cow in a patch of clover. All take a bow and the dance is over."

He looks around and finds my face and then smiles up at me. Then we play patty cake. "Patty cake, patty cake, baker's man, bake me a cake as fast as you can," I say. I hold his hands and move them to clap and rub his tummy. He can't do it himself yet, but he enjoys me helping him.

Bo comes in once or twice to check on us.

After a while, I stand up with him and look out the window. We check the weather. It's really nice. The wind has died down and the sun is out. I decide to take Jes outside. I tell Bo. She smiles and helps me get Jes ready. We bundle him up as best we can in blankets and snap his car seat into the stroller. Bo helps me arrange the ventilator and everything and carry his stroller down the flagstone steps of the porch.

In the front yard, Jes's eyes are wide and he looks all around. It's my job to bring him things. I bring him a dandelion. His eyes get even wider and he tries to grab it. I give it to him, and he pulls it apart. I get a pine cone, making sure it's an older soft one. He feels it and strokes it and tries to taste it. I pull it out of his mouth. He looks at me like *Mom, How could you?* Then he forgets and tries to put it in his mouth again. I laugh and trade him for a pink and gray rock. Then we sit for a bit in the sun. When he gets restless, I push the stroller all the way down the dirt drive. It's not easy. He bumps along looking this way and that, blinking at the shade and at the sun. We make it to the highway. We watch as a silver sedan streaks by, going way too fast. He almost misses it. He gets excited and cranes his neck. Then along comes a big red farm truck, and he loves it. His eyes are wide and he claps his hands.

With that, we turn around and go back to the house. Jes is getting tired. He rubs his eyes and yawns. When we get into the house, I hold him in my lap in the rocking chair and rock and sing "Koom-by-ah," my favorite because it rumbles down deep in my chest. He falls asleep against me and I sit with my arms around him and fall asleep too.

Maybe things will be all right, after all.

Jackdaw

I don't feel like going to a coffee place so I stay home and drink instead. I put bourbon in my coffee and sit on the couch and watch TV. I keep refilling the coffee and bourbon, till the pot is empty and I don't feel like making any more. So I just fill my cup with bourbon, no coffee, no ice, no water.

I'm at that point where you can't feel your nose, when I have to take a leak. I'm on my way to the bathroom and I walk by the bedroom where Maggie is giving the mutant a sponge bath. It's like something out of a bad hospital drama, all those machines. I can't see him because he's shielded by the machines, but I can see Maggie's face. She has this expression. It's like she's not inside herself at all but so focused on Jes she wouldn't notice if the world came to an end. Her soul is in him. She isn't smiling and isn't frowning. Her face is just totally open.

I watch her for a minute, looking around the door frame, trying not to bump the door. Then I realized what that look is. It's love, pure and simple. She loves that thing, even though it's mostly machines now. She loves it so much she's put herself inside it.

I think she used to look at me that way.

My face is wet. No fucking way I'm crying. Fuck that. But then I focus back at Maggie. There's something else in that expression. Something that makes me remember. A flicker from when I was thirteen, skinny and so spitting mad I felt like tearing the world out at the roots. I stood in the tiny bathroom and brushed my teeth at the porcelain pedestal sink, the hard bristles scraping against my gums. I hated the fucking toothbrush and I hated the fucking sink and the fucking bathroom and my pimply weak-ass face in the fucking mirror. I felt two-seconds away from exploding. I bent and spit and scooped water into my mouth and spit. I rinsed my brush and put it in the holder. Then I turned and glanced through the door into the bedroom across the way and there was my mom watching me. A mound of mom slumped on the bed. She had that look on her face. I knew she was obsessing the way she always did, dragging me closer to her in her quiet way in the never-ending battle that was my parents' marriage. So I look at her and she sees me looking at her and then I turn my back and clenched my fists. I turn my back on her and wish to hell she'd just fucking disappear. It was all I could do to keep from ripping the whole fucking place down. What did they want from me? I didn't even look at her as I walked out, grabbed my book bag, and went to wait for the bus.

That was the day Mom left, the last time I saw her.

But now, standing in the hall looking at Maggie, I recognize my mom's look for what it was. It was my mother loving me. She wasn't asking me for anything. She was just loving me so much she was beside herself, her soul was in me. But she also had to make a choice. All my dad's rage. All those bruises. The trips to the hospital for broken arms and collar bones and female trouble. Surgeries that were never explained to me. I never once stood up for her. I never gave her one bit of anything, in fact. What I saw as her asking for something was nothing more than her love. Now I know. Now I know she had to choose between dying and me. And she chose life.

Can I blame her? Blame her is what I've always done, but now, I'm not so sure. Maggie's put her soul in that thing that might have been a boy. She's giving up her life for his. I push away from the door and go down the hall and back into the living room. I fall onto the couch. My face is wet and my chin is wet. I'm crying like a little girl. What had my mother done? She chose herself instead of me, an ungrateful little prick who turned his back on her. Never tried to stop his father, never once took her side. He even wished she was gone, dead, something, so that he wouldn't have to deal with yet one more thing. He—I—am the one to blame, not her. And then I forgive her. I forgive my mom. Or maybe I forgive myself—hell, I don't know. But it makes all the difference. Things have changed.

I think of Maggie down the hall with her face wide open. I think I love her. I mean, not just think she's perfect or want to get into her pants. I think I really love her, you know, really.

Maggie

Jackdaw's sleeping off a hangover when Tibs comes over.

"I'm sorry, Tibs," I say. "Jackdaw's passed out in the bedroom."

He shakes his head. "I didn't come to see Jackdaw," he says. "I came to see you. Is Bo here?" He glances past me.

"Bo?" I say. "Yeah, she's back taking care of Jes." I nod that direction. "You came to see me?"

He looks past me and then nods back out the door. "Could you help me?" he says.

"Sure," I say, not knowing what to expect. I follow him, and he hands me a box. In it, I can smell food, something spicy. He grabs another box and kicks the door closed. "You hungry?"

"Sure, I guess."

We go inside and he puts his box on the counter and then takes mine and sets it next to the first one. "Sit down, oh sister of mine," he says, "and prepare to be dazzled." He walks over to the hallway and then turns back and says, "Is Jes sleeping?"

"No, he's awake."

"BO," Tibs calls down the hall. "Hungry? Something spicy, perhaps?"

Bo calls back, "In just a sec."

I don't know that I've ever seen Tibs like this.

Tibs starts setting the table and I get up to help. "No, no, Little Sister," he says, "you just sit."

"What's going on?" I ask.

"Can't I treat my sister to a special lunch?" he says as he glances at the hallway.

"Yeah," I say, "but why?"

"You've been pretty under the weather lately, you know, with Jes, and I thought you could use with some cheering up."

"You did not."

"Well, honestly, yes I did, actually. But it's an excuse too."

"An excuse for what?" I say just as Bo walks into the room.

Looking at me, Tibs shakes his head and turns to Bo and says, "Bo. How good to see you." He says it in the exaggerated way people use when they're talking around kids and don't want them to know what's really going on.

Bo laughs. "What's this?"

"Well, Maggie was hungry …" He looks at me.

I shrug. "Sure."

He continues, "And you have to eat too?" He looks at her expectantly.

She smiles and nods.

"So here I am! Today's menu is Mexican." He starts to unload the boxes. There's quesadillas and tacos and nachos and burritos. There's potato things and drinks. It fills the table. He shrugs. "I didn't know what you liked." He's looking at her.

I haven't had enough sleep, so I'm a little slow, but now I can tell what's going on.

Maggie

We eat, and throughout the meal Tibs tries to make jokes in his awkward way, but Bo laughs even though they aren't really funny. It's sweet, the way Tibs tries so hard.

Bo gets up from the table. "Time to check on Jes," she says.

I get up. "No, let me," I say and glance at Tibs. A grateful look comes into his eyes.

"You sure?" she says.

"Sure," I say. I walk down the hall and check Jes. He's doing fine. He's awake but just lying there. I lay my hand on his head for a minute. Then I walk down the hall to our bedroom, where Jackdaw is passed out on the bed. He's uncovered and just in his underwear. He looks flabby and pale and he's snoring. The room smells like farts.

It's him that smells, really. He isn't kind. He doesn't do the things he used to. He hasn't spoken to me in days. He treats Jes like less than an animal. I don't think he's ever even said Jes's name. He doesn't care about family or taking care of other people—the most important thing, *the* most important thing in this world. It's like he's dead inside. I look at him and think of Tibs, so alive in the other room, trying so hard to make Bo happy.

Then I realize: I don't love this man.

Tibs

A Saturday and I'm so jazzed about Bo I cannot sit still. I have papers to grade and laundry to do, but instead I sit down at the kitchen table with a blank legal pad and a pen—a blue Levenger, heavy between the fingers and thumb but weighted so that it balances. Its ink flows evenly, no blotting, no matter which way I hold it. The seat is cold against my butt and the table's a little high so my elbow props at an odd angle. But I'm going to do it this time, I swear. I'm going to get some words down, any words. I'm hoping the momentum of my mood will pull me through the impediment to my creativity.

I decide to write about that fishing trip to the Big Horns with Jackdaw. It'll be a short story. I'm unsure what it'll be about, what the change in the protagonist will be, but if I can just begin. Its theme will be friendship.

I decide to open on that first morning. I think for a minute and write, *The day began early.* I cross out *began* and write *dawned.* Then I think, that's silly, sophomoric. Days dawn when they dawn, and that's usually early by most people's standards. *The day dawned early*—what am I thinking? I scribble it out and write, *The sun peeked above the ridgeline* and then immediately crossed it off. The sun doesn't peek. It isn't a person. It doesn't have a consciousness. Sheesh.

231

What kind of mood am I trying to set? Optimism, freshness, hope, beauty. What animal might that be? A bird. Too predictable. A fish? Yeah, it's a fishing trip. So I write *The sun slipped up over the horizon like a rainbow chasing a deerfly*. It feels too wordy, but it's the best I can come up with. Then I think about the verb again. It doesn't feel right, the sun slipping, so I cross it off *slipped up* and put *broke* but that sounds even worse so I change it back to *slipped up*.

What do I have? *The sun slipped up over the horizon like a rainbow chasing a deerfly*. Well it does get the feeling of rushing into the day. Maybe I should add *joyously*? No, adverbs are not our friends. The feeling should be in the verb. Back to the verb again. *The sun surged*? But then does *horizon* work? How about *lip of the world*? *The sun surged over the lip of the world like a rainbow chasing a deerfly*. I like it better.

But Hemingway would call it self-conscious crap! He would write, *The sun rose*. Period, end of statement. So that's it. I rip the page out of the notebook, wad it up, and throw it on the floor. At the top of a blank page, I write, *The sun rose*.

How can simple language convey the plethora of meanings? How can I write it simply yet have it transcend its seeming simplicity? I don't know.

What will be the names of my characters? Two guys. The protagonist will be a kind of an everyman, say John, and with him his charismatic friend. Jeremiah?

Maybe this should be in two time periods, the present and then back then, to contrast the two. Then we could see the change in the friendship. But Hemingway would not do that. He would go moment by moment in one time period. Period.

Okay, I've got *The sun rose*. Fuck. What kind of a start is that? *The sun rose*. The sun rises every day. Nothing special in that. Fuck!

No wait! Maybe that's it. Maybe it's just like every other day. It's in the ordinariness of it, the details. That's what makes it special. But it felt extraordinary at the time. Or am I just looking back with rose-colored glasses? Cliché alert.

What if I go with it? *The sun rose*. What happened next? I woke up. *John woke up*. No. More specific. *John pushed his arms out of the sleeping bag and felt the wet slick dew that gathered there*. Yeah. *He found his pants in the bottom of the bag and slipped them on, contorting to put on first one leg and then the other*. I almost write, *like a caterpillar in a cocoon* but then stop myself.

What the fuck? Why am I even doing this? I'm not a writer. I'm an imitation claptrap tinhorn fucking fuckity fuck. This is crap. Every impulse I have is wrong. It's not clean and clear and crisp. It's muddied and flowery and Latinate and it sucks! I rip the page off the pad and rip it into tiny shreds. I throw it across the kitchen and it sprays out like a little yellow firework and settles toward the floor. I go to the other room and plop down on the couch and turn on the TV.

CJ

Bo's place is on the third floor of the modern glass and brick apartment building. I can hear music from behind the door as I knock. It's Ella Fitzgerald and Louis Armstrong singing "Let's Call the Whole Thing Off." I hear laughter. No one comes to the door so I knock louder and then find the doorbell and ring it.

I almost didn't come. What the hell am I doing? I don't know Bo at all. It's probably a bad idea. But I sat there in my apartment. There was nothing on TV. I couldn't focus on anything. I almost decided to just get trashed by myself, but then, what the heck. I'm not Tibs. I got balls.

Bo answers the door. Through it comes the smells of tomato sauce and oregano. Bo's wearing a little black dress and southwestern sandals. Her hair is spiked. "CJ! You made it. Come and join the orgy."

"An orgy?" I say. "You should have told me. I'd've worn my orgy clothes." I hope it doesn't sound like I'm trying too hard. I'm wearing jeans and a Native American ribbon shirt my mom picked up on her travels. It's white with an open neckline and red ribbons on its sleeves and bodice. It's as close as I get to dressy.

Bo laughs and grabs my arm. She tilts her chin down and looks up at me, all serious. "We'll just have to improvise, CJ."

There is a couple sitting on the couch and two other men, one sitting on a chair and the other lounging on the floor. She introduces the man and woman on the couch. The man has one of those ordinary faces that's hard to pick out in a crowd. The woman has long dark hair with bangs and lots of expertly applied makeup. "This is Charlie and Greta. Charlie is into investing, and Greta—what is it you do, Greta?"

Greta puts her hand on Charlie's knee and says, "Charlie."

Charlie nods vigorously,

The man on the floor laughs and says, "Put it away, Greta."

These people are my kind of people. Like a bar crowd. They're not afraid to let it all hang out.

Bo gestures to the two other men. The one sitting in the chair is tall and pudgy but clean-shaven and well-groomed. He's wearing a blue collared shirt with long sleeves, an expensive watch, dockers, and nice leather shoes. The one on the floor is small and slender. He almost looks like a schoolboy with hair carefully parted on the side and styled. "This is Jason and Jason," Bo says. Both men wave. "If you want one of them, just holler and you'll get one of them."

"Well, you won't, Bo," says the Jason who's a little heavier and sitting in the chair.

Bo opens her eyes wide and says, "They say they're *muh-nog-a-mous*."

"Damn straight," Jason in the chair says.

"Well, not straight, exactly," Jason on the floor says, which brings hoots from Greta and Charlie. Jason in the chair nods.

"Have a seat, CJ. Charlie, move over and give CJ a seat. Treat her nice while I get drinks. Beer, CJ?" I nod. "Anyone else?" A few takers.

"So, CJ, what do you do?" Jason on the floor asks. "CJ said something mysterious about purveying illicit substances."

"My official title is Corrupter of the Youth," I say. "Or is it Homewrecker?"

"My kinda gal," Greta says and laughs. They all laugh. It makes me feel good.

"Hear, hear," Jason in the chair says.

"Freeform corruption?" Jason on the floor asks. "Or just of a sexual nature?"

"Nothing that exciting," I say and nod. "Bartender."

"My good man," Jason in the chair says and lifts his drink.

"Not that I'm not up for a little corruption too," I add.

Bo comes back with the drinks. "It's my party and I'll be the only one corrupting anyone around here." She hands out drinks. "CJ, you just sit there and look pretty, darling, and let Charlie and Greta and Jason entertain you. Jason, come mangle the lettuces."

Everyone seems to know which Jason she's talking to. Heavier Jason in the chair gets up and follows her around the corner into the kitchen.

We continue talking about bartending. Greta was a cocktail waitress at one time, and Jason on the floor has bartended, along with a lot of other jobs.

"My Jason, he's a lawyer, so he keeps me in the manner to which I'm accustomed," Jason on the floor says.

"Well, Charlie hasn't worked an honest day's labor in his life, have you dear?" Greta says.

"Honesty gets you nowhere," Charlie says. "At least moneywise."

"Glad to know I'm in good company," I say and raise my bottle.

"Hear, hear," Jason on the floor says.

Soon dinner is ready. It's really good spaghetti with lots of vegetables and Italian sausage, with red wine, peasant bread, and a salad of butterhead lettuce and tomatoes. There is vanilla custard topped with frozen raspberries and honey for dessert. We eat and laugh our way through dinner.

It's such a great feeling to be here with them. It feels comfortable, like being in a bar, but not tired and worn out and worn down. It's new and I feel more alive than I've felt in years.

After dinner, Charlie suggests we play Pictionary.

"It's his competitive streak," Greta says.

"Well," Bo says, "it's my house. We have to play by my rules. Dirty Pictionary."

"Yes," lawyer Jason says.

"I've never played Pictionary," I say.

Bo smiles and turns to me. "We don't have the board game. It's just two teams, draw a word out of the hat, one person draws picture clues for her team for one minute while they try to guess, ten points every time you guess right, first team to one hundred wins. We all write down words for the hat." She says to everyone, "Rules: dirty words only, but you can't draw sexual organs as clues." She tips her head toward me, "We have a Pictionary virgin."

Bo sets up a white board against the wall and Greta hands out pens and pieces of paper. "Three each, so we'll have enough for a hundred." I think for a minute and put on the papers "no-tell motel," "finger fuck," and "horizontal bop" and fold them and put them in the bowl. Bo and Greta pick teams. Greta picks Charlie, Bo picks me, Greta picks lawyer Jason, and we get the other Jason.

"This could backfire on you, Greta," Bo says. "You got the two competitive bastards."

Greta smiles knowingly.

Bo and Greta guess a number to start, and Bo wins. She pulls a word. "It's a person, place, or animal," she says and starts the timer.

"Sure she's not just an object?" Jason on our team says.

"Hey, hey," lawyer Jason says, "no prompting."

Bo draws a stick figure with short hair.

"A man," Jason says. Bo points to him and then continues drawing.

"No organs," Greta warns.

Next to the man's leg Bo draws a stick.

"Masochism," I say. "Bondage."

Bo shakes her head.

"But I like the way you're thinking," Jason on our team says.

Bo puts little marks on the stick all the way down.

"Notches," Jason says. Bo shakes her head.

"Marks," I say, and Bo circles her hand in the air for more.

"Uh, marks, ticks, measurements," I say.

She points to me and nods.

"A measuring stick?" I say. She nods. Then she runs her hand all the way down the measuring stick and waggles her eyebrows.

"Show measurements?" Jason says "Long?"

Bo points to him.

"Fifteen seconds," lawyer Jason says.

Our Jason looks at me. "Now who do we know that's long legged? Known for being long legged?" I shake my head. I can guess, but I'm not sure what they're talking about.

"John Holmes," Jason says, "the porn star."

"Yes!" Bo says.

Our Jason points to lawyer Jason. "You put that one in there." Lawyer Jason grins and nods.

Bo hands the marker to our Jason, who pulls another slip of paper out of the hat. "An action," he says. We play. It turns out to be my "horizontal bop" and we don't get it. There's just too many possibilities. Then it's their turn. They don't get their word because Charlie and lawyer Jason spend all the time arguing about each other's guesses. "I told you, Greta," Bo says. We get up to fifty, while they have only ten. They go into a huddle to discuss strategy, while we gloat. They decide to quit bickering and then they come back and smoke us. We end the night, 60 to 100.

"Losers bring the wine next time," Greta says, as she and Charlie leave. Then the Jasons leave, singing "If You Ain't Got That Swing."

Bo sighs. "Take a seat in the living room," she says and grabs the bottle from the kitchen. She sits beside me on the couch and refills my glass.

"Whew," she says. "I love those guys, but they're a lot of work."

"I can see that," I say.

"But worth it."

"Yeah. I can see that too." I become aware of her perfume. It's an earthy scent, almost like a man's. It smells good. "What is that that you're wearing." I sniff. "It's nice."

Bo blushes. She's got that fair skin. It's weird. She's this combination of sassy and forward but she blushes easily. "My mom's musk."

"It's nice," I say.

"So, what did you think of our little group?"

"They're a lot of fun. Known them long?"

Bo sips her wine. "Oh, yeah. Greta and I met in school, and I think I met the Jasons at a party. They've been together forever."

"I really like them. How often do you get together?"

"We have a standing first Saturday of every month. There's a few more friends who usually come too. You met Tory at the bar."

"Yeah." I feel so welcome with Bo, like she brings out the best part of me.

Bo kicks off her shoes and tucks her feet up underneath her. She says, "Your family's really nice. You guys are close."

"Yeah. Our parents spent a lot of time away when we were kids. We had to kind of look out for each other."

"Where were your parents?"

"Away. You know, Indiana Jones, only not as exciting."

"What? Teachers?"

"Archaeologists. Dad dug up arrowheads and pots. What about your parents?"

"Oh, my mom raised us. I've got a sister back east. I never knew my dad." She reaches out and rubs her fingers on the ribbons on my sleeve. "I really like your shirt. I've never seen one like it." Her fingers warm my skin through the shirt and it feels nice but odd. My first impulse is to pull my arm back, but I hold it still so I won't offend her.

"It's a ribbon shirt. Indian. Crow or Cheyenne, I think."

"It's nice."

"So," I say, "I have a question for you. Sorry to bring up your work. What do you think about Jes?"

"Oh, he's such a wonder. He's got such a strong spirit. He's had a hard go." She's holding back.

"No, really. What I'm asking is, is he getting worse?"

She doesn't say anything for a minute, just traces the rim of her wineglass with her finger. "I don't know what to tell you. I've only seen one other case of SB."

This irritates me, and I suppose that shows on my face. "Bo, don't be like that. Tibs and I have talked about it. We know he's getting worse. We're just not sure how long he has."

Bo shakes her head. "I'm not a doctor." She hesitates a little longer. "But I'd say his functions are deteriorating. No one can predict exactly how long." She looks me in the eye like she's checking to see if I really want to know. "I'd guess he won't live a year. Probably less, maybe even a lot less. I'm sorry." She looks away as she says it and then looks intently back at me.

"That's what we thought," I say. "Thank you." I put my hand on her arm and squeeze. She smiles sympathetically and nods.

We chat for a while longer and then I get up to go. "I had a great time, Bo. Thanks for having me," I say.

"I …" Her voice trails off like she's about to say something but then changes her mind. "I was just going to say, I had a great time too."

Maggie

It's one o'clock in the morning on a Saturday night. I try to drag myself up from the heavy pall of sleep. It's dark except for what's reflecting into the kitchen from the hall light. I sit at the table drinking strong black coffee and hold Jes next to my chest. He fusses. He can't make any noise with the ventilator, but he waves his arms and scrunches his face, and tears reflect little spots of light on his cheeks. I sit forward and rock and sing, "Hush, little baby, don't say a word. Mama's going to buy you a mockingbird." I'm too out of it to be frantic. You can get used to being scared out of your mind, you know? Adrenalin's already coursing through your system, so when another crisis builds, your body reacts by being resigned, rather than another spurt of juice. "You can get used to hanging, if you hang long enough," as Jackdaw says.

I hear a noise. At first I think it's just a car out on the road. But it gets louder and comes through the wall and it's in the room. It's got that in-motion quality like a fly buzzing around and around. It's a humming and then it's a gravelly voice singing one note and then it's a voice talking very very slowly, so slowly I can't make out what it's saying. The sound dips from in front of the sink down to the floor and then picks up speed. It moves along the floor and then speeds up more, zipping up and past my head and behind me. I turn my head and try to follow it. There's nothing there, absolutely nothing, but if I close my eyes, I swear that it's real, substantial, and getting bigger. While it's behind me, it splits into two, and one of it zips back past my head on the other side and the other stays behind me, first going high and the falling low, to my left, to my right.

I'm too tired to be alarmed. One part of me says, this isn't right. No way this is real. You should be afraid. Another part totally accepts it, believing the evidence of my ears.

Then they split again, first the one in front of me and then the one behind me. They morph into voices talking slowly and then faster, but they're all talking at once and I can't make out what is being said. I think I hear the words "dog" and "she's going." They're splitting and forming voices and buzzing into a mass of sound above me, a cloud of zipping voices like locusts buzzing and weaving above my head. The Ms meld with the Os and the Ss. I close my eyes, but that makes things worse. The only thing I can sense are those voices and the hardness of the chair underneath me and the warmth of Jes in my arms.

I open my eyes and focus on Jes. I turn so that what little light there is shines on Jes. He's stopped crying now, and his eyes are on my face. I wonder if he can hear the voices too—loud, insistent, buzzing round and round and covering the ceiling. I focus on the white circle of Jes's face and put my fingers in my ears to block out the sound, but it doesn't block anything out. Then I realize that the sound is inside my head. I can't block it out because it's not something that's outside my ears. The buzzing is louder now, louder and in my ears. I clutch Jes to me and start singing the song again, louder and soon I'm shouting, "MAMA'S GONNA BUY YOU A MOCKINGBIRD!" over and over. It doesn't block out the sound, though. It's there and I can't hear my own voice. "MY GOD!" I yell, and the voices cut out. There's nothing. The hum of the refrigerator, the soft whoosh of the ventilator. Jes lays in my lap, his face scrunched up to cry again, but the voices are gone.

I hear something moving down the hall and I'm afraid it's the voice again. But, no, it's the tall shape of Jackdaw.

"What?" he says. "Are you okay? Is everything okay?"

"I'm singing," I say.

"You were shouting."

"Go to bed."

He looks at me for a minute and then shakes his head and turns back down the hall.

I start rocking Jes again, shushing him. God, I had said. God made the voices go away. "God," I say again like a talisman. "God? God." I rock Jes. I say, "God."

I put Jes into his stroller and then go into the living room. I find the Bible on the mantelpiece that belonged to Grandma Rose and I go back into the kitchen. I flick on the light. Then I sit with Jes in my lap and read until morning comes. I read the story of Jesus, over and over as it's told by the different apostles.

Jesus's whole story, including the birth story, is in Luke. I decide Luke's version is my favorite because he talks about Mary and Elizabeth and Mary Magdalene. Not like John who says women are cheaters and shrews. Poor Mary. She was supposed to be a virgin when she got married but she was pregnant. I can't imagine how hard it was for her. The Bible talks a lot about Jesus trying to convince people that he was the son of God. Imagine what it was like for Mary to tell people that she was pregnant by a miracle and have everybody laugh and sneer. "Yeah, right," I bet they said. It even says somewhere that Joseph was going to divorce her because he didn't even believe her. I bet it was hard, being married to Joseph.

And then Jesus denied her. I felt so bad when I read that part. When she and his brothers were standing outside, he said that the disciples were his mother and brothers and that he didn't even know his mother. Can you imagine how Mary must've felt, when her own son said he didn't know her? But when he was on the cross, Jesus made sure that she was taken care of. I think in those days women had a hard time when they didn't have husbands or brothers or sons to take care of them. When he was on the cross, Jesus had someone take Mary into his home so she was taken care of. And can you imagine what it was like for Mary to see Jesus on the cross, naked, all black and blue from being beaten by the soldiers, blood draining down his face from all the thorns poking into his head and pouring from around the spikes in his hands and feet? Not being able to help him or give him water. Not being able to even touch him. I bet she wanted to die, too. I bet she just wanted to die. To remember that little baby in your arms, his warm hugs and the smell of him, and then to see his grown-up body torn and dying?

I'm so alone. There's Jes needing me and I'm giving all I can. CJ helps out, Tibs too, Bo's a godsend, but, really, the weight's on me. I feel the pressure descend on my head and then reach to my stomach and grab it like a fist. I feel like I'm going to throw up.

CJ

Bo and I start to hang out together a lot.

Some days she shows up at the bar, and when I get off shift we sit in a booth and talk. Or sometimes we go to the bar at this Mexican place, El Patron. It's a good restaurant, but then they've got this small bar. We get a table off to the side to avoid all the guys watching ESPN on the big screen. Sometimes, if there's no one in there, we'll get the bartender, a nice older lady with frizzy orange hair, a lumpy body, and a smoker's voice, to give us quarters, and we'll pump them into the old juke box and choose a whole bunch of songs. I tend toward the blues and country songs. Bo picks rock of all stripes and even has a soft spot for bubble gum rock. We both like Rufus Wainwright.

We sit at the table and talk about things. She spent a summer in Central America nursing for a private charity. It was life-changing for her. She realized that she'd never want to live there but that her life was not so bad. It came at just the right time, she said, a time when she was in a serious depression and running with the wrong crowd. "Not that my crowd's the right crowd now," she says and laughs. "Just the right crowd for me."

Sometimes I drop by her place. That's one of the things that's so great about her. She doesn't mind me just dropping by. I try to call first, generally, but I sort of know her schedule, and I can bring a bottle of wine and some munchies and just show up. It's so comfortable. Or we'll decide to cook something. She's a fabulous cook. We'll have lamb chops with a sour cream mint sauce or Italian caprese or whatever strikes her fancy. I specialize in the drinks, so I'm always trying something new. She likes them sweet, and I'm more toward the hard stuff, but between the two of us we figure it out. Once, I made martinis out of vanilla vodka, Chambord, and pie cherries and she said they were out of this world. They were okay—I tasted them, but I was drinking Bombay Sapphire gibsons. And she's not afraid to boss me around. Most people hesitate, but she doesn't. So she's got me cutting things up and flipping stuff on the stove, whatever she needs me to do. She doesn't apologize, she just says, "CJ, the jalapenos need chopping, really fine, take out the seeds, and don't put your fingers in your mouth or you'll regret it."

One afternoon, I'm sitting at her kitchen table drinking red wine when I realize I've never had a girlfriend like this before. It's so comfortable. When we aren't together, I think about things she'd like and things I'll tell her the next time I see her. She doesn't mind if I pop by at a moment's notice. She stops by my place too, but hers is much more comfortable so we usually hang out there. She's introduced me to her friends and she knows the names of most of the regulars at the bar. Who knew that CJ Jordan was capable of such a thing? I'm a brand new woman. A tiger can change her stripes.

Jackdaw

My wife is way too thin, and she's developed this nervous habit of touching her forehead. It's like she's about to cross herself, only she's not Catholic. Especially when she's nervous, it's touch, touch, touch. She's started talking to herself, too. Mumbling, like praying, under her breath. And the boy obsesses her. She's never away from him if she can help it. She hardly sleeps. The nurse is here to help, but she's always in there too.

This wounded creature. Yes, he probably is my son, even if I blamed Maggie. He's more of a promise than he is a person. He's a shell kept alive by machines. Maybe he could've been a boy, a good man, even, but he's gone. He's died in all but body. Who knows how long this could go on. With modern medicine, months, years probably.

It's like old Palance, my blue heeler. He grew old and got cancer of the eye and stunk to high heaven. God, I loved that dog. I tried everything to save it. Read about cures and put on poultices and everything. Even slept with him. But nothing worked. Of course nothing worked. And he was in so much pain, the grouchy old bastard. Dad finally made me take him out and shoot him. The single hardest thing I've ever done in my life—till now. Only I don't love the boy the way I loved that damn dog. But I do love Maggie.

Yes I love her, I didn't know it, didn't know what love was, really. How can I explain it? It's like the whole world has changed. It's like all I want to do is make her happy. For the first time in my life, I feel like I could spend my life with someone, just bask in her presence for days and days. It's like I'm outside myself suddenly, and I don't matter anymore. I would do anything to protect her, anything.

And she's being torn down. It's not the boy's fault. It's all just destroying her. She'd give her life for him, and she's well on her way. He's dying and taking her with him.

Then my insides curl in self-loathing. I need to step up. Make up for all my shittiness before. This is where I need to be a man and do what needs to be done. It's not shooting him that's stopping me though—that I can do. That's doing the boy a favor. It's the fact that I'm going to have to turn the gun on myself next. It has to be a clean break. I can't still be there to tear Maggie down. I can't be a vegetable, or in prison. It has to be done, and done well. It has to be perfect. I have to step up. I have to be a man.

Tibs

Bo and I are out on another date. It's a sunny day, so I take her golfing. I'm not very good, but I like to get out and whack some balls. She's never been before, but she's game.

It's early in the year, but patches of green push up through the brown mat. The course is fairly flat but has mature stands of trees and water hazards. It is a green space, a Shakespearean woodland.

First we practice driving, whacking the balls as far as we can. Neither of us can make much distance. The pro is beside us, propelling balls into the stratosphere. He glances at us and then comes over and checks our grips. He says, "It's your follow through. Both of you need to work on not just connecting with the ball but swinging past it, on and around."

I nod and try again. This time I manage a bit farther. Bo still struggles.

"Why don't we try a round?" I say. We begin. The rough greens affect our play, but it doesn't matter because neither of us is any good and, besides, we are not playing by the rules. We play to the third hole and then find a bench in the shade of a cottonwood. It doesn't matter that we're both playing horribly. All that matters is she's here beside me.

"Why'd you become a teacher?" Bo says, tossing a ball back and forth between her palms.

I don't really know how to answer. It doesn't sound right to say I just happened into it. People want you to say you have a lifetime calling, especially for something like teaching, and then when you say it, they get this gleam in their eye like their assumptions have been confirmed. You see why it doesn't work to say, oh, I don't know, I didn't have anything else to do.

"Is it a hard question?" Bo asks because I'm taking so long.

"Well," I say, "I was taking English classes, which I dug, so I thought I'd teach it."

"I bet you're a good teacher," she says.

"Why?"

"Because you pay attention to people. Because you're kind."

She means this as a compliment, but it seems as if she's calling me "a nice guy," as in who'd want to go out with the nice guy when there's someone more exciting around. So I shrug. Then there's silence. I think it would've been a comfortable silence, only I'm in that frame of mind that undercuts everything that anyone says. You know the one. Someone says, let's have Chinese for dinner, and you say, what's the matter with Mexican?

So, to cover, I say, "Why did you become a nurse?"

"Well, I suppose because I like to help others and all that claptrap. Another word for codependent. But really I think it was because most nurses are women."

What she says and the way she says it fits my mood, so I feel a little less cranky. "Enabler," I say and push her shoulder.

"Yeah. I couldn't have been an engineer. Something like ninety percent of engineers are men."

"An enabler and a man-hater. Where does that leave me?" I say. I want her to say something sappy, like "in my heart," or something snappy like "I'll enable you."

But instead, she says, "Oh, shut up. I don't hate men. I just grew up around women. I feel more comfortable, you know?"

"Yeah." At least she's being honest, but it's too late for honesty. Someday I'll tell her about writing. Not today though. The sun is out, and the subject feels too much like rain.

CJ

One night I pick up *The Life of Brian* and go over to Bo's. You know the one, a Monty Python spoof of the life of Jesus where the crowds in Jerusalem mistake this regular guy Brian for Jesus and follow him all over the place. He tries to get rid of them by throwing his shoe at them, but they pick it up and say, "A shoe! A shoe! It's a sign. It means we should all wear only our left shoe." "No, it means we should throw our shoes." And so on. It ends with "Life's a piece of shit, when you look at it, so keep on the sunny side of life," that song. I've never been religious, but it's a funny show.

We're sitting on her couch. She's leaning back propped against some pillows with her butt scooted down, legs extended onto the coffee table. I'm sitting next to her toward the middle of the couch. All through the show, I'm conscious of her bare foot. It's almost touching my sock. When she laughs, she curls up just a little so that her leg bumps me. After a while, our legs rest together, and I hold mine very still, hoping she won't move, wanting to feel her touch. One part of me thinks it isn't odd at all, perfectly natural. But another part does. I've never felt so conscious of a woman before. She doesn't seem to notice the touch. When she pushes herself up to get drinks or to go to the bathroom, I scoot her direction a little, so she's closer when she sits back down. I feel weird about doing it, but that doesn't stop me. At no point do I think, what you're feeling is out of line. It just feels natural and right.

When the song "Always Look on the Bright Side of Life" comes on, we both start singing. She laughs and jumps up and grabs my hand and pulls me to my feet. We're dancing and bobbing our heads side to side and singing at the tops of our lungs, "Life's a piece of SHIT! when you look at IT!" and then we try to whistle along. I can't whistle but hers is pretty close. We form a two-person conga line, her hands on my waist, and we bop around the living room whistling and laughing.

As the song ends, her hands close on my hip bones and she pushes me around to face her. She looks at me for just a second and then kisses me. I tighten stiff as a board—I'm so shocked I don't move. But it feels so good, her soft lips on mine, her arm around my neck, I kiss her back. It's license to put my hands on her body, to feel the muscles in her shoulders and the bones of her spine. We kiss some more. She runs her fingers into my hair and the grabs it by the roots. My hands wander, feeling the softness of her belly and then the curve of her breasts. She's not wearing a bra. Her arm is around my neck and her other hand is on my butt. Her lips move to my neck. Then she grabs the bottom of my shirt and tugs it over my head and then pulls off her own shirt. Her breasts are small and high but round against the curves of her rib cage. I play with them and then lick them and then we're naked on the sofa, a tangle of arms and legs and my eyes are shut and my body is nothing but sensation and I can't tell where my body ends and hers begins. I can't explain it. It's like I've been doing it wrong my whole life.

It's not until the next day that I think of Tibs.

Tibs

I do my laundry at the laundromat amid the odor of warm clothes and detergent. I slouch back in the uncomfortable orange plastic chair watching *Oprah*. It's her book club, and she's interviewing Elie Wiesel, who wrote *Night*, about his time in World War II concentration camps. The sound is turned way down, and flashing across the screen are images of people stacked like so many corn stalks laid in for fodder. I watch, and I'm struck by the inadequacy of words. Imagine starving to death. Imagine watching your father starve to death and taking his last piece of bread because you, too, are starving to death. Words are nothing but pale reflections of experience, yet they're all we have. I'm also struck by the optimism of words, Little Engines That Could, trying to bring one wounded soul closer to another. They are at once futile yet hopeful, foolish yet pragmatic.

My cell phone rings, its upbeat song drowning out the scrape and hum of the dryers. I see that it's CJ, so I pick up.

"Hey," CJ says, "what you doing?"

"Laundry. You?"

"Not much. Thinking about quitting my job." Her voice is soft.

"What? I can hardly hear you."

"Quitting my job," she says more loudly.

"Really?"

"Naw. But Peter and I broke up."

"That's too bad," I say, thinking that for the first time in my life I'm the one with a significant other and CJ isn't. I try not to let it come through in my voice but my insides flip at the thought of Bo.

"It isn't really an issue, though," she says. "You know Peter."

I don't, not really, but it doesn't matter. "Hey, I'm just finishing up. Want to grab a bite somewhere?"

"Naw," she says. "I'm going out later."

"Mmmm," I say, phone propped on my shoulder, checking the dryer. "Well, was there something you needed?"

"Not really," she says.

"Well, then," I say and start to hang up.

"Wait. Tibs. I need to tell you something."

"Yeah?" How odd. CJ doesn't beat around the bush.

"I'm sorry about it too."

"Whatever, sis. You regularly piss me off, so don't worry about it."

"Bo and I slept together."

At first I don't understand what she's saying. My mind hears the name "Beau." I try to think of a guy named Beau but can't. "You what?"

"Bo. Jes's nurse? She and I ..."

"She? And you?" Then it sinks in. For a split second I think it's a mix-up, that she doesn't know about Bo and I, but then I remember telling her. That means she knowingly and Bo knowingly ...

At first I'm not even angry. I'm shocked. How does a person handle something like this? The more I think about it, the madder I get. I feel just like I would if some other guy had slept with Bo. I feel betrayed by Bo and by CJ. CJ of all people. She should've known better. She doesn't even like girls. Or does she? She knows how long it's been since I've had a girlfriend. And Bo. What was all that?

There is pain, but then my emotions flash-freeze. Anger crystallizes the world's complications into right and wrong. So that's the way it's going to be. I pull the phone away from my ear and press end. When it rings again, I shut it off.

Later in the week, I arrive at Jackdaw and Maggie's, and the sun is just coming up. Jackdaw and I are going camping. It's Saturday, and I aim to get an early start. Yesterday evening after work I packed the tents, chuck box, fishing poles, sleeping bags, steaks and eggs, beans, and spaghetti and everything else.

I go in. Maggie's up with Jes and a cup of coffee. She appears as if she's been up all night—in her pajamas, her hair oily and tousled. She rouses Jackdaw. He stumbles out and pours coffee into a Loaf-n-Jug mug. He gathers up a few things. He and Maggie don't say two words to each other, and when we leave, they don't kiss. We transfer the gear to his pickup. He tosses the keys to me and gets into the passenger side, so I drive. Once we're on the road, he huddles over his mug half asleep, sunglasses masking his eyes. We don't talk as we drive west into the foothills and then up into the mountains.

On the way I ponder Jackdaw: he's got the cajones. He's writing a book. That takes guts. It's just like him. He lives his life that way too. He lives large. He puts himself out there.

That's why Maggie loves him. That's why we all love him. His girlfriend wouldn't cheat on him.

The blacktop winds all over the place, so it's slow going. I never get above forty-five. We finally make it to the treeline and turn down first one then another dirt road. We luck into the perfect spot—the road meanders past a long string of beaver ponds that ripple and dazzle in the light and ends at a camping spot. This will be perfect, I think. This trip is always just perfect. It'll take my mind off things.

Jackdaw takes off his sunglasses, squints his eyes, and then puts the glasses back on.

"Happy birthday," I say.

"Fuck you," he says, shouldering the door open.

"There's some Tylenol in the first aid kit."

He starts to rummage through the bags as I unload and pile things at the base of a tree. His head flips back as he gulps pills and coffee.

"I'm going to scout the fishing," he says.

I nod. I set up camp, putting up the tent, laying out the fire pit, starting the fire, assembling the camp table, and stowing supplies. I heat some grease in a cast iron skillet and chop potatoes and onions and add them to the spitting grease. I open a can of corned beef and put a couple of slices of bread on the edge of grill to toast.

It's a cold day, so the fire feels good. I pull the hash off the fire and put a lid on it to keep warm. The sun is high in the sky and warms the chill air. I sit on a log with a tin cup of coffee. I try to live in the moment, to live the simplicity of simply being.

As I sit, a chipmunk pops his head around the base of a tree. It's a small one, but his stripes are dark. He's timid, but he really wants some food. I sit still as he walks a few quick steps and then stops. I pull the corner off some bread and toss it to him. The movement startles him, and he runs back behind the tree. Soon, though, he's out again, tentatively making his way toward the bread. He stops and sniffs, his head drawn toward the bread. Slowly, carefully, pausing often, he makes his way to it. I stay still. He knows I'm there, but as long as I'm still, he's reassured. After one long look around, Dark Stripe makes a dash and grabs the bread. He dashes back beside the tree, stops, and looks around for a long time. The he drops his head and takes a nibble of the bread in his paws.

Another chipmunk pops his head out from behind the tree. This one is big and fat, so fat it looks like a hamster. It waddles quickly over to Dark Stripe and grabs the bread. Dark Stripe lets out a long *cheep-cheep-cheep*, bobbing his head and thrusting his small chest toward Biggie. Dark Stripe tries to grab the bread back and run away with it, but Biggie wrestles it away. He turns his back on Dark Stripe and hunches over and stuffs the bread into his mouth. Dark Stripe looks back and forth for a minute, sniffs the ground, and then gives up.

Just then, Jackdaw comes back into camp, scattering chipmunks. His sunglasses are off, and he grins. His eyes are bright. He pulls the top of his Loaf-N-Jug mug and reaches for the coffee pot. He sloshes coffee over his hand as he tries to pour.

"WHAT THE FUCK?" he says, dropping his mug and whipping his hand back and forth, cooling it.

I don't say anything.

He blows on his paw and then places his mug on the camp table. He pours himself another mugful, carefully this time, and picks it up. He begins pacing back and forth on the other side of the fire.

"Hey, let's eat," I say.

We dish the hash onto plates and sit next to the fire. I take a big bite. The softness of the potato, the sweetness of the onion, the saltiness of the corned beef. Hmmm. Something about the mountain air makes the appetite keener. Food tastes better. This is the best hash I've eaten in a long time.

"What is this crap?" Jackdaw says.

"I don't know," I say. "Something your bitch whipped up while you were out seeking inspiration."

He shook his head and took another bite.

"Did you find any?" I ask.

"No, but I found your mama."

I snort. "You always were a mother fucker."

He laughs.

We eat in silence. He grips the spoon in a fist. It's a backhoe, digging into the pile of steaming hash, scooping and curling, and then dropping its load into the pit of Jackdaw's mouth.

The urge comes on me to smack him. Instead, I say, "How's the book coming?"

Jackdaw frowns. "Do me a favor," he says, "change the subject."

I shake my head back and forth. "What? The mighty Billie Boulder can't get it up?" Billie Boulder is his pseudonym. "Your pen a little limp?"

He doesn't say anything.

"Your keystroke a little weak?" I'm enjoying this, but at the same time I hate myself.

"Shut the fuck up," he says.

"The mighty man of words. Where is he? Where are these words?"

"So," Jackdaw says, "has old Tibs put pen to paper yet? Has he written the Great American Novel?"

I glance at him but don't say anything.

He pulls a flask out of his jacket and pours the last of the contents into his coffee cup.

I hesitate and then say, "No, but I'm not the only one."

His turn to snort. "You never did have the guts to put it out there."

He has a point. What can I say to that?

He continues, "You were going to be the next Hemingway. What happened to Indiana Jones and the Temple of Self-absorption? Dig itself into a hole, did it? Maybe two hundred years from now, some bone digger'll discover it." He makes a chuff-chuff-chuff imitation of a laugh. "No, wait. He can't. Because it hasn't been written."

His lips are curled, and his face is ugly. Raw aggression that is inward-looking too. He has that haunted look teenagers get when they feel alienated and have no place to turn, rebellion masking insecurity and self-loathing. The anger drains out of me.

"Let's just drop it," I say.

He grunts.

We go fishing. As we start walking upstream, he says that he'll take the feeder stream that issues from a narrow side canyon.

"There aren't any fish in that," I say.

He just shrugs.

I walk up the main stem and start fishing my way down. The fishing sucks. They aren't rising to the dry flies. I try a Royal Coachman and then a Light Cahill. I keep catching my backstroke on the bushes and having to stop and untangle the line. I snap leaders and have to restring. I get skunked.

While I'm walking back I hear shots, *pkoo! pkoo! pkoo! pkoo! pkoo! pkoo!* one after another after another. Silence. Three in a row, then a pause, then one more, then a pause, then two more.

Jackdaw is in camp when I get back. He doesn't have any fish either, but he does have a pistol in his lap. It's a heavy thing, shiny metallic and blocky. He isn't doing anything with it, just resting his hand on it and running his fingers over the textured metal of the grip. He hasn't started supper, but he's been working on a bottle of Ancient Age. He sits staring into the fire. He sways a little as he sits on the log.

We don't say anything the whole evening, just stare into the fire. He polishes off the Ancient Age and passes out with his back against the log. The gun falls off his lap onto the ground. I unstuff his sleeping bag and toss it over him and go to bed.

The next morning, Jackdaw's hands shake as he pours a little whiskey into his coffee. The whole day passes and we're quiet, not wanting to prod the beast. We fish and I catch a few. Jackdaw doesn't. In the evening, we nod to each other and then go to bed.

The third day is unseasonably warm. We decide to fish downstream and then walk back up.

It's Jackdaw's turn when we come to a deep pool under a huge fallen log where the bank overhangs. The perfect hole. I stop to watch. Jackdaw is a little drunk but not so much that his cast is affected. He sets a Mosquito pretty as you please on the top of the water next to the log. It drifts downstream. He recasts and this time we both see it, a huge trout weaving in the current. The fish moves toward the fly. On the third cast, it strikes, and Jackdaw pulls and sets the hook. The fish is on the line. Water splashes as it struggles. Back and forth across the stream the fish weaves and turns and slides, pulling and jerking on the line.

Jackdaw has the fish close to the shore when his reel jams. He cusses and jerks at the slack. The fish takes the slack in its teeth and runs, hitting the end of the line. The leader snaps, and the fish is off to the shadows under the bank.

"Fuck! Fuck! Fuck!" Jackdaw yells and in one vicious motion throws his rod up the bank. It lights high up in a tree. I move to get it down. He says, "Leave it be," so I move off down the stream and fish the next hole.

It's hot in the afternoon and after I fish out a big hole I shuck my clothes and let my body down into the water. At first, I shrink from it. It's so cold. But inch by inch I lower myself into it. After a minute, the chill feels good after the heat of the air. I lie back, propped on my elbows, and close my eyes. The air and the sun heats my face and chest, and the cool soothing pressure of the water flows past my legs. I can hear the *kinkle-kinkle-kinkle* of the stream and the lazy chirp of a bird. Far off, a squirrel lets out a loud chatter.

Why can't I write this? This experience and every other experience. Why is it so complicated? Why could Hemingway and Jackdaw, but not me?

When I get back to camp, Jackdaw is in high spirits. He's turned on the radio in the pickup to a jazz station, and he's eating a baloney sandwich and bobbing around camp.

"Tibs, my man," he says, "do you ever listen to jazz?"

"Not really," I say as I pull at the laces of my soaked tennis shoes.

"It's amazing. Listen to that clarinet." He paces back and forth.

I make myself a sandwich.

"Those sly old bastards," Jackdaw says with a smile. "You think they just make this stuff up on the spot. And they let you believe it, don't they? But they don't. They practice and practice. Rule their backup players with fists of steel."

"That's the way it is with a lot of art," I say.

"Yeah, but with things like writing you get to fiddle with it as long as you want. With jazz, you just get one shot at it. Do or die."

"A lot of work either way."

"No, Tibs, you're not getting it. They have to practice and work, sure, but then there's the moment that they have to take the bit in their teeth and run, man." He walks over to me, weaving and bobbing. "They're not just by themselves in a studio. They're up in front of people. Do or die."

"Tennyson, right?"

"What?" he says.

"Tennyson. Isn't ours to wonder why but only ours to do or die."

"Whatever. You're missing the point. The point is, art's about doing, not trying to do."

I want to argue with him, not because I've thought about what he said but because he's moving and pushing and because he's written a book.

"That's the thing," he continues. "That's where the rubber meets the road, where the bullet strikes the bone, where the rock meets the hard place." He grins to himself, a grimace really.

"If you believe this, where's the book?" I want to get to him, to hurt him.

He refuses to take offense. "That's just it, man. It's there. It's all there in my head. But everybody's got a book in their head. It's the man who actually does it."

"So where's the book?" I persist.

"It's like that old joke: What's the difference between an Imam and a terrorist?" He smiles.

I don't say anything.

"The ability to fly a plane," he says.

"What's your point?"

"Point is, imagine the guts it takes to fly a plane into a skyscraper. The shear will, like that English writer—What's her name?—deliberately putting a rock in her pocket, walking into a river, and then ducking her head under the water. I'm talking about taking the action before the whole world and having the strength of your convictions." He looks at me. "Having the fucking strength of your convictions and putting it down on paper, Tibs, ol' man."

"Fuck you."

"Fuck you," he says and starts stuffing his sleeping back into its nylon sack.

"No, Jackdaw," I say, "you fucking listen to me." I want to hit him so badly. I stand there with my fists clenched. Finally, through gritted teeth, I say, "Pull your head out of your ass," and break camp.

We drive back to town in total silence.

Jackdaw

My limbs are liquid. My l-l-l-limbs are l-l-l-liquid. Liquid. Liquidity.

What? What the fuck?

Oh, yeah, nothing.

Focus, my boy, focus. Writing is the world, I mean the word. Take a drink. Drinking is writing. Ha ha ha ha ha.

No that's not true. You're lying.

WHAT THE FUCK! You still here? I'm trying to write. The least I can do is write.

Where was I? Oh, yeah. Write write write write. One word. *The*'s a good word. Yeah. *The*.

Don't be a fucking idiot. Just because you have *The* doesn't make you a writer—I mean it doesn't mean you're writing. It's got to be a sentence, any sentence. And it better be a doozy, Jackdaw ol' boy, because it's got to make up for the fact that you're a shit writer.

No, it doesn't. It can be anything. I can change it later. I can always change it.

No, you can't. Once you put it down, it's there in concrete. It's there, and you might move things around but it's still there, a blemish on the perfect vision of the book.

FUCK!

Why can't I just jump in with both feet? Run with it. Chase my muse naked through the living room and catch her up and throw her on the couch. She's got the bit in her teeth and she's running off and I'm not on her back.

The fucking slut! She's a whore!

Take a drink, take a drink, take a drink. The burn … aaah. The jolt to my brain, there it is, the relaxing slide. Aaah.

Another drink, and then write. Write something, for God's sake!

Then I realize, even as drunk-ass as I am: I'm never going to fucking write another word. I'm never going to be that guy up there on stage, the guy that everybody wants. I'm always going to be fucking me.

CJ

"You up for this?" Maggie says. Her face used to be soft, but now it's thin and hard.

"Up for this?" I say. "Fuck, I was up for this the day he came into our lives."

Maggie doesn't say anything but nods.

"Tibs?" I say.

"He knows, but he's not coming."

I snort. "Yeah."

I follow her down the hall to their bedroom. Bo is in with Jes so we won't have to worry about him. The blood is pumping like when I have to throw out a belligerent drunk, and I'm carrying the baseball bat that we keep at the bar just in case. We walk into the bedroom and stop. Jackdaw's on the bed asleep with his clothes on—good, that'll make things easier. He's drunk by the smell of things. I lean in to Maggie and say, "Pack him a few things." She grabs a gym bag and throws some things into it and then zips it closed.

"Ready?" I say.

She nods once, twice.

"You stay back," I say. I walk over to the bed and grab his arm and pull him out and onto the floor.

"What the fuck?" he says.

"Get your mangy ass up and out of my sister's house," I say loud and clear.

Jackdaw shakes his head and then looks up at me. "What the fuck?" he says.

"You heard me. Get your fucking lazy ass out of my sister's house."

He's starting to wake up a bit, and he pushes himself up and then sees Maggie. "Maggie?" he says.

She was behind me but now she steps out to the side and crosses her arms. She looks a little tight around the jaw, but she's holding firm.

"Maggie?" he says. "Maggie, what are you doing?"

"Talk to me, asshole," I say. "You're not dealing with her, you're dealing with me. And I never liked you." I smile.

Jackdaw's starting to get mad. His head thrusts forward and he's staring at me. He keeps his eyes on me but then says, "Maggie, listen to me. I know I haven't been the best husband—"

"Damn straight," I say. "No use chewing our hash twice." I take a step toward him and raise the bat. Wouldn't be the first time I made a drunk see the light.

"Don't! Don't interrupt me," he says. "Don't you see I've changed? I'm different?" I'm about to say something when he says, "God, and I'm a fucking cliché too." He looks at Maggie again and says, "You don't believe me but everything's different now. Everything." He puts his hands down by his sides and opens them and widens himself out and just looks at her. It's like he's laid open his belly to show everything.

Then he says, "Maggie, I love you. I *love* you. Do you hear me?"

I hear a small intake a breath behind me and then silence. Then she says, "But, Jackdaw, I don't love you, not any more. I don't even like you anymore. I wish I did." This last part is almost a whisper.

The tone in her voice makes me think she might be wavering, so I step in and raise the bat. "You heard her. Get going, NOW." I take another step forward and I hear Maggie move around behind me.

Jackdaw tries to look past me, forward on his toes and his eyes wide, but then he looks at the floor. Something about Maggie makes him give in. "All right, all right," he says.

"Pick up the bag with your undies," I say.

He picks it up and moves on past. But just as he's past me, he swings the bag with his right hand. But I'm ready for it and I swing the bat for all I'm worth at his shoulder. I don't want to kill him, so I don't aim for his head, but I misjudge the distance and hit with his right forearm. It connects with a frightening crack. The bag goes flying.

"Fuck!" Jackdaw says and curls forward, his arm tucked into his belly. "Fuck fuck fuck!"

"Yeah? The next one's to that pretty little noggin." I poke him to get him moving and then I pick up his bag as we go past because he doesn't.

He's curled forward.

I glance back at Maggie. Then, to find out whether I had, I say, "I hope I broke it."

"You fucking wish," he says and then straightens up a little as he walks. Well, it can't be too bad. He heads for the door. "Keys," I say as he walks through the kitchen. With his left hand he reaches out and retrieves them from the counter. Then he stops and turns.

I take a step forward. "Just fucking try me, pretty boy," I say. "I've been wanting to do this since the day we met."

He looks at my face and then he shakes his head. "You don't understand," he says.

"Oh I understand," I say. "I understand you're an asshole."

He turns and walks out the door. Maggie stays in the house as I follow him out to his truck. He opens the truck door with his left hand and reaches across with his left to grab the steering wheel and pull himself in. I toss the gym bag into the bed. He starts his truck and drives away. When I go back into the house, Maggie is turned with her back to the kitchen window so she can't see the driveway. She has a cup of coffee in her hands. She takes a shuddering breath, lets it out, and then looks at me. I go over and put my arms around her.

Maggie

Jes and I are at the spina bifida clinic in a room with tan walls—one painted with a blonde pony-tailed girl three feet tall jumping for a blue balloon and another painted with a black-haired Asian boy, shorter, younger than the girl, crouching down looking at a short sunflower. Most of these are flat areas precisely painted, but there's just enough highlights and accents to give it life.

I sit on crinkly white paper on the examination table with Jes in my lap. During clinic, the patients stay in one room and the doctors and specialists rotate room to room. It's easier on the kids, and you get to see them all in one day.

"I have some papers I'd like you to consider signing," Dr. Erickson says, his concern stretched tight across his forehead. "I'll give you some time to read them over. Go ahead and take them home."

The papers are a Do Not Resuscitate order, a DNR. A DNR means that if Jes can't live without the aid of machines, if he has no future, they would turn off the machines. A DNR means that they can turn them off and Jes dies.

I feel like I'm going to throw up. I swallow hard.

How can I sign these? How can a mother kill her son?

If God's like they say he is—kind and fair—Jes deserves to live. He has to live. Someday he's going to kick a soccer ball and kiss a girl. He's going to be as tall as I am—no, taller, like Jackdaw—and he's going to have to stoop when he puts his arms around me to hug me.

I'm not ready for this. Besides, he's nowhere near this stage, not even close.

All I see is my little boy with a smile as open as his heart, his arms reaching for the world, alive with his whole body. I don't see a severe case of spina bifida. I see Jes.

I call Bo on the way home, as we'd arranged, and she's there when we arrive. Jes and I are both so tired we take naps, and since Bo is here I put Jes in his room. After a couple of hours, I wake up in a panic. I'm sure that Jes is dead. I've dreamed something horrible, like he's in a car with the windows shut in the boiling sun. He isn't attached to machines or anything, and I can see him through the glass. I kept thinking, oh he's all right. See, he's moving, playing. But then when I open the car door he starts to shrivel and gasp and sort of mutate backwards, like he's turning into a fetus. I stand there helplessly, knowing that it's my fault because I left him in the car.

I wake up sobbing. I run into Jes's room to check on him. He's fine, but Bo's eyes get really big when she sees me. I go over to him and lay my cheek on his hair.

"You all right?" Bo asks.

"I just—" I shake my head. How can I explain?

A day passes, and then another. I feel like under water, my movements slow, all sensation muffled.

Then, the week before Easter, I color eggs. The kitchen is hot and steamy from boiling water, and the smell of vinegar scrapes the insides of my nose. Jes lays in his car seat at the kitchen table, and Bo massages his hands. I put one egg after another into the little wire holder and dip them in cups of color and then place them back into their cartons to dry.

I just don't know what to do. It's all getting away from me. Jes is getting away from me. His eyes are trains disappearing down tunnels. The lights and sounds are getting smaller and smaller and farther away. There's just a spark left I can only see every once in a while. I keep trying to call him back. I move his arms and legs. But it doesn't do anything. He's slipping through my fingers.

"How are his hands?" I ask, dipping an egg half in blue.

Bo glances at me. Then she says, "He's lost a little muscle tone."

I dip the same egg half in red and hold it as it drips. "Have you noticed anything wrong with his eyes?"

"Like discharge?"

I can't seem to find the right words for this. "No. Not like a medical condition. More like, well, I don't know …" As I shrug, I accidentally tip the wire holder sideways and the egg, half blue and half red, drops and splats. Shards of eggshell skitter across the floor. Bo puts down Jes's hand and helps me bend and gather them up. I wipe the floor with a wet paper towel.

I try again. "It's like, like … his eyes, they don't focus well."

"Focus?"

"Like he's not noticing things he used to. Used to be, I could tell what he's feeling. I can't tell anymore."

"Well," Bo says and picks up Jes's hand, "have you talked to the doctor about it?"

"Yeah, of course. He says it's part of the progression of his condition."

"Did he say anything else?"

"No. Just that."

Bo stops massaging Jes's hand for a minute and then starts to say something and then stops. Then she says, "Come here a minute."

I wipe my hands and walk over to Jes and sit.

"No. Closer. So he can smell you." Bo moves behind my chair and helps me scoot it right next to his car seat. "Now put your face right next to his, so he can feel your heat." I bend and scoot my arms underneath him and around him and hug him as best I can around the machine hookups. "Now think of a happy time and say his name."

I close my eyes. At first, I just feel the warmth of his body. Then I feel his bulk. His body looks so thin, but when I lift him, he feels there, solid, weighty. He looks only half in this world, but in my arms he's real, solid, here. A sob bubbles inside me.

I think about when he was two months old, before he was attached to the ventilator and all that. How he fell asleep in my arms, the way he just relaxed into me, the solid weight on my chest, how peaceful he looked. How in that moment the future didn't matter and the past didn't matter. Just there, in that moment, him feeling me and me feeling him and him asleep, at peace.

Then I say, "Jes. Jes, my love, my baby doll. Jes."

"Look," Bo says.

I pull my head back and look into his face. He isn't looking at me, but it's like he's listening really hard, like a satellite dish pointed in my direction. "Jes, oh Jes," I say. Then he moves just a tiny bit, turns his head my way, and a flicker of a smile comes on his lips. His eyes aren't focused on me, but his whole body is.

It's then that I realize that he's almost gone. It took him coming back to me for an instant to see how far he's declined, to realize how he can go all day without recognizing anything or anybody, how the only thing he really registers is pain.

CJ

I come into Maggie's kitchen, Maggie holds Jes, and Bo's arms wrap around them both.

"Is everyone all right?" I ask, trying to keep the anger at Bo out of my voice.

Bo hasn't called or answered the phone since that night. At first I told myself to let it slide. What did it matter? But it matters. I told myself she was probably regretting it and maybe she wanted just Tibs. Then I started to miss the time we spent together, afternoons just hanging out. Then I got pissed. What right did she have, playing with people's lives like that?

"Is Jes all right?" I say.

Maggie looks at me with her head cocked to the side. "He's dying," she says, like she's just realized this.

"Right now?" I say and feel stupid.

Bo shakes her head and motions me to the table. She goes over and pours me a cup of coffee and refills her own and sits across from me.

Maggie turns to me again and says, "CJ. He's dying."

"I know, Maggie," I say. "I'm sorry." There's nothing else to say. I start to get up to go to her but then stop when Bo looks at me.

Bo leans across the table. "I'm sorry I haven't called, CJ."

"I didn't know what to think," I say.

"I know. I'm sorry."

"Is this what you usually do?"

"CJ! No. Not at all. There's just a lot …" She looks over at Jes. "I was trying to play it straight." She laughs. "Straight. That's a funny one. I mean I was really trying to do it right. Do it how you're supposed to, you know. I mean, with Tibs. But then you came along."

"Yeah. I came along. What was that? I've never been"—I lower my voice to a whisper and glance over at Maggie—"with a woman."

"Oh, CJ. Really?" Bo wrinkles her brow. "Really? I'm sorry. And there I had to go and screw it up. My first time … well, never mind."

"What is this, Bo? What are we?" I say, trying to keep the desperation out of my voice.

"CJ! I thought you knew. I thought I was explaining. It's just with Tibs—"

Whatever she's going to say is cut off by the door banging as Tibs comes in. He's mad, too. You can tell because his shoulders got all hunched up, his collarbones next to his ears.

Tibs

"CJ and Bo. Perfect," I say. And I mean it. It is perfect. All screwed up, like *Garden of Eden*.

Maggie sits with Jes. She turns to me and says, "Tibs. He's dying."

"I know, Mags," I say and go over to her. I pat her shoulder and say over her head, "People are going to shit all over the place."

"No, Tibs. He really is. I thought he was getting better. I didn't see it. But he's dying."

"We'll get through this, Maggie." My eyes never leave Bo and CJ. "Maggie. I'm glad you're here, too," I say. "We can just get it all out."

CJ says, "You're right, Tibs, but now? Can't we—"

"Yes, let's get it all out," Bo says. "Like the fact that I'm pregnant."

"Pregnant?" I say.

CJ's head flips around to Bo. So she didn't know either.

Maggie isn't following and isn't trying to. Her back is to us.

"So there's somebody else, too?" I say. "How many is that, Bo? Five? Six?"

"Fuck you," Bo says. "I've only had sex with two people in the last six months, and only one of them could get me pregnant. Ironic. The only time in my life I have sex that can result in pregnancy, and it happens."

CJ looks back and forth between us. "Bo?" she says. "You're pregnant?" As soon as she says this, she gulps air like she's going to cry. My sister CJ. The last time I saw her cry was when she crashed her bike when she was eight. "You're going to have a baby?" she says.

Bo looks at CJ. "That's why I didn't call. I had to figure it out. I thought I was going to get rid of it, but I couldn't. This may be my one chance, and I want to have this child."

"My child? You're sure?" I ask.

"Yes. Either that, or immaculate conception."

A kid. My son or daughter. I think of all those kids at school. Maybe I shouldn't have been a teacher, but I genuinely like the kids. They're so in the world. Underneath the put-on coolness, they have miles of good will and hope. I can't imagine what it would be like if one of them was mine. They're so, I don't know, like adults only better. Worse, too, I suppose, but better in so many ways.

Before I know it, I drop to my knees in front of her. "Bo, will you marry me?" I say it before I've even thought it, it seems, but once I say it, I really really mean it.

"Tibs," Bo says. "Oh, Tibs. I'm sorry. You really are the sweetest person, and if I was going to marry a guy, it'd be you." She reaches out and slaps my cheek, just a little too hard.

She leaves me there on my knees clutching at air and stands and turns toward CJ. "I can't marry you," she says back over her shoulder to me.

"A child, a baby?" CJ says.

At that, Maggie turns around and says, "What?" Her green eyes loom at us like eggs sunny-side. "What's going on?"

But then there's Jackdaw. He's standing in the entry door. His black pants and black t-shirt and his black hair makes him look white as a ghost. He looks drunk, the way he's standing and swaying slightly. But then I see his face. He's not drunk. I've seen Jackdaw drunk. Jackdaw drunk is Jackdaw larger than life. Outgoing kicked into overdrive. Now, instead, he looks like a pile of fall leaves, gathered right now, but one gust, one puff of wind, and he'd be all scattering motion. He's just keeping it together, his body focused on Maggie and Jes.

At first I don't see his hand down by his pants leg. Then I see it. He isn't trying to hide it, but his face draws your attention. There in his loose fist is his gun.

It sounds corny, doesn't it? Like a B western. Like something Jackdaw'd write. You want to laugh. Only, you don't laugh. Jackdaw isn't laughing. My stomach knots with adrenalin, and my bowels rumble.

He looks at Maggie and then tilts his head. "I'm so sorry, Maggie," he says. "I love you. I mean, I really love you."

"Jackdaw," I say, "look at me! Jackdaw. What's up, ol' buddy?" I step toward him.

CJ reaches for Bo's arm and yanks her onto her lap and they both topple backwards in the chair onto the linoleum floor.

Jackdaw glances in their direction but then looks back at me. "I'm sorry, Tibs." He turns back to where Maggie sits.

"Jackdaw!" I yell, trying to draw his attention, but Maggie doesn't stay still. She's come out of her daze, and her face is tight. I put my hand out for her to sit, but she shakes her head and slides out of her chair to come between Jackdaw and Jes.

I move toward Jackdaw, fast, talking in low tones. I don't think I'm making sense, but Jackdaw doesn't seem to be listening, so it doesn't matter. I say things like "Hey, Jackdaw, it's ok," and "How about a beer?"

"No, Tibs, I'm sorry," he says. He says this low and steady, a voice frozen in an ice box. "Sometimes a man's got to take care of things, you know?" As he says this, he points the gun at me, and I think, this is it. He's going to shoot me.

He's going to shoot me? Shoot *me*? But instead of being scared, I'm calm. In fact, I'm mad and getting madder by the minute. What's kept me from hauling off and smacking him all these years? Was it fear? Maybe. But it was also because I thought he was my friend. Friends don't shoot you.

He holds the gun on me for a minute and then points it Maggie's direction. He doesn't say anything, just raises the barrel. He's going to pull the trigger.

I launch myself at Jackdaw just as the gun goes off. I don't think about the consequences. I don't hesitate. I just aim for the gun arm. I tackled him back against the entry doorframe. We're half in and half out of the kitchen, my arms wrapped around Jackdaw's gun arm and my hands around his wrist.

CJ

The gun goes off, and then there's a horrible sound like an animal caught in a trap, half-groan, half-cry. It's Maggie. Then it's quiet except for the wheeze of the ventilator and the grunts and thumps of Tibs and Jackdaw in the doorway. There's the smell of gunpowder.

Bo and I are on the floor in a heap. I scramble to try to push Bo back out of the way while craning backwards to see where the gun is. I'm ashamed that it's not Maggie I tackle to save. In that split second, my priorities became crystal clear. Bo is the most precious, most delicate thing in the world—she must be protected, and the baby, the unborn child, blood of my blood.

Why does it seem like it's always Maggie who gets left in the cold? Maggie deserves so much better, a better family. I have failed her ever since our parents died.

"She's hurt!" Bo says and scrambles up and over to Maggie. I don't know where the gun is, so I try to pull her back. Bo yanks her arm away.

She has Maggie's shirt up and there's a little oozing round hole in Maggie's side. Maggie doesn't seem to notice—she's looking back toward Jes. Bo wipes away the blood. "Sit down, Maggie, sit down," Bo says. Maggie's face is white. Her eyes start to roll upwards in their sockets. I make it just in time to grab her other side to guide her into the chair. Bo pulls her down so she's lying on the floor. She pushes against Maggie's bloody belly, applying pressure. "Call 911," she says.

I glance over at Jes. He's the same, hasn't even reacted to the gunshot sound. For a split second I wonder if he's been shot, but he seems fine.

I turn and stop. Tibs and Jackdaw are pulling against each other in what looks like slow motion. Their muscles strain. They're back in the kitchen. Jackdaw thrusts Tibs back toward us as he lurches to his feet. Tibs stands. Jackdaw points the gun at Tibs. He says, "I'm sorry, Tibs. I'm so sorry." Then Jackdaw jerks the gun up under his own jaw. Tibs launches himself at Jackdaw and tackles him out into the entry. The gun goes off a second time. I can't see what's happened, if anyone's been shot, but I can hear them struggling. Then the gun comes skittering back into the kitchen. I run over and grab it and then run to the phone and place the gun on the counter and dial 911. Then I pick up the gun again and aim it toward the floor by the entry.

Tibs

It's been a week since Jackdaw's incarceration. I should've let him cap his own ass, the asshole. I believed he was better, larger than life. I believed—well it doesn't really matter what I believed, does it?

CJ phones me. Then she phones again. I think she calls four or five times. I don't pick up. But then she arrives at my house. Bangs on the door. I ignore her. But, of course, she lets herself in. I sit on my sofa grading papers.

"Little Brother," she says and plops down on a chair. "Big bad wolf at your door."

"Go blow," I say not looking at her.

She seems about to retort but then she stops. "You can fucking hate me. I deserve it."

I don't say anything.

She comes over and sits next to me on the couch, right on the papers I'm grading. I pull them out from under her and put them on the coffee table. She moves closer. "What you doing?" she says.

I move farther away and ignore her. She moves closer again. "Any of 'em any good?" she says as she cranes her neck at the papers in my lap.

"Get off," I say and push her away. She pushes me back. I turn so that my back is to her and she reaches over and pulls the papers from my lap and throws them into the room like an eruption.

"CJ! Knock it off."

"Oh come on, Tibs."

"Get the fuck out of my house."

She sighs and stands, her arms across her chest. "Okay, you can hate me. Go ahead. But you can't hate Maggie."

I look at her.

"Maggie needs us, Little Brother."

"Yeah, I know," I say. "That's why I'm doing all I can to help her."

"Do you know that she hasn't slept in three days? Nights, I mean? Luckily her side isn't too bad, but she prays under her breath continuously. She doesn't eat anything. Frankly, I don't think she's all there. How could she be?"

"Yeah, and?" I don't mean this to sound callous, but I'm doing everything I can.

"She's living for Jes, and Jes is dying, so that means you and me, Little Brother, got to step up to the plate."

"I have, CJ. I'm there for her."

"But you didn't know that, did you? Did you know she's going to sign the papers so they shut off the machines?"

I didn't. If they shut off the machines, Jes'll die. That's all there is to it.

The fire drains out of me.

"I know I'm a schmuck," CJ says, "and I know that you hate me, but we have to put it aside. You can kill me later, but Maggie needs us now. You and me, us as a family."

She's right. I shake my head at her, not a denial. She comes over and slaps my cheek a bit too hard. "I'm so proud of you, Little Brother," she says.

CJ

Isn't it funny that they have you go the hospital to die? Begin life there, and end it there. It would suck working there. It would take a special kind of person. A special person like Bo.

They've put Maggie, Tibs, and I in a private room with Jes. How it's decorated makes me wonder if this is a special room just for dying. Wouldn't that be odd? But very practical I suppose. Why not? It's got to happen.

The room looks like a regular hospital room but its decorations are blues and greens instead of maroons and greens. It has an area with a little round table and more chairs than usual, and the chairs—instead of being those hard uncomfortable ones with the thin padding—are deep armchairs. It's got all the hospital equipment but the whole room is more formal—heavier blue drapes to block out the light, lots of fake plants, and textured wallpaper with blue and brown vertical stripes, kind of like washed-out wrapping paper. And it has classical music playing in the background.

Maggie sits in a chair holding Jes, Jes's stroller with all its equipment beside her. The bullet wound in her side was superficial, in and out, but I'm sure it hurts. Not that you can tell. She's so focused on Jes, and she probably hurts so much in other ways, I don't think she differentiates, or notices.

I sit in the chair next to her. Tibs stands looking out the windows opaqued with hard water stains. Jes's doctor comes in, the one who's been there through it all, trailed by a nurse and another woman in a beige pantsuit with a clipboard of papers.

"How are you doing today?" the doctor says. It doesn't sound all syrupy when he says it. It sounds real, like it's something he means and wants to know.

I stand and say, "Pretty much sucks, doc, but we're holding it together."

He nods and then introduces the beige woman. She's a social worker. "She'll take care of you," the doctor says. "She's got a few things she needs to talk to you about, and then I'll come back in." He walks over to Maggie and Jes and bends and puts a hand on Jes's head and just stands there for a long time, longer than I expect him to. Maggie holds Jes up as he does this. Then he puts a hand on Maggie's shoulder and Maggie looks up at him, her face drained of expression. Then the doctor turns and leaves.

I don't know how Maggie's holding it together. The procedure lulls me like it's supposed to till I look at Jes and remember what we're here for and my chest squeezes like a fist.

"Please," the social worker says, holding her hand out toward the chairs. I sit back down next to Maggie, and Tibs comes over behind Maggie and stands.

"We have a few things to do," she says, "some papers to look over." She looks at Maggie, her head thrust forward. "Are you ready? Do you need more time?"

Maggie looks down at Jes and then back at the woman and then slowly shakes her head.

I say, "We'll need a minute, you know, before ..."

"Yes, of course," she says. "You'll have all the time you need."

Then she explains all the paperwork, handing each piece to us as she talks. There's the explanation of ours rights—well, Jes's rights, really. There's other papers—what's going to happen, support services for after, information about the hospital. She has Maggie initial a few things. It feels a little like getting a loan.

"As an extra precaution," she says, "we need to verbally confirm that you are aware of the consequences of this procedure. Do you consent to having all life-sustaining equipment and procedures withdrawn from the patient?"

Maggie nods.

"I'm sorry," the social worker says, "but we need to have you verbally confirm."

"I'm sorry?" Maggie says.

"We need you to say yes or no."

"Uh, yes," she says.

The woman continues, "As the responsible party, do you consent to withholding all other life-saving measures?"

"Yes."

"Do you understand that the procedure we are about to perform will most likely result in the decease of the patient?"

You can hardly hear Maggie's voice as she says yes.

The woman pauses and then goes on. "There's just one last form for you to sign. It's the written consent. But we're going to wait to have you sign that till right before the procedure, okay? That way, the doctor'll be here, and he'll witness it." She looks at us and nods slightly. "Now, I'll leave you alone. When you're ready, just come get me. I'll be right there at the nurses' station. Okay?" She stands and hesitates, "If you need anything in the meantime, let me know." And then she walks out.

I glance up at Tibs and then we both look at Maggie and Jes.

Looking first at me and then at Tibs, Maggie says, "Do you want to hold him?"

I hold out my arms and Maggie places Jes in them. In the past, he's always felt heavy compared to his size, but today he feels light, like he's already partway gone. He smells of diaper rash ointment. Today of all days, Maggie put on diaper rash ointment. He's wearing a baby blue sleeper with a green frog on front that's unsnapped where the tube from his belly comes out. There's the ventilator tube coming from his throat. His dark spikey hair reaches down past the tips of his ears. His eyes are closed. It would be like he was asleep, but it's not even that. You know how when babies sleep they twitch a bit or have color rising in their cheeks? That part, whatever it is, it's just not there. When I really look at him—not through all the memories I have of him—he looks like a doll or a plastic sculpture.

He's not there anymore.

I feel the water spring to my eyes, and I take a big shuddering breath. I hold him to my chest tightly, and then I hand him to Tibs. Tibs takes him but doesn't even look at him. He just holds Jes to his chest and closes his eyes and takes deep breaths. Then he hands Jes back to Maggie.

Maggie takes him back into her lap and just sits, staring into his face. Tibs and I don't say anything. Maggie starts whispering under her breathe. I can't tell what she's saying, but it's got a rhythmic quality, like she's saying the same thing over and over. She holds him close, stares into his face, and whispers. It's 15 minutes, then 45. Then she stops.

Her face white, Maggie says, "All right."

Tibs goes out and comes back in. After a minute, the social worker comes in, and then the doctor and nurse. We all stand.

"Are you prepared?" the doctor asks.

Maggie ducks her head once, and then again more slowly.

"Would you like to lay him on the bed, or would you like to hold him?"

"Hold him," Maggie whispers, and then clears her throat. "I think he needs to be held," she says louder.

"Okay, one last form to sign. You ready?"

Maggie nods. He looks at us and we nod. He holds up the clipboard. Maggie doesn't want to put Jes down on the bed, so the doctor and I support the clipboard as Maggie shifts Jes to her left arm and grabs the pen. Tibs puts an arm under Jes. Maggie signs. It's more of a uncontrolled scribble than a signature.

"Doctor Erickson, can we take all this away?" Maggie's voice is loud and firm.

Tibs and I glance at each other and then at Maggie.

The doctor looks at her and tilts his head.

"What I mean is, I want just my little boy. Can we take all of it, this, out"—her voice catches—"away from him?" She points to the tubes.

"Yes of course. As we're doing the procedure, we can remove all attachments."

Maggie doesn't say anything, so I look at her and she looks at me and I say, "Well, then, I guess we're ready."

Maggie holds Jes and I put my arms around Maggie and Tibs puts his arms around both of us. The doctor and nurse go through their procedure, turning off machines and reaching into Maggie's arms and unhooking things. There's a long high beeping. They do it quickly and efficiently. Then they step back. There's silence and then I become aware of the soft music that's still playing in the background.

We all hold each other tight. I watch Jes's face for any sign of change, any sign of struggle. There's no change of expression, just one moment he seems to stiffen a little, like his body that's so used to taking that next breath tries to follow with the habit. And then nothing. Maggie lets out a loud sob, and we stand and hold each other. Maggie's crying, I'm crying, and Tibs is crying.

Jackdaw

"Your son is dead," Tibs says, not looking at me. *And I wish it were you*, he says without talking.

He's pissed, you can tell by the hunch of his shoulders. I can hear him: *What the fuck am I doing here?* In fact, his whole attitude is different than it was. When he walked into the visiting area, he had a chip in his shoulder the size of Texas. *I'm only performing this hideous task for Maggie. Because she wanted him to know. God knows why.* When he sits in the chair across from me at the table, he doesn't face me but instead turns his chair so he's looking out the window. *At least they have metal mesh on the windows, keep assholes like him in their little loony bins.*

I'm so happy at the news about the boy I can't keep the smile off my face. At last, Maggie is free! The killing weight of dying has been lifted!

"Nice way to respond, Ace," Tibs says when he catches my grin. "In fact," he says with spite in his voice, but then he sinks back in his chair and shakes his head and shuts up. *In fact, why DID you shoot your wife while trying to kill you own child? What was that? You're one sick fucker, you know that? If I had the guts of a deer mouse I'd shove your fucking head up your ass so far you'd never see daylight.* He glances around the room at the other patients. *Well, at least there's this.*

"How's Maggie?" I ask.

Tibs's face slides a little. And then tightens again. "She's doing fine. Well, as fine could be expected, considering the circumstances." *No thanks to you.*

"I'm writing," he says.

"That's great, Tibs. Really great. You always did want it more than me."

He looks surprised.

"No, you did. I was only in it for the glory. I know that now." I want to make it into a joke but then I don't. Because it's true. I've been thinking a lot about what's true. "Glory don't mean squat when you're a failure."

Tibs's face twists. You can see the conflicting feelings pull one way and another.

I say, "No, you don't need to say it. I am."

"How? Specifically, in what way?" he finally says.

"Not how you think. I failed to save the love of my life. The fact that she is saved after the fact does not change the fact that I failed." I smile. "Too many facts."

Tibs shakes his head and says, "Yeah, you failed all right." Then he turns his chair to face me, and for the first time since he came in he looks in my eyes. He says in a low voice, "If you only knew what you had, what you squandered, in Maggie, hell, in me, in all of us."

"But I do. Don't you see?"

"Whatever." He looks at my face one last time, shakes his head, and gets up. "I'll be seeing you," he says. *Jackdaw.*

"No you won't," I say. Because first chance I get, I'll be dead.

Maggie

Glorious colors! The green has the texture of velvety grass, the blue is the cool of shifting water, the yellow the warmth of a friend's hand, but the red, ah, the red. It burns. It burns through me like the mind of God. Like the love of God. I'm so glad the pew is made of dark wood, solid and supporting as the earth. I couldn't take it otherwise. God's love goes through me so harshly.

The smell though. It is the white smell of Grandma Rose's house at Eastertime. How did the smell of Grandma Rose's house get here? Did someone put it in a box? Or chase it down with wild flailing arms and catch it in a ziplock bag? A van full of ziplock bags, brought here by the armful and opened to release the smell like so many butterflies.

The voices lap over me, over me, over me. They aren't saying anything, they're just humming nonsense syllables louder, and softer, louder, louder, peaking, then receding, softer now, softer. A low voice. A high voice. All the voices together.

In front of me is a wooden box. I wish it didn't have the brass fittings. The brass is too tight and holds the wood squeezing it, so much so much it can't breathe. It can't breathe! Can't you see that? It's squeezing the life out of it, binding it tight so that it can't get away. I wish I had a hammer, a chisel—I would break it apart, pull it away. I would get at that box and smash it apart, don't you see?

Something touches my arm. Aah, it's CJ. Her face is pitted with concern and the bones of her fingers meld and pull at the bones of my forearm, bones of my bones. She's sitting next to me here on this hard wood, but everything, everything shifts and I'm not where I was and she's not where she was but sitting next to me on a huge scratchy brown couch, not a wooden pew, that's worn smooth by the hands and feet of children and rubbing bodies of adults. She's young and beautiful in her denim mini skirt and blue-flowered t-shirt and I wish I had breasts like she does. I'm not even wearing a training bra yet. But it shifts again, everything, and now her breasts have sagged and she's sitting next to me on a couch of maroon and green flowers. She's happy. She's holding something squirming and warm and round, something that smells wonderful, something like something I used to have but have lost, somehow.

No! Something's piling up inside me. Something, I can't let it out, I can't. It comes out, it'll keep coming out and rising from within me and coming out of my mouth and my nose and I won't be able to stop it. It's been there coming and trying to get out for so long, seeping out at odd moments, trying to push out of me, always, always.

I close my eyes and open them. On my other side, a body close to me, an arm around my shoulders. There's Tibs, on my other side. Tibs—the red burning love of God is in him and all around him! It pulses from his eyes—don't you see it? It's coming from his mouth and licking his lips. It's propelling him forward, pushing him outside himself. He can't keep it inside himself anymore, he has to, has to let it out! It will consume him if he doesn't. He's angry, but the anger helps him. He raises his right hand and brings his thumb together with his first two fingers, and streaming from them is a cold and fluid light. It's the only way to draw off the horrible love of God!

Time passes. The light changes. Now it's not one light tossing colors everywhere. It's dispersed, evened out, a shadow of light all around us. The air is heavier here. There's the sound, *plock! plock! plock!* of raindrops on canvas, and the real grass seems dead next the neon green of carpet grass around a square hole at my feet. The hole is being filled with the box. It's as if the hole was made for the box, so tightly does it nest.

"Please, God," I whisper and close my eyes. I open them again.

The box is still there but it isn't a box. It feels like a real box, only instead of being square, it's curved and sinuous. But, while everything else in this world feels with a life of its own, this box docs not. It is nothing more than a container. It is not too tight. It is not too loose. It supports. It fits. It cups. What it cups I can see now, and it is beyond words. It is all colors. All colors shifting, melding into white. It is lifting from the cup, shifting shape and size, expanding, contracting, lifting from its vessel. Threads of it start drifting off, one for each shadowy person standing around me. The threads seek each person out and enter them caressingly, and then disappear into the darkness that is the person. There are more and more threads, and they reach farther and farther to more and more shadow people, farther and farther away. More and more come past me, so a fast I can't see them all, more and more and more.

303

Wait! There is one for me. It is a radiant blue and it comes toward me. It gets bigger and bigger as it approaches and then it enters me. As it does, I hear a sound that is both a whisper and the voice of every person past present and future.

I look around me and see that my thread is attached to the thread of every other person. It's a vast sticky spider web of threads that pulls all of us together and pulls each of us apart. This thread pulls a woman to toss quarters in a red Salvation Army pot. That thread pulls a man to say, "Well, I didn't love you anyway." This thread pulls a woman to knife open another woman's belly for the life inside. That thread makes a man walk into a burning skyscraper to rescue the people inside.

I look back at the small sinuous box. Where once there was the mass of writhing colors is left a single thread of light. It is the most beautiful thread of all. It's the thread that means the most, the one I want the most. It hovers and then begins to rise, slowly at first, but then faster. I follow it as it streaks toward the sky. It gets smaller and smaller. And then it is gone, but I still feel its tug on the web. It pulls. God, it pulls.

The End

Acknowledgements

There are so many people to thank.

First and foremost, I would like to thank Alex and Kelly, whose love inspired Maggie's story.

To my agent Rachel Stout and everyone at Dystel & Goderich Literary Management, I so much appreciate your help and support. I would also like to thank those who edited *Deep Down Things* in various capacities: Julie Doughty, Rachel Oakley, Stephanie DeVita, and Judy Clain.

My friends have given me invaluable feedback, particularly Jessica, who had the unfortunate experience of reading *Deep Down Things* right after having a baby. I apologize now and forever and am so glad she's still one of my closest writing BFFs! I would also like to thank all my writing friends from the bottom of my heart: Nina, Mary Beth, Ken, Pierre, Rashena, Kerry, Patty, April, Meg, Daisy, and many more. You make writing bearable.

I would like to thank the many doctors and medical professionals who have made it possible for Steve and I to have our happy ending. And to April—you are our heart, you are our life. Now and forever, thank you.

I would like to thank my family—the official ones and the unofficial ones—and most of all Steve, Eli, and Elizabeth. I love you with all my heart.

– Tamara Linse, Laramie, Wyoming, 2014

Reading Group Guide

Deep Down Things
Tamara Linse

Deep Down Things, Tamara Linse's debut novel, is the emotionally riveting story of three siblings torn apart by a charismatic bullrider-turned-writer and the love that triumphs despite tragedy.

From the death of her parents at sixteen, Maggie Jordan yearns for lost family, while sister CJ drowns in alcohol and brother Tibs withdraws. When Maggie and an idealistic young writer named Jackdaw fall in love, she is certain that she's found what she's looking for. As she helps him write a novel, she gets pregnant, and they marry. But after Maggie gives birth to a darling boy, Jes, she struggles to cope with Jes's severe birth defect, while Jackdaw struggles to overcome writer's block brought on by memories of his abusive father.

Ambitious, but never seeming so, *Deep Down Things* may remind you of Kent Haruf's *Plainsong* and Jodi Picoult's *My Sister's Keeper*.

Like the characters in *Deep Down Things*, the author Tamara Linse and her husband have lost babies. They had five miscarriages before their twins were born through the help of a wonderful woman who acted as a gestational carrier. Tamara is also the author of the short story collection *How to Be a Man* and earned her master's in English from the University of Wyoming, where she taught writing. Her work appears in the *Georgetown Review*, *South Dakota Review*, and *Talking River*, among others, and she was a finalist for *Arts & Letters* and *Glimmer Train* contests, as well as the Black Lawrence Press Hudson Prize for a book of short stories. She works as an editor for a foundation and a freelancer. Find her online at tamaralinse.com and on her blog Writer, Cogitator, Recovering Ranch Girl at tamara-linse.blogspot.com.

Letter from the Author

Dear Reader,

Oh, what I wouldn't have given to be able to give Maggie a happy ending, to have Jes grow into a happy and healthy young man whose only scars are those left by his troubled father. It wasn't to be, however. The logic of the story inexorably pulled me to where it ended.

That's not entirely true. The first ending actually had Jackdaw successfully shooting Jes and then killing himself. So maybe I did pull back a little—at the behest of an editor friend. The conversation went something like this. "The ending is too unremittingly dark." "But Jes has to die. Otherwise no one will buy it." "Yes, but does his father have to kill him? AND THEN commit suicide?" Point taken. That same friend said she bawled in public in NYC at least four times while reading it. Now THAT is a compliment. I think.

The inspiration for this story is a friend and coworker who is one of those ideal mothers. If I could have chosen to have any mother in the world, she would have been at the top of my list. She had two boys, and then her third boy was born with severe spina bifida. Watching what she went through was heart-wrenching. When I decided to write this book, a few years after the darling boy had died at age six, we sat and talked through what had happened. She said that most people act as if it never happened and so it was good to talk about it. I hope so, and I hope I've in some small way been able to honor what she went through.

Another inspiration for this story is my history of infertility. My mother had seven kids including me, and one of my sisters had seven, and so I never considered that I would have problems having children. Then, my husband and I had five miscarriages, the first at six months. Medical rigmarole ensued. I'm so glad for it, though, because we were able to have our happy ending. A wonderful amazing woman—whom I'd trust almost more than I'd trust myself—acted as gestational carrier for us, and our twins were born. Our son was also born with a severe cleft lip and palate, and so more medical procedures. As much as we've been through, though, I can't express how thankful I am to medical science and the wonderful doctors who made it all possible.

The first scene of *Deep Down Things* that I wrote, I was actually staying in a residential hotel in Denver undergoing IVF procedure for the twins. All those shots. That was August 2005. The first scene I wrote was where Maggie walks into the room and Jes just lights up. He makes her feel wonderful, despite everything, just by the way he beams at her. I finished a first draft by June 2009. I remember because I completed it for a Tin House writers conference mentorship with the legendary Little, Brown editor Judy Clain. The manuscript was an unqualified mess— four points of view with two timelines going concurrently. Bless Judy's heart for first of all agreeing to do the mentorship and second of all giving me such great advice. Help your reader out. Chronological, chronological! More reflection to let the reader know what to take away from a scene. Her talking with me was simply the best encouragement I could have had.

So I went back and majorly rewrote it. Because of how I'd written it—two timelines—the beginning and the end were basically written and I had to write through the middle. An odd experience, to say the least, but a good one. It shaped up nicely, although I distinctly remember having writer's block and thinking, this is the most horrible thing I've ever read. I do that when I write—I go through periods of loving the work and then hating it. Especially when I'm not writing, I think about all the flaws.

Having four points of view presented its own challenges. If you have a point of view, you must have a character arc. Something has to happen to that person. They have to change. And therefore all the stories have to be coherent in their own right, yet they have to meld together into this unified whole. "Ambitious," someone called it, and at the time I don't think they meant it as a compliment. My initial inspiration for form was the movie *Love Actually*. I was fascinated with how that movie was able to have all those different story lines yet work. I still love that movie. It strayed pretty far from that, though, didn't it? Another big inspiration was William Faulkner's *As I Lay Dying*, one of my favorite books. All those points of view tied together in a country setting. Believe it or not, I didn't actually read Kent Haruf's *Plainsong* till late in the writing process. Without knowing it, I had mirrored a lot of that wonderful book, and so when I did finally read it I was a bit thunderstruck.

I deliberately try to have all kinds of people in my books. I regret that I don't have more diversity in this one, but I am glad I was able to have CJ work through her sexuality. Race and ethnicity and gender and sexuality are not binaries—they exist much more on a spectrum—and I find myself continually fascinated with the complexities of these subjects.

Finally, I often have an extended metaphor or theme that I'm thinking of when I write a story or a novel. In the case of *Deep Down Things*, it's the story of Jesus. Many readers would not pick up on it, I think, but Jes's story riffs on it with details large and small. I'm a spiritual person—though I'm not a religious one—and the ideas underlying the story of Jesus are complicated and compelling and timeless. Self-sacrifice, family relationships, being a good person—these all are just as relevant today as they ever were. And I find by using something like this as a framework, an extended metaphor, I can explore these subjects more deeply. I don't think of this as a religious book or a Christian book, but I am very invested in the ideas that Christianity presents to us. I am happy, however, if this book helps someone affirm his or her faith or think more deeply about the issues presented. We all need help sometimes in being good people.

My finally confession is that the ending still makes me bawl like a baby. I don't think writers are supposed to admit that.

– Tamara Linse, Laramie, Wyoming, 2014

Discussion Questions

1. How does the title *Deep Down Things* reflect what the novel is about? Would you have chosen a different title? The title comes from a poem by Gerard Manly Hopkins entitled "God's Grandeur" (printed above before the text)—how does the novel relate to the poem?

2. The original title of *Deep Down Things* was *Loveland*, reflecting the importance and resonance of place and landscape. Would you have preferred the title *Loveland*, or would it have had the wrong connotations? In general, how does landscape shape the characters in the novel?

3. The characters have odd names. Does this lend itself to their characterizations or detract? How do these names reflect their characters?

4. Very little backstory is given about the characters. We know a few major life events, and there are a few flashbacks. Do you think the story would have benefited from more history and more flashback? You don't hear much about Bo, in particular. What backstory would you imagine for her?

5. What do you imagine is Jackdaw's pig story that Tibs tries to get him to tell early in the book?

6. Tibs's story parallels Jackdaw's in relation to writing. CJ's story parallels Maggie's in relation to having children. Compare and contrast these stories and their outcomes.

7. There are a number of sex scenes throughout the book. Are the scenes convincing? Are they necessary? Would it be a different book without them? There is also some bad language. Would the novel be as convincing without it?

8. Which of the four points of view was your favorite? Your least favorite? Whom did you like the best? Was the most likable character the same as your favorite character?

9. Jackdaw does what he thinks he has to do. What in his past brought him to this decision? Should euthanasia ever be an option?

10. How is the medical community portrayed in the novel? Do you think the novel accurately shows what it's like to deal with an illness or with the death of a loved one?

11. Does having both members of a gay couple named Jason play with stereotype, or reinforce it? Are there other stereotypes in the book? Do some points of view call for more stereotyping than others? Which characters would be more apt to stereotype?

12. The three siblings are close because they were first abandoned by their parents and then their parents were killed in a plane crash. In what ways are they "functional" and in what ways are they "dysfunctional"?

13. How would you describe the town of Loveland, as depicted in *Deep Down Things*?

14. The story of Jesus is an extended metaphor that inspired the author. In what ways does *Deep Down Things* riff on the story of Jesus?

15. Does the climax scene at Easter—where Maggie realizes Jes is dying, CJ confronts Bo, Tibs confronts CJ and Bo, and Jackdaw shoots Maggie— seem contrived? Did the author convincingly lay the groundwork for the scene earlier in the book?

16. Both Maggie and Jackdaw have "gone crazy" at the end of the book. In what ways are they crazy? How might the author have portrayed this differently? Do you think their mental illnesses are justified?

17. How would you have ended it?

About the Author

Tamara Linse grew up on a ranch in northern Wyoming with her farmer/rancher rock-hound ex-GI father, her artistic musician mother from small-town middle America, and her four sisters and two brothers. The ranch was a partnership between her father and her uncle, and in the 80s and 90s the two families had a Hatfields and McCoys-style feud. She jokes that she was raised in the 1880s because they did things old-style—she learned how to bake bread, break horses, irrigate, change tires, and be alone, skills she's been thankful for ever since. In high school, she was rodeo queen, placed in a poetry contest, and waitressed.

She put herself through the University of Wyoming as a bartender, waitress, and editor. At UW, she was officially in almost every college on campus until she settled on English and after 15 years earned her bachelor's and master's in English. While there, she taught writing, including a course called Literature and the Land, where students read Wordsworth and Donner Party diaries during the week and hiked in the mountains on weekends. She also worked as a technical editor for an environmental consulting firm.

She lives in Laramie, Wyoming, with her husband Steve and their twin son and daughter. They went through five miscarriages before the twins were born with the help of a wonderful woman who acted as a gestational carrier.

Tamara writes fiction around her job as an editor for a foundation. She is also a photographer, and when she can she posts a photo a day for a Project 365. Please stop by Tamara's website, www.tamaralinse.com, and her blog, Writer, Cogitator, Recovering Ranch Girl, at tamara-linse.blogspot.com. You can find an extended bio there with lots of juicy details. Also friend her on Facebook and Google+ and follow her on Twitter, and if you see her in person, please say hi. She really means it.

Find Tamara Linse on the web:

www.tamaralinse.com
tamara-linse.blogspot.com
@tamaralinse
fb.com/tlinse

Your Turn

If you enjoyed *Deep Down Things*, it would be tremendously helpful if you would spread the word—stop by your favorite online book site and review it! It's the one thing you can do to really help an author. It doesn't have to be anything elaborate, just a sentence or two if that's all you're up for.

Here are some sites you might visit to leave a review:
- Amazon
- Barnes and Noble
- Goodreads
- Booklikes
- LibraryThing
- Shelfari

You can also visit www.tamaralinse.com/writing_deep_down_things_review.html for direct links to these sites.

If you'd like to sign up for Tamara's newsletter, stop by her website (www.tamaralinse.com). There you'll also find some freebie content as an incentive.

And, if you liked *Deep Down Things*, you might also enjoy other works by Tamara Linse. Her short story collection, *How to Be a Man*, is available online at Amazon, Barnes and Noble, iBooks, IndieBound, and possibly at a bookstore or library near you. It's also in audiobook, read by P. J. Morgan.

Here's a synopsis of *How to Be a Man*.

"Never acknowledge the fact that you're a girl, and take pride when your guy friends say, 'You're one of the guys.' Tell yourself, 'I am one of the guys,' even though, in the back of your mind, a little voice says, 'But you've got girl parts.'" – Birdie, in "How to Be a Man"

A girl whose self-worth revolves around masculinity, a bartender who loses her sense of safety, a woman who compares men to plants, and a boy who shoots his cranked-out father. These are a few of the hard-scrabble characters in Tamara Linse's debut short story collection, *How to Be a Man*. Set in contemporary Wyoming—the myth of the West taking its toll—these stories reveal the lives of tough-minded girls and boys, self-reliant women and men, struggling to break out of their lonely lives and the emotional havoc of their families to make a connection, to build a life despite the odds. *How to Be a Man* falls within the traditions of Maile Meloy, Tom McGuane, and Annie Proulx.

13076015R00198

Made in the USA
San Bernardino, CA
09 July 2014